Praise for **C**

"*Cascade Vengeance* takes ~~dual worlds of drug dealing and big-game hunting deep~~ Washington's Cascade mountains. Rob Phillips uses his extensive knowledge of the region to tell the fast-moving tale . . . on the way to the story's harrowing and heartbreaking conclusion."

–Scott Graham, National Outdoor Book Award-winning author of *Mesa Verde Victim*

"Luke McCain and his wonderful yellow lab Jack are back for another fast, fun read in a series you won't want to miss. The big Mexican drug cartels have moved into the Cascade Mountains of Washington State where thousands of miles of forests provide endless opportunities for illegal marijuana grows, and the men doing the growing and harvesting are being stalked and killed. Luke must use all his experience and knowledge to help his girlfriend FBI Agent Sara Sinclair discover who is doing the killing. This is crime fiction at its finest – the perfect blend of a compelling mystery, a fabulous setting, the best dog ever, and a very likeable hero you won't forget."

–Christine Carbo, award-winning author of the Glacier Mystery Series

"Rob Phillips delivers another page turner. *Cascade Vengeance* is full of murder, intrigue and suspense. And just when you think the case is solved, Phillips throws you a curveball. If you enjoyed *The Cascade Killer*, you'll love Phillips's latest in the Luke McCain series."

–Pat Hoglund, publisher of *Western Hunting Journal*, *Traveling Angler*, and *Salmon & Steelhead Journal*

"*Cascade Vengeance*, the second book in the Luke McCain series, is another hang-onto-your-hat, nonstop action episode with Luke, a Washington State Fish and Wildlife officer, his FBI girlfriend Sara, and Jack, his loyal yellow Lab. I felt like I was riding shotgun in Luke's Ford pickup, bouncing along forest service roads where very bad guys might be lurking."

–Susan Richmond, owner of Inklings Bookshop

"Another fast-paced, exciting chapter in the Luke McCain series that remains true to the Pacific Northwest. Phillips leaves readers with a splendid conclusion, helping us wonder when the next Luke McCain volume will be out. I am truly a fan of Luke and Jack!"
   –Vikki J. Carter, host & producer of *Authors of the Pacific Northwest Podcast*

"Rob's knowledge of the outdoors, his attention to detail, his main characters – Luke McCain, FBI Agent Sara Sinclair and their yellow Lab, Jack – all come together for another quick-paced, fun, hard-to-put-down novel."
   –Steve Raabe, author of *Patrolling the Heart of the West: True Tales of a Nevada State Trooper*

Praise for **THE CASCADE KILLER**

"Real! Captivating! Once you start, you can't put it down! *The Cascade Killer* is VERY well done!"
   –Scott Haugen, host and producer of *The Hunt* and author of numerous outdoor books

"Rob Phillips' intimate knowledge of Washington State's outdoors scene and recent newsworthy events is on full display in this fast-paced novel. Featuring a smart, hard-working fish and wildlife officer, a demented serial killer, an attractive FBI agent and a scene-stealing Labrador retriever, this is a great read and if you are like me you'll have a hard time putting this book down!"
   –John Kruse, host and producer of *Northwestern Outdoors Radio*

"The author's knowledge and love of the outdoors and the bounty it provides shines through in this fast-paced, fun and thrilling story. *The Cascade Killer* captures many of the attributes important to those within the rural, outdoor community."
   –Buzz Ramsey, author, outdoor personality and Hall of Fame angler

CASCADE VENGEANCE

CASCADE VENGEANCE

A LUKE MCCAIN NOVEL

ROB PHILLIPS

LATAH
BOOKS

Book design by Kevin Breen
Cover image derived from Adobe Stock photos

ISBN: 978-1-7360127-1-0
Cataloging-in-Publication Data is available upon request

Manufactured in the United States of America

Published by
Latah Books, Spokane, Washington
www.latahbooks.com

The author may be contacted at yakimahunter@yahoo.com

DEDICATION

To Bob and Boni Phillips, my parents. My dad was the person who introduced me to the outdoors, and I will be eternally grateful to him for that. And my mom always believed I had a book in me. Unfortunately, neither of them are with us today, but I believe they'd be proud of this book.

Vengeance is Mine, and recompense;
Their foot shall slip in due time;
For the day of their calamity is at hand,
And the things to come hasten upon them.
– Deuteronomy 32:35

PROLOGUE

The first sliver of light was just visible in the east when Shane Wallace parked his Ford Explorer in a pull-off high up on Manastash Ridge. He waited for it to get a bit lighter and then shouldered his pack, marked the spot on his GPS, grabbed his rifle, and headed out for the day.

His plan was to walk up to the top of the ridgeline, then work down it toward a drainage he had circled on the map. There were a few clear-cuts in the area, and with water nearby, he hoped the area would hold a few deer. During the first couple hours he saw a few deer, but besides a small forked-horn buck, which wasn't legal to shoot, there were only does and fawns.

He was sitting up against a tree eating a mid-morning snack when he spotted a bigger buck move through a saddle about four hundred yards away. He quickly found the deer in his binoculars and saw that it was definitely legal. The buck had three points on one side of his antlers and four points on the other. Shane's heartbeat spiked, and the adrenaline started to flow.

He knew the deer was too far to shoot at with his primitive black-powder rifle, but being new to the sport he wasn't too sure what to do next. He decided to just sit and watch the deer to see where it headed. The buck slowly worked its way through the saddle, feeding on leaves as it moved along. After a few minutes, it disappeared over the hill.

Wallace made his move. He walked as quickly as he could, trying to make as little noise as possible. As he approached the spot in the saddle where he'd last seen the deer, he slowed his pace and searched for the buck. When he finally spotted the deer, he was amazed that it was still at least three hundred yards ahead of him. The animal wasn't running and showed no indication it knew Wallace was stalking him. But the buck was covering some ground.

Wallace watched the deer for a couple minutes until it disappeared into a dark green patch of vegetation. As soon as the deer was out of sight, he headed that way. When he got to the edge of the dark green foliage, Wallace stopped and looked at the plants a bit closer. He wasn't a pot smoker, but he knew marijuana when he saw it. What the heck was all this pot doing up here, he wondered. It didn't take him long to figure out the plants were being grown illegally, and based on what he could see, the pot field was a substantial one.

He had just taken out his GPS unit to mark the spot so he could report it when he was hit with a burning hot punch in the chest. A split second later he heard the crack of a rifle, and he realized he had been shot. He was trying to understand why this was happening as he sunk to the ground, blood pouring from his body.

CHAPTER 1

Autumn in Central Washington was Luke McCain's favorite time of the year. As an avid hunter, it meant there would be some hunts to enjoy in the weeks and months ahead. And as a Washington State Fish and Wildlife police officer, he would be very busy at work. He liked to be busy.

At a little under six feet, five inches tall and a very athletic 224 pounds, McCain was in excellent shape for thirty-eight years old. He loved being in the mountains. A veteran wildlife police officer, McCain worked out of the WDFW Region 3 office in Yakima which was responsible mainly for the central part of the state. The area he patrolled was huge, with much of it encompassing hundreds of thousands of acres of National Forest Service and state-owned lands.

McCain spent some time in the office filling out reports and going to meetings, but usually he was in the field checking on hunters and anglers. On occasion, he and the other wildlife officers, still called wardens by many, would be asked to assist other police agencies in investigations and disturbances.

McCain frequently had his big yellow Lab, Jack, with him

when he was working in the field. The dog loved to ride along with McCain. Jack had, on more than one occasion, assisted in the search and location of injured animals.

The year prior, Jack had helped find the body of a woman who had been partially eaten by a bear. Then he helped track down the woman's killer who had also murdered several other women before dumping their bodies along the eastern slopes of the Cascades.

It was the last Monday in September, a day off for McCain, so he was planning on taking Jack up into the mountains to hunt for blue grouse. He had worked all weekend, checking on deer hunters in the mountains and anglers fishing for salmon on the Columbia River. He was ready to do some hiking and hunting.

McCain and Jack were just climbing into his Tundra when his phone rang.

"Yeah, this is McCain," he answered.

"Hi Luke," a woman replied. "This is Deputy Hernandez with the Kittitas County Sheriff's office. I assisted you last year on a call to run down a poacher who had escaped from the Yakima County Jail."

"Sure, deputy. How are you?"

"I'm fine. Listen, we've been called out on a lost hunter. We've located his vehicle, but we haven't been able to find him. We're hoping you and your dog might lend us some assistance."

"I'm off duty today, but if you can clear it with my boss, I'd be happy to help."

"I'll have the sheriff make the call now. He's pretty persuasive. Any chance you can head our way?"

"I'll grab my gear and start your way now. Text me the coordinates."

The deputy said she would and thanked him.

"No grouse hunting for us today," McCain said to the yellow dog.

Jack turned and followed McCain back into the house.

"We're not going hunting after all," McCain yelled into the kitchen. "There's a lost hunter up in Kittitas County, and they want my assistance. Well, not so much *my* assistance. They want Jack."

"Well, that doesn't surprise me," came the voice of his girlfriend. "He's the star in my book, and he's a whole lot cuter too."

Sara Sinclair and McCain had been dating ever since he and Jack saved her from the mass murderer who came to be known as the Cascade Killer. There was an almost immediate attraction between the two before Sinclair was abducted, but after McCain and Jack had rescued her and then caught the killer, a real love had grown. She had moved in with McCain a couple months later.

"What's up?" Sinclair asked. She was tall and slim, with the body of a person who worked out regularly, because that's exactly what she did. Her straight black hair fell to her shoulders, and her dark brown eyes were flecked with the tiniest of orange spots. She was the FBI agent in Yakima and was always more than interested in the daily activities of her fish and wildlife police officer boyfriend.

"Not sure," he said as he grabbed his service utility belt and vest. "They found the hunter's rig but can't seem to locate him. That's all the deputy told me."

"Well, if anyone can find him, Jack can," she said as she rubbed the dog's ears.

Sinclair had been eating a bagel with cream cheese before heading to her office in downtown Yakima, and Jack was sniffing around for any crumbs that had maybe hit the floor. He paused in his search to allow Sinclair to pet him, then looked up at her to see if his big brown-eyed puppy-dog stare would entice her to give him a bite.

As usual, it did.

"Come on, you chow hound," McCain said to Jack. "It's time for you to go earn your keep."

McCain kissed Sinclair goodbye, and then he and Jack loaded up in his state-issued Ford F-150 pickup and headed toward Ellensburg. He had put the coordinates Hernandez had sent into the GPS map app on his phone and, while he didn't really need the directions, the app told him the quickest way to reach the hunter's truck.

During the drive up to the ridge, McCain took another call from Hernandez.

"Your boss cleared you to come assist," the deputy said. "We'll meet you at the missing hunter's rig?"

"How'd you find out the guy . . . I'm assuming it is a guy . . . was missing?"

"His name is Shane Wallace. His wife called it in late Saturday night when he didn't come home. He's muzzleloader hunting for deer, and he is hunting alone. She said he was new to hunting and was very worried he'd gotten lost."

"When did you find the rig?"

"Not until late yesterday. Some hunters noticed it had been sitting there for two days and called it in. The plates matched. We called in our search and rescue team. They searched through the night but have had no luck in locating Mr. Wallace."

"Okay, I'll be there in less than an hour."

McCain clicked off and then, as he had promised, called Sinclair and gave her the details.

"Hopefully, Jack and I can find this guy and be home by dinner."

"I hope so too. Good luck and be safe."

McCain had been involved in a few other lost hunter searches. Elk hunters in Yakima County often got lost in the rugged terrain of the Cascades. Most of the hunters were found alive within a day or two, but on rare occasions a hunter would be found dead. A couple of the missing had died of heart attacks or from other medical problems, but one, McCain remembered, had succumbed to the elements.

In general, hunters don't plan on getting lost, so they rarely carry enough supplies to survive a few nights in the wilderness. Especially during elk season, when the weather can be very unpredictable and often well below freezing at night, being prepared with the right items can mean the difference between life and death.

But this was a little different. The late September temperatures had been typical of Central Washington. Daytime highs in the mountains had reached the upper 60s, with nighttime temps dropping to near freezing. And it was dry. Even if Wallace was unprepared to spend a couple nights in the woods, the elements were such that a person should have no problem surviving for a while, even without food.

McCain wondered if Wallace had wounded a deer, then followed it around the mountain and gotten so turned around he didn't know which way to go. That happens sometimes. Or he could have been injured in a fall. Still, McCain thought, if Wallace was somewhere in the vicinity, he should be able to hear the search and rescue people who would be whistling and making plenty of noise as they looked for him.

When they got close to the coordinates Deputy Hernandez had given him, McCain spotted four rigs parked near a pull-out. There were two Kittitas County sheriff's units, a dark gray Chevy three-quarter-ton pickup and a gold Ford Explorer.

McCain recognized Hernandez right away. The deputy was short and stocky, and as McCain remembered from their meeting the year before at a bear poacher's cabin in Cle Elum, she was tough, smart and capable.

He pulled up behind the other rigs, and McCain and Jack jumped out.

"Hey, Luke," Hernandez said. "Thanks for coming. This is Deputy Ryan Barnes, and this gentleman is Vern Kennedy. Kennedy is the head of the Kittitas Search and Rescue group."

McCain shook hands with the two men and asked Kennedy, "Your people are still out looking, I assume?"

"Yes," Kennedy said. "But we've found no sign at all of Mr. Wallace. Of course, we have no way of knowing which way he went. We've been searching in ever-increasing circles around his rig here."

"We got the spare key to Wallace's rig from his wife and have looked around in it, but there's not much in there that might tell us which way he went," Barnes explained.

"Any clothing items?" McCain asked.

"Yeah, there's a hooded sweatshirt in there."

"Okay, I'll grab that and let Jack give it a good smell. I'll get my gear, and we'll see what we can do."

Jack was not a professionally trained tracking dog, but he had an incredible nose, and somehow he knew what or who he needed to follow when McCain asked him to do so. The serial killer was the first person Jack had tracked, but he wasn't the only person he'd located.

Earlier in the summer, McCain and Jack had been called in to help find a three-year-old boy who had disappeared from his family's campsite near Lost Lake. McCain let Jack smell some of the little guy's clothes, and after he found a couple tracks leading away from the campsite, he let Jack go.

As it turned out, the boy was only about five hundred yards from the camp once Jack found him safe and sound. Evidently, the youngster had crawled into the end of a big hollow log and fell asleep. Jack found him in about fifteen minutes, much to the joy of the boy's very frightened parents.

The search for Shane Wallace, McCain knew, was not going to be as easy.

CHAPTER 2

Jack was an excellent tracker with his nose, but McCain was a pretty good tracker with his eyes. He'd spent much of his youth learning to track animals, and in his work with the WDFW he had become an excellent tracker of people too.

After getting his gear loaded and ready to go, McCain spent a few minutes around Wallace's rig, hoping to identify any tracks that might be those of the lost man. McCain discussed with Kennedy which way his team members had gone and then followed one track from the rig that went nearly straight up the hill. It was difficult to follow in the long grass and rocky terrain, but every now and again he'd find a partial or even a full print. When he was confident it was Wallace's tracks he was following, McCain had Jack take a good snoot-full of the sweatshirt and then put him on the track.

Scents, depending on humidity and the type of foliage in the area, can be detected up to sixty hours after the fact. Being that this area hadn't had rain in weeks, McCain was dubious about just how much of Wallace's scent would be available for the dog to follow. Occasionally, as he followed Jack, McCain would find a boot track, and it told him Jack was on a human scent. McCain was pretty sure it was Wallace they were tracking.

McCain and Jack worked slowly up to the top of Manastash Ridge and then turned and followed it down for a couple miles. Around the base of a tree that overlooked a saddle, Jack stopped and concentrated. This would be the perfect place for someone to sit and watch for deer, McCain thought. As he looked around, he found the freshly torn corner of a miniature Baby Ruth wrapper. Someone in the past couple days had eaten a candy bar here.

Jack soon left the tree and began slowly working through the saddle and down the other side. McCain found boot tracks in the dry dirt where a man had stood, feet together. Jack then worked down the hill toward a big patch of bright green vegetation. It didn't take McCain long to figure out what he was seeing.

Even though marijuana became legal in Washington late in 2012, illegal pot operations were still a problem around the state. Much of the pot was being grown on public land which created all kinds of issues as the illegal grows impact the soil, water and wildlife. The growers use heavily concentrated fertilizers and pesticides, and rely on generators that leak oil and gas into the soil and eventually into the creeks. The pot farmers come in, make a huge mess that is never cleaned up, then move on.

McCain had been in on a few different pot-grow busts over the years, and while the number of growers was down, there were still illegal grows out there. He was looking at one now.

As they got to the edge of the pot plants, Jack slowed down and worked a very small area. McCain walked over and looked closely at the grass and other surrounding vegetation. Splattered on the leaves of some brush, and in more concentrated amounts on the grass, was blood. It was dark red, almost black after two days, but McCain was sure it was blood. The question then became what or whose blood was it.

McCain pulled out his cell phone and dialed Deputy Hernandez.

"Have you found him?" she asked.

"No, but we've tracked him to a big illegal pot grow. And we found blood."

"Aw, crap," Hernandez said. "Do you think it's his?"

"The odds are it's from a deer he hit, but we need to check it out for sure. And we need to let the State Patrol know about this grow."

McCain pulled out his GPS, got the coordinates and passed them on to Hernandez.

"I want to keep trying to track Wallace," McCain said. "Do you think you or one of the other deputies can get in here and get a sample of the blood for testing?"

"Yeah, we'll get in there right away."

"You might want to get something with Wallace's DNA from his wife. It will freak her out, but I think we need to be on top of this. We can tell her we don't think it's her husband's, but we need to rule him out, just in case it is human blood."

"Not a call I want to make, but we'll do it," Hernandez said. "Hope you find him."

McCain hung up, pulled a roll of bright orange surveyor's tape out of his pack and marked the area around the blood. Then he went about looking for more boot prints. He found some a few minutes later, but they weren't Wallace's.

"Oh boy," he said to Jack, who was still sniffing the bushes and grass covered in blood. "I'm not getting a good feeling about this."

After searching for another few minutes, McCain found more boot prints. He found a partial print here and there and then he found more drops of blood along the trail. He followed the tracks around the outer, lower edge of the pot plants until they cut into the middle of the field of marijuana plants.

The marijuana plants were huge. Most were over ten feet tall, and they were as full as a small pine tree. McCain had no way of estimating how many plants were growing here, but there had to be hundreds.

He and Jack cut through the field of cannabis, following the tracks for ten yards, twenty yards, thirty yards, and then McCain saw something that made his gut turn. There, in the middle of millions of dollars of pot plants, was what looked like a newly covered grave.

"This is not good," McCain said to Jack who was now very interested in the freshly covered hole in the ground.

McCain grabbed his phone and tried to dial Hernandez, but he had no service. So, he called Jack, told him to heel, and they carefully walked out of the marijuana and back up the hill to where he had last called Hernandez.

She answered by saying that Deputy Barnes was on his way to the location of the blood to get a sample. She had talked to Wallace's wife, and she was having his toothbrush and a hairbrush set out for someone to pick up.

"Okay, that's good," McCain said. "But we might need the coroner up here. In fact, go ahead and get him rolling. I believe I found a grave in the pot plants. I haven't dug into it yet, and won't. That's for you guys to handle. But if I was to make a prediction, I would say we may have found Mr. Wallace, and he most likely was killed because he stumbled into this marijuana grow."

"Shit," Hernandez said. "Shit. Okay. Well, stay right there, I guess. And if someone is killing people around the pot plants, you might keep your eyes open."

"Roger that," McCain said, looking around for where the person might have taken the shot at Wallace, if that is what had happened. "I guess someone could have buried their old dog in there or something. But I have a bad feeling about this."

"Me too," Hernandez said. "Thanks, McCain. Hang tight. Barnes should be there shortly."

Instead of sitting and waiting for the deputy, McCain decided he would try to backtrack the other set of tracks that had led him down the hill and into the marijuana. He picked up the tracks at the blood and started following them through a small draw and up the other side. He was concentrating on the tracks but also keeping in mind what Hernandez had said by diligently looking ahead for anything or anyone who shouldn't be there. He kept Jack close by so he didn't have to worry about where he might get off to. One less thing to worry about if there was a killer around.

Slowly, McCain worked the tracks back up the hill until they led to another draw, this one bigger and with water running down it. He marked this spot, too, with the surveyor's tape and sat down. From here he could see where he had found the blood, and he could look down the other draw. If someone had shot Wallace, or another person, this would have been an excellent ambush spot. McCain looked around the area, and as he searched through the grass, a flash of brass caught his eye. Sure enough, there was a spent cartridge, and it was bright and shiny new.

Again, he pulled out the orange tape and marked the spot where the spent shell was sitting. He was searching for anything else out of the ordinary when he caught movement below. Through the saddle came Deputy Barnes who was staring at something in his hand. McCain assumed it was a handheld GPS unit.

McCain whistled, and Barnes looked up at him.

"You're on the right track," McCain hollered. "I'll come down and meet you at the blood. See where it's marked by the orange tape?"

"Yep, got it," Barnes said and kept walking toward the spot McCain had marked.

Barnes was collecting a blood sample as McCain joined him.

"We may not need that," McCain said.

"Why's that?" Barnes responded.

"I've followed some tracks into the pot field, and I believe I've found a grave. I thought I'd leave it alone until you got here. If this is a crime scene, and I have a bad feeling it is, this is Kittitas County Sheriff's crime scene."

"Geez," Barnes said.

McCain figured the deputy wasn't more than twenty-five years old, meaning he had to be fairly new to police work. Fair-skinned, with short blond hair, very fit and about six feet tall, it was easy to see why Hernandez had let the young officer make the hike in to the blood.

Barnes immediately called Hernandez on his radio.

"What do you want me to do?" he asked after she responded to his call.

"We need to know exactly what or who is buried there," Hernandez said. "You and Officer McCain go back in there and see what we're dealing with. Try not to make too big a mess. The crime scene unit will need to be there if it is Wallace or some other person."

"Ten-four," Barnes said. "We'll let you know as soon as we know."

CHAPTER 3

The blank, dead stare of Shane Wallace looked up at McCain and Barnes as they moved the fresh dirt from his face.

"Damn," Barnes said. "Poor guy."

"I don't know for sure this is Wallace, but based on his description and what he's wearing, I'm guessing it's him. Better let Hernandez know."

Barnes radioed Hernandez, and she told him to stay at the scene. She said the coroner and the crime scene crew were on the way. She asked if McCain could stick around too.

"Tell her I'm happy to, but I want to do a little looking around. Let her know I believe I found where the shooter was when Wallace was killed."

Barnes relayed the message, and McCain heard her say "ten-four."

"I won't be too far away," McCain told Barnes as he and Jack headed back up the hill. "Holler if you see anything or need me."

"Will do," the young deputy said.

From the experience McCain gained during a couple raids he'd been in on with the Washington State Patrol, he knew most of these grows were overseen by two or three men who basically lived on site. They were the boots-on-the-ground pot farmers. They fertilized, irrigated, and when it came time, harvested the crop.

Usually they were on the payroll of a bigger organization, which recently had been a big Mexican drug cartel. They used public land for their grows and planted the marijuana in spots that were surrounded by trees and other vegetation, making the fields difficult to see from the air.

In their infinite wisdom, the federal government seemed to believe that because pot was legal, the illegal grows would go away. The Feds cut funding for air patrols of National Forest lands, and now there were more and more illegal grows popping up again around the state.

McCain figured there had to be a shack or tent or supply shed somewhere in the vicinity. He and Jack dropped down into the next draw and followed the creek past the northern border of the pot field. He worked slowly, keeping an eye peeled for any movement or anything man-made.

First, he found a pump in the small creek at the bottom of the draw. Green PVC pipe snaked up the hill and into the marijuana plants. He was looking at the pump set-up when he heard some brush rustling in the distance. He sure wished he'd brought his state-issued Springfield Armory .223 rifle with him. He had his Glock .45 caliber pistol in a holster on his service belt, but if someone was going to start a long-range gun battle, the pistol was essentially useless. McCain slowly moved his head toward the sound and peered through the trees. He was relieved to see a mule deer doe and her fawn browsing in some buck brush. He watched the deer for a moment and then went back to checking out the pump. A second later, the deer started stomping their feet and blowing, the noise they make when trying to identify the smell of danger.

McCain looked at the deer again, figuring he and Jack had been pegged, but he was wrong. The two deer were looking in the opposite direction, farther down the creek. A second later, they'd had enough and turned and started bounding up the creek, right at McCain and Jack.

The deer ran within ten yards of McCain and Jack before they turned and bounded up the hill. Jack had never been a deer chaser, but if he was ever going to do so, this would have been the time.

"No," McCain hissed at Jack. He didn't want to speak too loudly until he identified what it was, or who it was, that had spooked the deer. If one of the pot farmers was prowling about, McCain wanted to make sure he wasn't the next shooting victim. And, if it was one of the pot growers, McCain wanted to try to get the jump on them to make an arrest.

As they continued, McCain watched Jack's ears go up as the dog looked down and to the right of the creek. McCain dropped to Jack's line of sight and saw a big male coyote slowly working up the creek.

"Just a coyote, huh boy?" McCain whispered to Jack. McCain was a bit disappointed, hoping it had been one of the marijuana farmers. It would be great to have an arrest in the case so quickly.

They continued down the creek, and as they reached the bottom of the grow, McCain spotted a couple camouflaged tents big enough to house two or three people. He and Jack stopped to listen. The two stood dead-still for three minutes, watching for movement and listening for voices or any other sounds that might indicate there were people in the small camp. When he was convinced there was no one around, McCain patted his hip which indicated to Jack to fall into place at heel. The dog followed obediently as McCain eased down to the tents. It was eerily silent.

"McCAIN!" Barnes yelled from the grave site in the marijuana.

McCain jumped about a foot off the ground, which in turn

spooked Jack. He was trying to get his pistol out of the holster while looking around for anything that might want to do them harm. It took a minute or two for his heart rate to get back down into double digits, and then he hollered back at Barnes.

"YEAH, WHAT?"

"CORONER IS FIVE MINUTES OUT. THOUGHT YOU'D WANT TO GET BACK OVER HERE."

"OKAY, THANKS! I'LL BE ALONG SHORTLY."

"Stuff like that will age a fella," McCain said to Jack, who was not paying attention but instead sniffing at one of the tents.

As McCain drew closer to the tents, he started to smell something too. It only took him a second to figure out that something, or someone, was dead in the tent. He'd been around dead and decaying animals all his life, and while a dead human smelled a bit different, it was still very obvious when he smelled it.

For the second time in two minutes, McCain pulled his pistol and stepped closer to the tent.

"State Police! Anyone in there?"

No answer. McCain went to the zipper on the door of the tent and opened it.

The smell of death was doubly bad, as there on their cots were two dead men. One was shot in the chest, and the other was shot in the head. They were lying on sleeping bags on top of the cots, and there was blood everywhere.

"This isn't good," McCain told Jack.

He removed his phone and took a few photos of the scene, then he zipped the door shut to help keep the flies away from the bodies. He started to dial Hernandez but still had no service down in the deep draw. Before he headed up to Barnes, he decided to look around a bit more. The two dead men weren't going anywhere.

In the other tent there was one cot covered with a sleeping bag, just like in the other tent. But this cot was free of dead bodies. There were a couple duffle bags with clothes scattered around, along with two Safeway bags loaded with packages of tortillas, bags of chips, cookies and other food.

In a third, smaller tent, McCain found tools. There were shovels, rakes, bags of fertilizer and other items, all evidently used to grow marijuana. McCain took photos inside and out of the other two tents and then scoured the area one more time. He found nothing more that told him what had happened here in the pot growers' camp.

He and Jack hustled up the hill, around the other side of the marijuana field, and found the trail back to Wallace's grave where Barnes remained.

"Give me your radio," he said to Barnes, half out of breath.

The deputy handed over his radio, and McCain said into it, "Deputy Hernandez, this is McCain."

"Yeah, go ahead."

"We've got a real situation here. I found the camp the pot growers were using and I've discovered two more dead bodies."

"What?"

Barnes echoed Hernandez as he looked at McCain in disbelief. "What?"

"Two Hispanic men. One shot in the head, and the other shot in the chest. It's pretty ugly. You better get some more folks up here."

"Yeah, roger that. Is the coroner there yet?"

"No, not yet. We'll get him down to the tents after he sees the body here. You might call his office and get another rig up here. I'm not sure his van is big enough for three bodies."

"Will do. Keep me posted."

"So you think Wallace shot those other two men before someone killed him?" Barnes asked.

"To tell you the truth, I'm not sure what happened. But Wallace was hunting with a muzzleloader. That's one shot, then you have to reload. And it's not a quick reload. Unless the men were drunk and passed out or drugged, it would be very hard to kill two people right next to each other with a muzzleloader."

"Maybe he had a pistol," Barnes said.

"I just don't think he was the shooter," McCain answered. "He was most likely in the wrong place at the wrong time. He stumbled into this deal, and it got him killed."

The coroner arrived a couple minutes later, and McCain told him everything that had happened. The coroner, whose name was Burt Jansen, cringed a little when McCain told him about the other two bodies located in the camp a ways down the mountain.

In his mid-50s with a bulbous nose and curly salt-and-pepper hair erupting out from under a black hat with KCC stitched in white letters on the front, Jansen was not designed to be hiking up and down any mountain. The man was at least forty pounds overweight, and when McCain saw him cringe, he wondered if he was upset by the two additional bodies or by the added hiking.

"Let me take care of a few details here, and then we can go look at the others," Jansen said.

"I'm going to hike up the hill to get some cell service so I can send a couple photos I took down at the camp to Hernandez," McCain said to the coroner. "Holler when you're ready to go to the camp."

Two investigators from the crime scene unit showed up as McCain was walking back down to the Wallace grave. He pointed out the surveyor's tape marking the spots where the blood was and where he had found the spent shell casing. Then he led them to the body in the pot field.

One of the crime scene folks stayed at the Wallace body, and McCain led the other, along with Coroner Jansen, down to the camp. He told the investigator everything he saw and did and then asked if he could be dismissed.

"Give me your card in case I have any questions," a female

coroner requested.

McCain eagerly obliged, called Jack, and they headed up the hill, hopefully for the last time that day.

On his way out, McCain ran into Kittitas County Sheriff Mark Anderson, who had also worked up a pretty good sweat walking into the crime scene. The two chatted for a few moments, and McCain told him everything he'd found. Anderson thanked him for all his help and then headed down to the pot field.

McCain counted three more deputies and two men who were packing stretchers into the site as he and Jack hiked out. McCain assumed they were from the coroner's office. They all had a long day and maybe night ahead of them.

CHAPTER 4

That evening, McCain and Sara headed to their favorite Chinese place, Taeka Wok. McCain always found humor in the name and wondered if the person who owned the restaurant was actually named Taeka or if someone was simply having fun with the play on words.

"Poor Mrs. Wallace," Sinclair said after listening to the events of the day. "I can't imagine what she's going through right now."

"Yeah, it's pretty sad," McCain said. "I really think her husband was in the wrong place at the wrong time, and there is something much bigger going on with this thing."

Sinclair had worked a drug-smuggling investigation two years prior, so she knew a little about it.

"You think it's the Sinaloa drug cartel that's driving all this?" McCain asked.

"I'm not sure, but it wouldn't surprise me," Sinclair said. "I know our offices along the west coast have been trying to keep track of them. They've been very active in Los Angeles, and stuff has been moving up and down I-5 pretty regularly."

"Do you think they would get involved in growing pot around here?"

"I think they have their hands in just about anything that involves illegal drugs, money laundering, sex trafficking and who knows what else."

"Nice bunch," McCain said as his order of General Tso's chicken arrived.

When the check and the fortune cookies arrived, Sara broke hers open and read it. She started laughing.

"Okay, read it to me," McCain said.

"It says, 'Confucius say: Man who drive like hell, bound to get there.'" She laughed again.

McCain loved her laugh. He didn't think the fortune was all that funny, but he laughed too.

"So, what's yours say?" she asked.

"Mine says: 'You'll be hungry in an hour.'"

Sinclair laughed.

As they were driving home, Sinclair's cell phone rang. McCain listened as she answered "yes" and "no" a few times. Then she said, "we're on it" and clicked off.

She turned to McCain and said, "Evidently, the Kittitas County Sheriff believes your discovery today is too big for his department, and he is asking for help from the FBI."

"And you're jumping in?"

"I need to talk to my boss, but I believe we will, yes. But let's not talk business tonight. Can you come into the office in the morning and share everything you saw and did?"

"I've already told you all that. Twice."

"Well, we're going to do it again, officially."

* * *

McCain was at Sinclair's office at nine o'clock the next morning, and he told her everything he did from the time he took the call and kissed her goodbye the previous morning until he arrived home at a little after six o'clock and fed Jack. He had sent her all the photos he'd taken at the field, the grave and the tents before he headed to the meeting.

"Okay, Officer McCain, I think that is everything for now. Can I call you if I have any more questions?"

"You know where to reach me. I'm the big guy sleeping on your left side."

She smiled at him but said nothing. He winked at her and closed her office door behind him on his way out.

Since he'd worked all day yesterday, a day that was supposed to be his day off, McCain decided he'd go grab Jack and do what he'd planned to do before he got the lost hunter call.

He drove home, changed out of his WDFW uniform, got into his hunting clothes and boots, grabbed his 16-gauge, double-barrel shotgun and headed for the truck. The second Jack saw McCain putting on his boots, he started to whine and could hardly sit still. Then, when the side-by-side shotgun came out, the dog started barking and jumping up and down.

"Take it easy," McCain said to the yellow dog. "You don't want to hurt yourself."

Jack didn't listen. He barked and jumped the entire thirty-foot walk from the front steps to the truck. McCain opened the back door of the truck, and Jack jumped in. After he fired up the rig, McCain put a Luke Bryan CD into the player, and in two minutes they were on State Route 12 headed west.

As he slowed to go through the little town of Naches, McCain checked his gas gauge. It registered a quarter of a tank. It was probably enough gas, he thought, but he decided to go ahead and fill up at the Chevron station next to the highway. He set the nozzle of the gas pump to fill automatically and went into the small store to get a soda and a candy bar.

He was just stepping up to the counter when in walked Jim Kingsbury. McCain could never quite figure out how old the gentleman was, but he was at least in his late 60s. A slender man with an impressive head of silver hair that flowed over his ears and shirt collar, Kingsbury was definitely retired. McCain would see him all over the place and often found him and a friend fishing on one of the local lakes or rivers. Kingsbury usually wore a Crocodile Dundee-style hat, and he always wore a shirt with some saying on it.

"Officer McCain. How are you today?" Kingsbury asked.

"Good, Jim," McCain said. He looked at the man's t-shirt. It was blue with bright yellow letters reading: "COME AT ME, BRO!"

"Sounds like you had an interesting day yesterday. I saw the report in the paper that a game warden with a tracking dog found the body of a lost hunter and two other dead bodies near an illegal marijuana field up by Ellensburg."

"Yep, Jack and I helped out up there."

"Any idea who did the killing?"

"Not a clue. The sheriff up there is on it. You been out doing any grouse hunting?"

"Yeah, me and Dugdale went by Jump Off Joe a couple days ago. We found a couple blues, but they flew up into a tree, and we never could find them. They were probably sitting up there just laughing at us."

Frank Dugdale, the man with three first names, was Kingsbury's hunting and fishing buddy. Normally, if you saw one, you'd see the other.

"They'll do that," McCain said. "Jack and I are headed up that way now."

"Well, good luck."

McCain finished gassing up, hopped in the truck, and said to Jack, "Finally. You ready to find a bird?" Jack wagged his tail and looked out the windshield like he was telling McCain to go this way and speed it up.

There is plenty of talk about the fall colors in the northeastern part of the United States, but McCain figured the higher Cascades in September would give Maine and Vermont a pretty good run for their money when it came to the beautiful colors of the deciduous trees and bushes. He loved this time of year. While the valley temperatures were often in the upper 70s, the mountains would be ten or fifteen degrees cooler. And if a bit of a breeze was blowing, you knew fall had arrived.

As he drove higher up SR 12, he noticed the western larches were turning yellow. The aspen, cottonwood and maple trees were also turning yellow and orange and red, with some of the bushes along the creeks already a brilliant red.

He turned off the highway and headed up the road to Bethel Ridge. The blue grouse, now called dusky grouse, liked to stay up on the ridges this time of year, and McCain knew a couple different watering holes where the grouse liked to hang out.

When they arrived at the first little spring that filled a small pond, he pulled off the dirt road, parked and let Jack out. As McCain put his shell vest on and grabbed his shotgun, Jack started working around the pond, nose down, tail spinning eighty miles an hour.

"Slow down," McCain said to the dog.

Jack obeyed. In fact, he stopped for a second and then took off faster than before. That told McCain the dog was hot on the scent of a bird.

Jack cut through a small stand of young pine trees, and as soon as he got on the other side, three grouse flushed. As often happens in grouse hunting, the birds had put the trees between themselves and the hunter, so McCain heard the birds flush but couldn't see them. Or he couldn't see them at first. One of the grouse made the mistake of curving to the right just enough.

McCain quickly found the bird over the two barrels of his shotgun, put a good lead on the fast moving grouse, and pulled the trigger.

"Fetch, Jack!" McCain yelled.

But it wasn't necessary. Just as the words were leaving his mouth, he caught sight of a yellow blur moving through the grass, and in an instant the dog had gathered the downed grouse in his mouth and was proudly bringing it back to McCain. He praised the dog for his work and tried to pet him, but Jack was having none of that. There were still two birds out there somewhere, and he immediately turned to go find them.

Even if Jack did find them, McCain wasn't going to take another shot. He had a nice young grouse for dinner, and it was plenty to feed him and Sara. He did follow Jack, though. He loved walking these mountains, and he and Jack spent the next three hours hiking and resting and just enjoying a perfect fall day in the beautiful Cascades.

CHAPTER 5

Sinclair and the Kittitas County Sheriff investigators weren't making much headway in the deaths of the three men near the marijuana grow. As McCain had suspected, Shane Wallace had been ambushed where McCain and Jack found the blood. Based on the shell casing and the entrance wound in the man's chest, the coroners concluded Wallace had been hit by a bullet from a smaller-caliber rifle. Investigators had yet to find the bullet, so trying to match it to a rifle was a dead end.

The two men found in the camp had IDs, but they were fakes. Officials assumed they were Mexican nationals who had entered the United States illegally. Sinclair ran fingerprints with the Mexican national police and found a match for one of the men, a Rafael Ortiz-Sanchez. He had served time in a federal prison in Mexico for kidnapping.

Kittitas County Sheriff deputies had done some checking at a house in Ellensburg that Ortiz-Sanchez listed as his address on his driver's license. They showed the dead man's photo around, but nobody would come forward to say they knew him.

The coroner had determined both men were killed by a thirty-caliber rifle. With two different caliber rifles involved in the killing of the three men, Sinclair and the sheriff's investigators were going on the belief there were two different shooters.

"Did the coroner nail down a time of death for the men?" McCain asked Sinclair as they were discussing the investigation one morning, a week after the bodies were discovered.

"He put Wallace's death most likely sometime mid-day on Saturday."

"And the two men in the camp?"

"He was less sure on that. Could have been as early as Friday evening or as late as Sunday morning."

"There was only one cot in the second tent," he said. "So, I'm thinking that since he had the tent to himself, he was the boss or foreman."

"You're assuming it was another man," Sinclair said. "What if the other person was a woman who had the tent to herself, and she was forcibly taken at the time the men were shot?"

"That's a possibility, but the brief look I got at the clothes in the tent with the single cot made me think they were all men."

"Yeah, that's what I thought too. Still we can't totally rule out the person staying in the tent was a woman."

"I agree. What did the DEA say about the whole deal?"

The Drug Enforcement Agency or DEA had agents in Central Washington full time, trying to keep track of where the different drugs were coming from and where they were going. Yakima had become a hub for much of the drug activity in the Northwest, so the DEA agents stayed busy.

"They are almost positive the marijuana was planted and farmed by the cartel," Sinclair said. "They know some of the main players and are keeping an eye on them, but so far there has been no connection to the dead men in the tent."

McCain asked her what they were going to do with the pot field, and she explained that Kittitas County deputies and several Washington State Patrol officers came in and, with the help of a bulldozer, removed all the plants, pushed them into a big pile, and had a giant bonfire.

"I hope they stayed upwind," McCain said.

"They were wearing hazard suits and masks, so their air was filtered."

"How in the world did they get a dozer up there?"

"Basically, they started at the trail down on the Forest Service road below and dozed a path up to the field."

"Hmmm, I would've liked to see that."

After chatting about the investigation for a bit longer, McCain announced he was going to finish a few reports at the office and then go check on some elk hunters with Jack.

"Sounds like fun," Sara said as she kissed McCain on the cheek. "I gotta run too."

* * *

McCain finished with his paperwork just before noon and was heading out the door when WDFW fish biologist Andrea Parker stopped him.

Parker was an attractive thirty-something with dirty dishwater blonde hair that was always wound up into a bun on the back of her head. She wore black-framed glasses and very little make-up. Today, she was in khaki slacks and a white blouse that looked to be at least one size too big. McCain always wondered if she intentionally kept an unattractive look.

"Hi Luke," she said. "You got a minute?"

"Sure, what's up?"

"I was up on the Little Naches yesterday afternoon, checking on some chinook salmon redds, and discovered a place where someone is driving vehicles across the river. They're destroying good nesting habitat for salmon and trout. Any chance you can take a look up there and see what's going on?"

"I'd be happy to," McCain said. "In fact, I was heading up that way right now, so I'll check it out."

McCain and Parker had some history. They had dated when he first arrived in Yakima, but after a couple dates McCain knew it just wasn't going to work, and he told her so. Unfortunately, Parker hadn't taken it too well, and she seemed to always be carrying a little grudge against him. Any chance she could get a little dig in on him, especially in front of their boss, she would. Parker was constantly hounding him about checking anglers in the streams in the Central Cascades that were home to the endangered bull trout.

In this case, she certainly had good reason to ask him to check out the illegal off-road activity. The use of four-wheelers and side-by-sides was becoming more and more popular in the mountains. Hunters used them to navigate the many Forest Service and old logging roads, and others just liked to get out of town and ride the ATVs. On any Sunday afternoon when the weather was good, there would be a parade of rigs pulling trailers loaded with various off-road vehicles coming down out of the mountains after a fun weekend of riding. Most of the ATVs would be caked in dried mud.

There were plenty of roads for the riders to use, some created just for them, but that never seemed to be quite enough for a few. It was illegal to leave the designated roads, yet drivers who weren't too concerned about that drove off the roads occasionally. It was especially egregious when they drove through the streams. While he didn't always agree with Parker's frequent hand-wringing and complaining, this time she was right – the ATVs were destroying good salmon-spawning habitat, and frankly, it pissed McCain off.

He left the office, took SR 12, and turned south near the town of Gleed, toward the house he shared with Sinclair. It wasn't a fancy house, but it was out of town, close to good fishing on the Naches River, and the fenced back yard was a perfect place for

Jack to hang out when he wasn't accompanying McCain in the field.

When he pulled into the driveway, he could see the big yellow dog peeking through a space in the fence.

"You ready to go to work, boy?" McCain asked the dog.

At that, Jack started jumping up and down and then headed to the back door. McCain let him in, and Jack shot straight through to the front door, ready to go.

"Slow down," McCain said. "Let me get a few supplies in case we're up there a while."

Once he had his to-go pack loaded with some water and treats, for both him and the dog, McCain threw it over his shoulder, patted his hip, and he and Jack headed to the truck for the drive into the Cascades.

There are two passes travelers can take to cross the Cascades from Yakima to the bigger cities of the Puget Sound area in Western Washington. State Route 12 goes over White Pass, and State Route 410 goes over Chinook Pass. White Pass circles around the southern side of Mt. Rainier, and 410 takes drivers around the north side of the big mountain. McCain and Jack had been grouse hunting up along SR 12, but today they were headed out on 410. And as glorious as the fall trees had been on White Pass a few days before, they would surely be even more spectacular on Chinook Pass.

McCain drove past a couple small restaurants on the way up the mountain, passing a few campgrounds along the Naches River. Quite a few cabins and summer homes sat near the river too, but the higher he went up the highway, the fewer and fewer settlements he saw. When he reached the spot where the Little Naches River fed the Naches, McCain turned off the highway and slowly began working his way up the road that followed the river. Parker had shown him on a map where she had seen the tire tracks crossing the little river, and he was concentrating on that when he met a couple side-by-side ATVs coming down the road.

The men on the ATVs were outfitted all in camouflaged clothing which told McCain they were most likely muzzleloader hunters. He pulled slightly off the road, rolled down his window and stuck his hand out, indicating to the drivers to stop.

"Fancy meeting you here," one of the men said. "We were just going to find some phone service to call you or the sheriff."

"Well, here I am," McCain said. "What's going on?"

"We're pretty sure we saw a guy shoot an elk with a rifle," the driver of the first ATV said. "We couldn't see the elk, but we saw him shooting at something, and it was definitely a rifle."

"It had a scope, a short skinny barrel, and it sounded just like a rifle," the passenger in the first vehicle said. "Scopes aren't legal on muzzleloaders."

"I'm pretty up to speed on the laws," McCain said. "So where was this and when did it happen?"

The men told him that it had happened about two hours earlier, and they were at least a couple miles off the road. They said they had parked their side-by-side on a small two-track logging road and had taken off to the west on foot.

"So, you didn't go over to try to see what the guy was shooting at or if he had hit anything?" McCain asked.

"No, but we marked the spot on our GPS, and we can take you right to it. If he has an elk down, he'll most likely still be in there dealing with the meat."

"Okay, I'll follow you. I don't think we all need to go," McCain said to the two guys on the second ATV. "If you want to keep hunting, there's no sense in you guys wasting good daylight. By the way, you all do have your licenses and tags, right?"

The men all confirmed they had all the appropriate paperwork, and without checking, McCain told them they were good to go.

"Lead the way," he said to the two men on the first ATV.

CHAPTER 6

McCain followed the ATV riders up the road about six miles. There, they pulled off, parked, removed their helmets, and walked back to McCain's F-150 patrol rig.

"We were in about two miles, due west," the ATV driver said. "We can lead you in if you want us to."

"I don't think that's necessary," McCain said. "Give me your GPS coordinates, and my Lab and I will go in and give it a good look."

The men each grabbed their GPS units and confirmed the coordinates where they'd seen the man fire his rifle. McCain punched the coordinates into his GPS, and a map showed him the path he needed to take to reach the waypoint.

"And tell me again what this guy looked like," McCain said.

"It was hard to tell, but he looked real fit," the ATV driver said. "And I think I could see some dark around his ears. He was wearing a camo hat, so I couldn't swear to it."

"His hair might have been more brown than black," the second ATV guy said. "Because he was so fit he looked tall, but again we were quite a ways away, so it was hard to tell. His legs looked long to me."

"What was he wearing?"

"Typical hunter gear," said the driver. "Camo from head to toe. He did have a small backpack on. And the rifle was black. The scope, the barrel, the sling – everything was black."

"He could have been Hispanic or Native American," the passenger said. "Or a guy with a really nice tan."

"Okay, thanks guys."

"I'm sure that describes about half the hunters in the woods right now, but hope it helps," the ATV passenger said.

Before he let the men go, he took down their information and gave each of them his card. Hunters who report a major game violation stood to receive extra bonus points toward special hunts in future years. McCain wanted to make sure these men got their points if and when he found the hunter who may have shot an elk out of season with his rifle.

"Thanks again, guys," McCain said as he sent them on their way. "I'll let you know what I find out."

With that, McCain shouldered his daypack, let Jack out of the truck, and they were on the way up and over a tree-covered ridge.

As they hiked in the direction of the waypoint, McCain let Jack run as much as he wanted. It was good exercise for the dog, and with the pheasant and quail seasons opening in a couple weeks, it helped him build some stamina. The hiking was good for McCain too, and he pushed himself as he kept an eye on his GPS to make sure he stayed on track.

He watched Jack run through the trees while keeping an eye out for any hunter or hunters who might be coming out with meat on their back. Shooting a bull elk and getting it back to a rig some two miles away is a massive undertaking. It definitely isn't a knock-'em-down, drag-'em-out situation. The animal would need to be, at the minimum, quartered and packed out by a horse, or on a person's back. Many hunters also would debone the meat, making the pack-out a little less burdensome.

When he arrived at the waypoint, McCain slowed and surveyed the surroundings. He also stopped and listened. If it was a hunter who shot an elk, and he had a partner, chances were they'd be talking. He looked at Jack to see if the dog had heard anything, but he was busy sniffing around some low brush, maybe looking for grouse. McCain knew from his many years of hunting that getting to a high point was the best strategy for searching with binoculars. He whistled for Jack, who fell in alongside him, and they headed to a small rise on the ridge some 250 yards away.

When they reached the small rise, McCain sat down, pulled his binoculars out of his pack, and began searching all around. It was unlikely the man could have gotten the whole elk out of the area in the time since the men had seen him shoot, but even if he had moved it some, McCain was hoping he could find a gut pile or some other evidence of a kill.

He searched one side of the ridge from the high point and found nothing, so he moved to the other side and immediately found something he wasn't expecting to see. There in a big draw, covered by fir trees, was another marijuana grow. The pot field wasn't as large as the one in Kittitas County, but it still was plenty big, and the plants were as tall as the ones he'd seen a few days prior.

"We'd better go check it out," he said to Jack.

Before heading that way, he thought about Shane Wallace and decided to take one more good look around the pot field. As he searched the edge of the field – inch by inch, foot by foot – he spotted something out of place. He wasn't positive, but he thought he was looking at a human hand. It was as if the hand was reaching out from inside the pot field, pleading for help.

"Okay, Jack," McCain said, still studying the hand. "Let's go check it out."

He took it very slowly down the hill, watching all around him as he went. He kept Jack at heel and watched the dog as they snuck through the trees. Jack always seemed to sense, hear, and see things before McCain did, and right now he was glad the dog was at his side.

When he got to the field, McCain confirmed what he thought he had seen from up on the hill. There was a hand sticking out of the pot field, and it was still attached to a man – a very dead man with a bullet hole in the center of his chest. McCain could tell from the blood and the lack of rigor mortis that the man had only been dead for a short time, maybe less than four hours.

McCain checked around the body and found a hoe and a bucket filled with fertilizer. The man, who looked to be Hispanic, was most likely one of the boots-on-the-ground growers and, like the two men McCain had discovered in the tent at the pot field in Kittitas County, this man had come to a very suspicious and untimely death.

McCain thought about it for a minute. The man the elk hunters had seen was shooting at something, but they hadn't seen what. They assumed, because it was elk hunting season, he was shooting at an elk even though he was using a high-powered rifle during muzzleloader season. But could he have been shooting at this man in the marijuana field?

McCain needed to call the sheriff's office and notify them of what he'd found. He had no cell service down in this draw, so he'd have to get to a high point in order to call out, or else hike back to his truck to get through on the radio. Before he headed out, though, he wanted to take another look around.

As he had done at the other pot field, McCain walked around the edge of the field. Once again, he found the camp where the man, or men, who were tending to the crops lived. There was just one tent, identical to the ones he'd seen at the other field.

McCain, with Jack at his side, stayed back and watched and listened. After seeing and hearing nothing, he moved forward to check out the tent. When he zipped the tent door open, he found a cot, covered by a sleeping bag. There were a couple bags of food and a few dirty clothes stuffed in one corner. Outside the tent, he found a cheap barbecue and some gardening tools.

Seeing nothing more of interest, McCain took photos of the small camp and then walked the lower perimeter of the field and up the other side until he was at the man's body again. One more time, he took out his bright orange surveyor's tape and flagged the area so that whoever came in from the sheriff's office could locate it. He also took several photos of the body and the surrounding area.

"We need to go make some calls," McCain said to Jack, who looked up at him. "Sara is going to want to see this too."

He and Jack worked quickly back up the hill, on high alert for anyone who might be hunting people. When he got to the same high point on the ridgetop, he checked his phone. One bar showed on the little service meter in the corner of his phone screen. He tried to call but couldn't get it to go through.

"We're going to have to go back to the truck anyway," McCain told Jack, who heard the word truck and headed back in its direction.

As he hiked back, McCain pondered the similarities between the two murder scenes. Could this just be a coincidence? Was one drug cartel trying to take out another? He really wanted to talk to Sara.

When he got to the truck, he dropped his daypack, peeled off a layer of clothes, drank a bottle of water, and poured another in a dish for Jack, who quickly lapped it up. He climbed in the truck and radioed dispatch.

"Wildlife 148 calling for Yakima County Sheriff's office," McCain said into the radio.

"Roger, Wildlife 148," said the woman's voice. "Patching you through now."

"Yakima County Sheriff's office," said a different woman over the radio.

"Yeah, this is Wildlife Officer McCain. I'm up the Little Naches and have discovered a dead body in an illegal marijuana grow. Need assistance from your office and the coroner."

"Ten-four," replied the dispatcher.

A minute later, a man's voice came over the radio. "Hey, Rifleman. What you got going up on the hill?"

It was Deputy Bill Williams. He was the only one who regularly called McCain the Rifleman. He did so because the sheriff in the 1950s TV western was named Lucas McCain, and the show was called *The Rifleman*. The fictitious McCain used a specially equipped 30-30 Winchester rifle instead of a revolver to keep his little town safe from scofflaws.

"Found a dead body in an illegal pot field up on the Little Naches. Just shot. I think some elk hunters may have witnessed the shooting, although we need to check it out further."

"Didn't you and Jack just find some dead bodies near a pot field up in Kittitas County?"

"Yes, and it's my guess this is related."

"Okay, tell me again where you are, and I'll get rolling that way. And I'll get the coroner headed that way too."

"I'll be waiting for you at my truck. Oh, and can you let Agent Sinclair know what is going on? If it is related to the murders up in Kittitas County, she'll want to be here to see this."

"Ten-four. We'll get there as quickly as we can."

CHAPTER 7

It took just over an hour for Williams to arrive. He pulled in next to McCain's truck, hopped out and started toward McCain and Jack, who was sleeping in some grass in the shade of the truck. Williams was a fit fifty-two-year-old guy with dark hair, dark eyes and a face that always seemed to be contorted into a look of someone who was half pissed-off. A twenty-five-year veteran of the sheriff's office, Williams and McCain worked several cases together over the past seven years, and had developed a friendship. When Jack saw Williams, he jumped up and went to greet the deputy.

"Hello, Jack!" Williams said and rubbed the yellow dog's ears. "You guys sure know how to find trouble."

"We figured you needed something else to do," McCain said. "We were up here to check on the muzzleloader hunters, and I had a tip from a biologist that some four-wheelers were running through the river where they shouldn't be."

"So, how did you come to find a dead guy and another marijuana field?"

"Long story. Is Sara coming?"

"Yep, she's about ten minutes behind me. Guess you might

40

as well wait to tell the story until she gets here. It'll save you from having to tell it twice."

The two men shot the breeze for a few minutes until they saw Sinclair roaring up the road, a cloud of dust trailing her.

"You made good time," Williams said as Sinclair climbed out of her big, black Chrysler 300 sedan. "I'm not going to have to issue you a speeding ticket, am I?"

"Put a cork in it, Williams," Sinclair said. "I'm in no mood for jokes. I got called out of a Zoom meeting with a bunch of department heads in DC. They weren't happy, but they'll get over it. So, what's up, Luke?"

"Gear up for the hike in," McCain said. "I can tell you what happened on the way."

With Jack leading, the three hiked the two miles back to the spot where McCain had first glassed the pot field.

"I'm pretty sure this is where the shooter was, based on the description from the ATV guys," McCain said. "I've done very little looking around for a spent cartridge, tracks, or any other evidence."

"Okay, let's mark a big circle around here and then head down to the body," Williams said. "We can give it a thorough search later."

Since it was yet to be determined if the shooting was related to the ones in Kittitas County, the FBI was not officially on this case, and the Yakima Sheriff's Office was currently in charge of the investigation. Williams took the lead taping off the area on the top of the knoll, and then they all headed down the hill, searching for boot tracks or any other evidence.

When they reached the body, McCain and Jack stood back and let Williams and Sinclair take photos and assess the scene.

"The coroner was on another call in the Lower Valley," Williams said. "So it may be a while before he gets up here. And he'll need someone to lead him in."

"Jack and I can go back out and wait for him."

"That would be good," Williams said.

"Do you need to take us to the camp?" Sinclair asked.

"I don't think so. Just follow the edge of the field down, cut back around, and you'll run right into it."

"Okay," she said. "Go get the coroner."

Jack was sitting obediently up the hill a few yards, right where McCain had told him to sit and stay.

"Come on, boy. We've got some more hiking to do."

When they got back to the truck, McCain again radioed the YSO dispatcher and asked if she might have an ETA on the coroner.

"He said he'd be there about five o'clock. So, in a half hour or so."

"Received."

McCain turned to Jack and said, "We have a little time to kill. Let's go see if we can find where those ATVs were crossing the river."

McCain drove back down the Forest Service road and parked where Parker had marked the spot. He let Jack out, and they headed down a slight grade to the river. First, they walked up the stream a ways. Spotting nothing out of the ordinary, they turned and walked downstream. They had gone a couple hundred yards down the river when McCain spotted an obvious illegal crossing. The bank leading into the water was torn up, as was the other side. Because the water was shallow, the tire tracks in the gravel river bottom were easy to see.

"Damned idiots," McCain said out loud.

Again, he pulled out his phone and took several photos of both sides of the river and the tracks in the river bottom.

"Okay, Jack. I've seen enough. I can't wait to catch these guys."

Jack wagged his tail and made a happy face. He appeared to

be eager to catch the idiots too, although he was probably just happy hearing his name.

They were just getting back to their truck when the coroner's van came up the road. The driver stopped when he saw McCain's truck.

"Hey, Luke," Dan Duchovy said. "Is this the spot?"

Unlike the Kittitas County coroner, Duchovy, the Yakima County Coroner, was in pretty good shape for a man in his early 50s. He was average height, with the build of a man who either ran or walked regularly. Duchovy always wore a ball cap with YCO stitched on the front, so McCain had no idea if he had a full head of hair or was bald.

"No, we need to head up the road a few miles, and then it's about two miles on foot."

"Guess I'll get my steps in today. You think you or Deputy Williams can help me bring out the body? Nobody was available to help."

"Yeah, I'll be glad to. I will definitely have my steps in for today. But it's all good. I want to be in shape for hunting season. This'll help, for sure."

When they got back to the vehicles, Duchovy pulled out a portable stretcher and a backpack. He put the pack on and looked at McCain.

"Lead the way," he said.

McCain whistled for Jack, and for the third time that afternoon, he was off to the marijuana field and the dead body, its hand reaching out for help.

CHAPTER 8

When McCain got up the next morning, his legs were a little sore. He wandered into the kitchen, and when he didn't see Sara sitting in her normal spot, drinking her day's first cup of coffee, he called out to her.

"In here," she said from the spare bedroom, now a makeshift office.

McCain grabbed a cup of coffee and asked if Sara needed a refill.

"No, I'm good. I've already had two cups and I don't need the caffeine jitters just yet."

He went into the bedroom-slash-office and found Sinclair sitting at her laptop, scrolling through the photos she had taken the afternoon before.

"See anything of interest?" he asked.

"No, not really. Except that the tent, cot, fertilizer and some tools are exactly the same as the ones we found in Kittitas County. That tells me all this is related. The bigger question is motive. Why are the growers being murdered?"

"I've been thinking about that, and the only thing that really comes to mind is a rival gang or cartel that wants to shut this down. You've dealt with this drug stuff before. What do you think?"

"It could be that, but for some reason this seems too small and isolated. Hopefully, the coroner can get an ID on the dead man, and we can follow up on him."

"I take it you think you'll be overseeing this one too, once they determine it is related?"

"Oh, it's related. I told Williams so last night. He was going to run it by the sheriff this morning. I expect to be getting a call any time."

"Okay, well let me know if you need any assistance. I'm going to shower and head into the office. Then Jack and I are going to head back up and see if we can find the guys running their ATVs through the Little Naches River."

When he got to the office, McCain took out his notepad, picked up the phone, and dialed the number for the guy driving the ATV who had alerted McCain to the shooter.

"Yeah, this is Art," a voice replied.

"Hey, Mr. Duncan. This is Officer McCain of the WDFW. I just wanted to let you know what your tip helped us discover. I'd also like to ask you a few more questions."

"Sure, Officer McCain. I hope you caught that guy. It's not fair to be shooting elk with a rifle during muzzleloader season."

"That's just it. We now think the guy wasn't an elk hunter at all. We think he shot a man who was working in an illegal pot field not far from where you saw him shooting the rifle."

"No kidding? That's wild. We might have actually watched a murder?"

"I know you said the rifle was all black, but could you tell if it was a hunting rifle or what the news media is now calling an assault rifle?"

"I know what an AR rifle looks like. I have a couple myself. No, it wasn't an AR. It was a regular-style hunting rifle, just it was all black."

"Okay, did you see the man move after the shot? Did he head toward the direction he shot, or did he walk a different direction?"

"You know, we watched him for a bit after the shot, and he just stood there, watching through his scope. We thought he had dropped an elk and was making sure it didn't get up and run off like they sometimes do. Geez, maybe he was watching the man to make sure he didn't get up."

"That could be. So you never saw him go?"

"No, he was still standing there when we turned to head back to our ATVs to call the sheriff."

"Was he shooting right-handed or left-handed?"

The man thought about that for a second and said, "I'm almost positive he was shooting right-handed, but with the blue-sky background, it could have been an optical illusion, and he was actually shooting left-handed."

"Okay, well thanks, Mr. Duncan. If I have any more questions, I'll give you a call."

McCain next called Brad Clark, the man who was riding with Duncan, and asked him the same questions. Clark, like Duncan, was amazed they might have watched a murder take place. And he answered all the questions pretty much the same as Duncan had. The shooter never moved, and he looked like he was shooting right-handed.

When he hung up with Clark, McCain sat for a second and thought about it more. Could the man have been a hunter who mistakenly shot the worker in the pot, thinking he was an elk? It happens occasionally, where a hunter gets so excited he or she believes they are shooting at a deer or a turkey or a bear, and boom, they injure or kill a person. Or was it a hunter who saw the guy doing something illegal and, in the heat of the moment, decided to take the law into his own hands? Maybe he was just trying to scare the guy and hit him accidentally. But that didn't take into consideration the two Kittitas County pot growers who were killed in their beds. That was no accident, McCain reminded himself. He figured ballistics on any bullets found in the men might help tie the two shootings together. Or not.

"Did you get a chance to check out those illegal crossings up on the Little Naches?" a female voice asked as he was thinking about the shootings.

Andrea Parker was like a pit bull. Especially when it came to her beloved bull trout and their habitat.

"Actually, I did Andrea," McCain said as he spun around in his desk chair to face her. "I got a good look at it and took some photos. But as you might have heard, I was a little busy after finding a dead guy in an illegal pot field."

"Yeah, I heard about that. I didn't mean to push," she said, meaning to push. "That's pretty creepy. I don't know what I would do if I found a dead body."

"Sure, you do. You'd do what I did. Phone the sheriff and assist where you could. I am planning on heading back up to the place where the ATVs were crossing after I get done here. I'm hoping to learn some more when I get there."

"Great," she said and walked away.

"You're welcome," McCain mumbled under his breath, almost hoping she'd hear it. He thought maybe he'd get a thank you once in a while. He did notice that today, for some reason, Parker wasn't wearing her trademark bookworm glasses, and her clothes weren't quite as baggy.

Before he left, he had one more thought and dialed Art Duncan again.

"Officer McCain," Duncan said by way of answering the phone.

"Sorry to bother you again, Mr. Duncan, but I had another question, not related to the murder."

"Sure, what can I help you with?"

"I was up the Little Naches, investigating a report of some

ATV riders crossing the river there illegally, when I ran into you guys coming down the road. They're tearing up the riverbanks and messing up the river bottom. Have you seen or heard of anyone doing that in the area?"

"You know, I did hear some guys running off-road in that area a few days ago. I just figured it was a hunter who was going to haul out an elk."

"Elk or no, it is illegal to be running off designated roads, and crossing a stream is an even bigger violation."

"Totally agree," Duncan said. "I guess I should have called the sheriff at that point, but I was by myself, and it sounded like two or three ATVs. I didn't want a hassle. I will certainly call if I see or hear anything like that in the future."

"I would appreciate it," McCain said. "If you hear of anything from your other buddies too, you have my number."

After returning a few more phone calls, McCain ran home, picked up Jack, and they headed back up SR 410 to the place where he had found the off-road damage.

As McCain was driving up past Naches, he called Sinclair.

"Hey, Luke. What's up?"

"Just wanted to check in. Jack and I are on our way back to the Little Naches to check out the illegal off-road stuff. Did you get the call from the sheriff?"

"Yep, we're officially in charge of the shooting from yesterday, and while there's no concrete evidence the shootings are related, everyone I've talked with from the FBI and the DEA believes it to be so."

"Makes sense. I'm not planning on being up here all day, so we should be home by dinnertime."

"Okay, be careful, and no more bodies please. It's the last thing any of us needs."

He and Jack arrived at the illegal river crossing and spent some time looking around. They found nothing that might help them identify the culprits, so McCain decided to follow the tracks up the hill to see if they might end at a gut pile where a hunter might have killed an elk, as Art Duncan had speculated.

With Jack running ahead of him, McCain followed the tire tracks up the hill for about a half mile, and then back down the hill where they hit a spur road to the main Forest Service road. The riders – McCain could tell there were at least two based on the different tire tracks – had just made a loop after crossing the river, up through the trees and back around. They may have parked and gotten off at some point, but McCain didn't find any evidence of that.

He figured the ATV riders were probably not hunters, but just weekenders who were getting off the main road. McCain would call Williams when he got back down the hill and let him know what he found, so that maybe he could have the deputy that patrolled Chinook Pass keep an eye on the spot.

Because he would be here often during this and the other upcoming big game seasons, McCain would keep an eye on it too. And he had one other trick up his sleeve. WDFW had recently invested in some trail cameras, and in the next day or so he'd discreetly hang a couple in the trees along the illegal trail.

Before he headed back to town, McCain decided to drive up the Little Naches and check out some of the hunting camps set up there. The general hunting season opener was approaching, and he knew there would be some folks getting camps ready for the season. Many would keep the camps up through the end of the elk season in early November.

The first camp he came to was a hubbub of activity. There were three ATVs sitting next to two pickups. An older man who looked a little like Donald Sutherland was splitting kindling, and two other younger men were putting up a wall tent. They all stopped what they were doing as McCain pulled in next to their rigs.

"How's it going, fellas?" McCain said as he exited the truck. He told Jack to stay.

"Good," the Donald Sutherland lookalike said. "Just getting things set up for the next three weeks."

"What's the word on the deer populations?" one of the younger men asked. He was wearing blue jeans, a red plaid shirt and a camo hat with the Browning deer logo on it.

"Still not great, but they're doing a bit better," McCain said. "I actually saw a nice four-point buck up here about a week ago, and I'm seeing a few younger legal bucks around."

"We're mainly elk hunters," said the older man. "But we like to get our camp set up early so we can have our spot. We've been coming up here since 1988."

"I see you've got some ATVs," McCain said. "Just wanted to remind you to stay on the main and open roads. We've had some illegal off-road activity, and the county sheriffs and I will be up here really keeping an eye on things."

"For sure," said the second young camper, who looked a lot like the first but with a different-colored plaid shirt and a red hat with a Winchester logo. "Dad likes to drive the roads on his, but we mostly use the other ones to get to the spots where we take off to hunt."

McCain handed the older gentleman his card and said, "If you see anyone off the roads, please give me a call."

"Sure will," the older man said. "Say, we had kind of a strange conversation with a guy earlier this morning. He pulled in and asked if we had seen any illegal marijuana fields when we'd been out scouting. We thought he might be DEA or something, but he never identified himself as law enforcement."

"We've done a little scouting in the past couple weeks," the youngest of the three men said. "But we haven't seen anything like that and told him so."

"When he heard that, he thanked us, jumped in his truck

and drove off," the other young man said. "Kind of weird, we thought. Has there been a problem with illegal pot being grown up here?"

"There has been for years, but just recently we've had a couple of unusual murders associated with them here in Yakima County and up in Kittitas County. What did the guy look like?"

"He was maybe fifty or so," said the youngest man.

"His hair was light brown and cut real short," the older man said. "He was wearing sunglasses, so we couldn't see his eyes. Had a nice tan and kind of looked like a cop."

"How tall was he?"

"Might have been a little over six foot," the younger man with the Winchester hat said. "He was about my height, and I'm six-one. He probably weighed around 185. Looked to be in good shape."

"What was he driving?"

"A white Chevy pickup, real similar to mine," the Sutherland lookalike said as he pointed to the newer of the two white trucks sitting next to the camp.

"Anything on the truck that might make it stand out?" McCain asked.

"Nope, it looks like the other hundred thousand white Chevy pickups on the road today," the youngest man said.

McCain thanked the men, wished them good luck on their hunt, and jumped back in his pickup. He thought about the man in the white Chevy for a minute, until Jack snuck up and licked him on the cheek.

"Oh, sorry, boy. I guess I forgot about you for a second."

Jack gave him another slobbery lick and wagged his tail.

McCain drove up the road and pulled in to two other camps. The people in the camps told him the same story the first group of hunters had. The man in the white pickup had also talked to them, asking about illegal pot fields. None of the folks had been doing any scouting yet, so they had nothing to tell the man, and he drove off without much small talk.

"Was he a cop?" a young lady in the third camp asked McCain. "He sure looked like one."

"I don't know," McCain answered. "Could be, I guess."

As McCain drove back down the Little Naches Road, he thought about the man asking about the marijuana fields. He could be DEA, McCain thought. But he might just be the man shooting workers at the pot fields. He wished one of the campers had written down a license plate, but none had. The man at the first camp was right. There were thousands of white Chevy pickups around, and without tag numbers it would be next to impossible to find this one. He would check with Sara tonight to see if she knew of any DEA guys that fit the description the campers had given him.

McCain thought back to the meeting he had with the men on the ATVs coming down this very same road earlier. They had given a description of the man they saw shoot from the knoll above the marijuana field. But they were a long ways away, and the description was pretty general. They thought the man was possibly Hispanic. It could have been the same man, or any one of a hundred guys who were fairly tall, lean, tan and fit.

As he drove back down SR 410, McCain slowed as he passed Whistlin' Jacks. There was a restaurant, bar and mini-mart there – a popular spot with folks traveling Chinook Pass east and west over the Cascades. He scanned the rigs in the parking lot and saw not one but two white Chevy trucks. He quickly pulled into the lot.

McCain told Jack to stay and headed for the restaurant.

"Just one today?" asked a perky, little, red-haired hostess when McCain walked into the lobby of the restaurant.

"No, thanks," McCain said. "Just wanted to see if my buddy is here. I think that's his truck in the parking lot."

"Oh, okay," the young hostess said. "You're welcome to go

take a look and see if he's in the dining room."

McCain walked around the corner and took a quick look around at the few diners in the room. None fit the description the men at the camp had given, so he went around the corner into the mini-mart. There were only two people in there besides the man behind the counter, and since the shoppers were women, they obviously weren't who he was looking for.

While he was in the store, McCain grabbed a bottle of Diet Pepsi, started to reach for a candy bar, thought better of it, paid for his soda, and headed back to the truck. Jack was very happy to see him.

"You were just hoping for a bite of candy bar," McCain said. "Well, you're out of luck. It's too close to dinnertime."

Before he took off, McCain looked back around the parking lot one more time. When he saw that one of the white Chevy pickups was gone, he wondered how that had happened so quickly.

As McCain drove home, he thought more about the river crossing and the man asking about the pot fields. Then he thought it was a relief that at least another pot farmer hadn't died today.

He was partly right.

CHAPTER 9

Juan Delgado was a pot farmer for the Sinaloa cartel. He had come into the United States illegally, and because the cartel had helped him make it to Washington State, he felt he owed them. Actually, they worked hard at making him feel that way. He would have been happy taking an honest job working in the fields or the orchards, but when one of the officers in the cartel offered him a good wage to work in the mountains, tending to the marijuana, he decided there were worse things he could do.

As it turned out, Delgado had a knack for growing weed. He was good at finding spots to grow the pot where it thrived and stayed mostly camouflaged from the prying eyes of the police in their planes flying overhead. The more successful he became, the more responsibility the cartel gave him.

Now, eight years after his arrival in the United States, he was no longer one of the pot field workers. He supervised the different grows around the region. He'd help pick a spot for the field, then oversee the planting, fertilizing, watering and harvesting of the crops.

Delgado had never killed anyone before. But when he saw

the hunter snooping around the field, he knew he had to do something, because if the illegal pot was reported to the police, he'd lose a large potential bonus. He wanted that money. He needed that money.

He had just left the camp where he and his two field workers had stayed the previous night. He grabbed his AR-15 and a few other personal items and was starting to walk down the creek to his truck when he heard a shot just above the camp.

Delgado knew hunting season was open, but so far none of the hunters had ventured this far off the road. At the sound of the shot, he turned and went back up, past the camp. The two workers had come out of the tent and were looking around. Delgado told them to relax, that he'd go check it out.

He circled back around, up to the top of the field. When he looked down, he saw the hunter standing at the edge of the field. Delgado thought the man had his phone out, making a call. He couldn't let that happen. He raised his rifle, centered the man in the scope, and shot.

That's when he got scared. Now what was he going to do? He had to get rid of the body, and his thought was to bury him in the pot field, and then, when it came time to harvest the field, he'd pack the body out of the mountains and dump it in the Columbia River with a couple concrete blocks tied to the legs. Everything was going to work out, Delgado told himself. Then, someone had discovered the field and the hunter's body, and somehow, sometime after he'd left the camp, someone had killed his two workers. If he'd been at the camp when it happened, maybe he could have saved the men. Or maybe, he thought, he might be dead too, rotting and stinking in the tent next to them. The more he thought about it, the more he believed he'd been lucky.

It was a shame the workers had been killed, he thought, but it was even more disheartening to lose the big pot field. It was nearly ready to harvest, and if he and his crew had gotten the yield he thought they would, he would have been up for a tidy bonus. There would have been more than enough money to send home to Mexico to bring his wife and three other children to the United States. To know that the police had bulldozed the crop and burned it up was a huge disappointment.

And now, a third pot field worker had been killed. Several other workers had heard about the shooting and were starting to worry that their lives might be in jeopardy too. Delgado called a meeting of all the workers under his watch at the house where he lived in Yakima. There were eight men left, and four of them showed up for the meeting. The others stayed and watched over the pot fields.

It was a nice early fall evening, so the men met for a quick dinner on the back patio of the house where Delgado was staying. They were just finishing eating, enjoying a beer, talking about the man who had been killed the previous day when they heard a sizzling sound and the smack of a bullet. The men all looked around, and by the time they understood what was happening, Delgado was basically dead. His throat gurgled as blood poured from the hole in his neck. Ten seconds later, the life left his eyes.

Shootings in Yakima had become a common occurrence – if not every day, then at least every week. The two rival gangs in town, the Norteños and the Sureños, were banging away at each other. Most didn't die, but some did. The victims were primarily young Hispanic men, dying to protect some imaginary turf.

When the Yakima City police officers showed up to the Fair Avenue house, they chalked it up to just another senseless gang shooting. Police detectives knew the house, as they had been tipped off more than once that the people living there were somehow involved in illegal drugs. But the residents came and went with such regularity they couldn't keep tabs on them all.

Juan Delgado was known to the police because he was one of

the more permanent residents of the house, so one of the officers was able to identify him as soon as he saw the body. Although they hadn't heard Delgado was involved in one of the gangs – on this side of town it would have been the Sureños – they still just assumed his death was a gang-related, drive-by shooting.

There were a couple of oddities in the shooting, however. With the men all seated on the back patio, someone would have had to leave their car to shoot with any accuracy. And there hadn't been multiple calls about gunshots being fired to 911 around the time of the shooting. There were always multiple calls on the drive-by shootings, but not this one.

As the days went by and the investigation into the shooting of Juan Delgado puttered along, there would be no other conclusion but that it was just another needless death due to gang violence.

* * *

It was a few days after the muzzleloader elk season had closed. McCain was patrolling some country between White Pass and the Cowiche near Rimrock Lake. There would most likely be some camps in place as the rifle hunters were getting set up for the upcoming deer season, and there were a handful of special permit elk hunters in the area hunting now, so McCain wasn't surprised when he came upon a couple hunters dragging a six-point bull down the hill.

McCain saw what was happening as soon as he rounded a turn in the road. Nobody drags a big bull elk very far, so it was obvious that the men had killed the elk just up the hill a short ways and were now trying to get it down to the road.

He pulled up shy of the two men, climbed out of his truck and said, "Looks like someone was successful."

The men were not wearing the required hunter orange, and McCain noticed there was no tag affixed to the bull's antlers, or in an ear, or on a leg.

The men just stared without responding.

"Can I see your hunting licenses and permits?" he asked.

Again, stares and dead silence.

"Listen guys, I really need to see your licenses and permits. And I need your driver's licenses too."

Finally, one of the men decided to speak. "I think you should just load back up into your truck and move along."

This was one of the days McCain had left Jack at home, and now he was regretting not having the dog by his side.

"I can't do that, fellas. Now, are you going to show me your paperwork, or am I going to have to arrest you?"

"I don't think that's such a good idea," said a voice from behind McCain. "You need to do what the man said, climb back into your rig, and just move along."

McCain turned and saw an older man pointing a shotgun at him. Where he'd come from, McCain didn't know. But he looked like he meant business.

"Okay," McCain said. His brain was spinning about ninety miles an hour. "I'll be happy to. Put the gun down, and I'll be on my way."

"I'll put the gun down when I see your taillights disappearing down the road," the man with the shotgun said. "Now, get!"

"Okay," McCain said as he assessed the situation and started walking past the man, back to his truck.

The man with the shotgun was about five-foot-ten, thin, and had a week's worth of gray stubble on his face. McCain figured he was pushing seventy, if not older. The other two men were in their late forties or early fifties and both were slightly overweight. As McCain looked into their eyes, he didn't think the total IQ between the two of them would add up to 150. They had their rifles slung crisscross, bandolero-style over their heads and shoulders to make the dragging easier. And they were fifteen feet away.

As McCain walked past, the older man pivoted slowly. As he turned, he kept the gun barrel pointed at McCain's mid-section. But, while he was turning his body, the man wasn't moving his feet, which gave him a very unstable base. When the end of the barrel was just a foot or so away, McCain grabbed the barrel of the shotgun with lightning quickness and pushed it to the sky while simultaneously sweeping his right foot at the man's legs. In an instant, McCain had the shotgun in his hands. The older man had fallen to the road and was scuffling around, trying to get up. Before the other two men could get their rifles around their heads and off their shoulders, McCain had the shotgun pointed at them.

The older man was just getting to his feet, and McCain gave him a good shove with his foot and pushed him toward the two younger men. The old boy stumbled at the force of the shove and fell face-first back to the gravel.

"Now, let's see if we can try this again," McCain said. "First, I want to see your hands in the air."

The last thing he needed was one of the men pulling a handgun or knife. McCain decided that the shotgun in his hands was doing just fine at keeping the three men at bay, and as the men raised their hands, he noticed the bloody scrapes on the palms of the older man. Served him right, McCain thought. He had the three men lay facedown in the road, five feet apart, with their hands behind their backs.

"Don't move until I tell you to," he said with authority. "I haven't shot anyone this week, but this might be my best chance. Just give me a reason."

McCain carried two pairs of handcuffs and took extra care in cuffing the two younger men while keeping the shotgun at the ready. He sat them up and told them to just sit there in the bar ditch next to the road. Then he had the older man walk with him to his truck. Once there, McCain grabbed some zip ties and secured the man's skinned-up hands behind his back.

"You're a real asshole, you know that?" the man said to McCain.

"Shut up and go sit with those two," McCain said. "And just try to make a run for it. I'd love to see what this scattergun would do to a man at twenty yards. It might not kill ya, but it sure as hell would hurt."

McCain backed up to his truck, opened the door, and grabbed the radio microphone. His eyes and the barrel of the shotgun never left the three men.

"Wildlife Officer 148 requesting assistance," he said into the mic.

He gave the dispatcher his location, and she said she would send anyone she could as quickly as possible.

"No rush," McCain said. "These boys can wait."

"He's an asshole," the older man said to the other two. They looked blankly back at the old man.

"You'll really think I'm an asshole when we get done here. Now, I need to see your driver's licenses, hunting licenses, and the special permit for this bull, if you have one."

As McCain suspected, none of the men had the necessary permits to shoot a bull elk, so there would be poaching violations for all three, accompanied by a healthy fine. But the bigger violation would be for the older man, Clyde Collins. He'd likely do a little jail time for assault on a police officer with a deadly weapon. When McCain ran Collins's name, along with the names of the other two men, Joe Walker and Jase Collins, he discovered this wasn't the men's first bout with the law. All three men hailed from Morton, on the other side of the mountains, and each had been arrested at least once before for assorted crimes. The older Collins had done some time in his youth for fighting with a sheriff's deputy in Cowlitz County.

"Well, you boys sure know how to have fun," McCain said to

them after he got done running their information. "I see a little jail time in your near future, and some hefty fines. Where's your rig parked?"

The dullest looking of the two men, Jase Collins, started to say something, and the old man elbowed him and said, "Shut up, stupid."

McCain didn't know if the younger Collins was the older man's son, or some other relative, but the dullard stopped talking.

"No matter, we'll find it," McCain said. "I'm no judge, but from my experience in cases like this, you'll most likely lose your rig and rifles for today's little out-of-season hunt."

"Aw man," said Joe Walker to the older Collins. "I told you this was a bad idea."

"Just shut up," Collins said to him.

"Yeah, but I really like my truck," Walker said. "And that's my daddy's rifle. He's going to be really pissed."

"Shut up!" Collins repeated.

Twenty-five minutes later, Yakima Sheriff Deputy Paul Garcia showed up. He pulled his YSO rig up next to McCain's truck and got out.

"You're rounding them up in threes now, huh McCain?"

"Yeah, these fellas decided to open elk season a little early."

"What can I help with?"

"I've read them their rights, but if I can get you to transport them down to the county lock-up, that would help. I need to find their truck, and I need to deal with this dead elk. Hargraves is on his way and he can give me a hand."

Stan Hargraves was another WDFW police officer and often worked with McCain on bigger cases in the region.

Garcia started to help the men get loaded into his SUV. He had just helped the younger Collins to his feet when the man head-butted Garcia, pushed him aside with his body, and both he and the older Collins were off and running down the dirt road.

Walker just stood there and watched.

BOOM! McCain shot a load of buckshot from the old man's shotgun over their heads. At the sound of the shot, both men flinched, then stumbled and fell. As they fell, McCain ran at them. Once again, as the old man tried to get up, McCain pushed him in the butt with his foot, and the older Collins went face-first into the road. With his skinned-up hands behind his back, he had no way of stopping himself, and he ate dirt big time.

"I won't miss again," McCain said. "Now, on your feet and back to the rigs."

"What kind of idiots are you?" Garcia said as he came and grabbed the younger Collins by the arm. He was using his other hand to rub his eye. He'd have a dandy shiner in a couple days from where the man's head hit him. "Now you're going to have another assaulting-an-officer charge."

"They'll be in jail for a long time," McCain said. "A year or more is my guess."

Of course, he had no idea if they'd get jail time or for how long, but he wanted them to think about it.

"Man, I told you guys this was a bad idea," Walker said as Garcia stuffed the three men into the back seat of his SUV.

"Shut up!" Clyde Collins said.

CHAPTER 10

The next day, as McCain was driving into work, he received a call from one of the assistant district attorneys for Yakima County. The lawyer, Blake Franks, said that one of the men McCain had arrested for the elk poaching wanted to make some kind of a deal. Franks said the man had some information that might help solve some other poaching cases, and maybe even some drug stuff.

"The thing is," said Franks. "I'm not sure what kind of deal we can make. It sounds like you have a whole laundry list of violations on him and the other two men. Any chance you'd be available to meet with this guy?"

"Sure," McCain said. "I assume it's Joe Walker who's willing to talk?"

"Yep, it sounds like you've put the fear of God into him. I have no idea what he has, but it might be worth hearing him out."

"Just let me know where and when."

"Okay, I'll talk to his lawyer and then text you with a place and time."

"Sounds good," McCain said and clicked off.

As soon as he walked through the door to the office, the receptionist said, "Hey, Luke. There's a gentleman here to see you."

McCain turned and saw an impeccably dressed older gentleman sitting in a chair in the corner.

"My name's Ashford," the man said. "Walt Ashford."

"Yes, Mr. Ashford. I'm Luke McCain. How may I help you?"

"I know who you are, Officer McCain," the gentleman said.

McCain thought Ashford might be eighty, although he could be ninety. He was about five feet, five inches tall, with a full head of white hair and a thin white mustache riding just over his upper lip. He was in a brown suit with a bolo tie snug to the buttoned-up collar of his white dress shirt. The bolo tie featured a hand-carved wooden horse head as the clasp. The man had a cane, or more accurately, a walking stick, but when he stood and walked toward McCain, he didn't use it.

"You're the guy who caught that serial killer last year. I commend you for that. You and that dog of yours."

"Yeah, well, we were just doing our job. So, what can we do for you, Mr. Ashford?"

"Call me Walt, please."

"Okay, Walt, how can we help you?"

"I live up in the Nile, off 410. My wife Catherine and I built a cabin up there in the seventies, and when we retired, we moved up there full time. Catherine passed away in 2016, but I still love living up there. I'm ninety-four but I'm doing just fine on my own. I chop the firewood, mow the lawn and take care of the place the best that I can."

McCain wasn't sure how the Nile came to be called the Nile. After all, it had no resemblance whatsoever to the river in Egypt. The Nile in Central Washington was a nice little unincorporated community in a valley along the Naches River where a number of houses and cabins had taken root. The little community had a church or two, a fire station, along with a small restaurant and gas station. There was even a community library.

"I'm sorry to hear about your wife," McCain said. "So, are you having problems with some wildlife?"

"No. The wildlife and I have a deal. If they don't bother me, I won't bother them. I've had to shoot a few coyotes over the years that were killing my laying hens. And we had a cougar prowling around a couple years ago, but mostly I just enjoy seeing the elk and deer and turkeys."

"So, what is the issue, Walt?"

"Well, it started about four months ago. I'm an old man and I need to get up a couple times to pee, so I see things at night."

He paused again and looked at McCain.

"Yes, sir, go on."

"Well, I've been seeing some unusual traffic on the Forest Service road coming out of the mountains at night. You know the road up to Little Bald Mountain?"

"Yes, I know the road. What kind of traffic?"

"Big trucks. Not eighteen-wheelers or logging trucks, but bigger than a pickup."

"Like delivery-size vans or trucks?" McCain asked.

"Yeah, about that size, I guess. They're coming and going at all hours of the night. Now, I haven't been hearing any shooting, but I'm just wondering if someone is up there jacklighting elk and deer and using the trucks to haul the carcasses out of the woods."

"That's a possibility, I guess. Is there any writing or logos on the sides of the trucks that you could see?"

"No, I don't think so. At least nothing stands out."

"How about color?"

"They're kind of a brown or tan color. Almost like the color of the Army rigs you see in the convoys over by the firing center."

"And they're coming and going every night?"

"Well, no, not every night, but often enough to make me think something is going on. I just thought you would like to know. Since you solved that mass-murder case last year, I figured you'd be the man to check it out."

"Okay, Mr. Ashford – "

"Walt," he interrupted.

"Okay, Walt. Let me get your contact information, and I'll try to come up sometime in the next few nights to see what I can see. Are there any nights you've noticed that seem more active than others?"

"It seems that they are coming down from the mountains on Fridays, but not always on Fridays. Sometimes it's on a Thursday or a Saturday."

"Okay, then. I'll come up on Friday night, and we'll see what we can see."

"Thank you, Officer McCain."

"Call me Luke."

"Deal. Thank you, Luke. I'll see you Friday night." And with that, the nattily dressed Walt Ashford tapped his walking stick on the floor, bounced it up and caught it mid-stick, swiveled, and walked out the door.

McCain turned and saw the receptionist smiling at him.

"Well, he was interesting," the receptionist said. "If he was about fifty years younger, I'd see if he'd like me to come up and spend the night on stakeout."

McCain shook his head and chuckled as he walked toward his office. He didn't quite make it.

"Any luck figuring out who's riding four-wheelers through the Little Naches?" Andrea Parker asked as she walked over to McCain.

McCain had done some checking around up there after they found the dead man in the pot field, but he had very little to go on. The men in the side-by-sides who had reported the shooting didn't know much, and with so many hunters this time of year riding the roads on ATVs, it could have been one of a hundred people.

"I looked around and talked to several people, but no one had any information," McCain said. "I'll keep checking on it, but if someone doesn't witness it and report viable information, there's not much I can do."

Parker looked frustrated, but she didn't say anything.

"Listen Andrea, I'd like nothing more than to catch whoever did it. They need to be caught and pay for what they did. My next step is to requisition some trail cameras and set them up near the crossing. Hopefully, we'll get some photos that might help us identify the guys."

"Okay, thanks Luke," Parker said and wandered off down the hall.

Frankly, McCain had forgotten about the crossing, what with everything else that was going on. The murder in the pot field and having to keep an eye on about 20,000 square miles of country during the various hunting seasons had taken most of his time and attention. He didn't tell Parker, but the illegal river crossing was a low priority at the moment. Not to mention the pending meeting with the assistant DA and the meeting he just had with Walt Ashford. He had a lot on his plate.

It was just before noon, and McCain was about to grab a bite of lunch, pick up Jack, and head to the mountains to do some more looking around when his office phone jangled.

"McCain," he answered.

"Officer McCain, it's ADA Franks. I've set up a meeting with Joe Walker and his attorney for two o'clock at my office. Can you make it?"

"Yep, that'll work. See you then."

Instead of driving home to get lunch and Jack, he decided to call Sara and see if by chance she had time for lunch.

"Hey, Luke," she said answering her cell phone. "I hope you're calling to take me to lunch. I'm starving."

He laughed and said, "As a matter of fact . . ."

They agreed to meet at the little sandwich shop on Second Street, near the courthouse in downtown Yakima. Sara was looking at her phone when McCain walked in.

"I've already ordered for us," she said. "I hope you're okay with a club sandwich."

"Geez, I guess you are hungry. Yeah, a club is great. Did you get fries, or are you going to make me eat a salad?"

"No, I got you fries, but you have to share them with me."

"Deal. So, how's your day going?"

"Okay. We're still trying to make heads or tails of that shooting in Kittitas County. It's just so weird that three different men were killed with two different rifles. They're related, but we're still not sure how. The coroner believes Shane Wallace was killed by a .223 caliber rifle."

"That very well could be an AR-15," McCain said, even though he knew Sinclair knew that. "But not necessarily."

"It's what the cartel members shoot," she said. "But everyone and their brother has an AR these days. Unless we can match a bullet with something in our system, we have no way of knowing who might own the rifle, or even if it was an AR."

Their lunch arrived, and they talked a bit more about the shootings, including the one up by the Little Naches. As it turned out, McCain got about three of his French fries. Sinclair mowed through her big chef salad and most of his fries as McCain watched in amazement. He told her about his scheduled meeting with the ADA and about talking with Walt Ashford.

"Wow, I'd like to meet him," Sinclair teased after hearing about Ashford. "It would be great to see what a real gentleman looks like."

"Just for that, I'm ordering a piece of apple pie for dessert, and you aren't getting any," McCain quipped.

"Geez, you're awfully sensitive. Order it a la mode, please."

CHAPTER 11

When McCain arrived at the district attorney's office, Franks met him at the door.

"Walker has his attorney, and they're looking for a reduction in fines," Franks said. "He wants his truck and his dad's rifle back, and he wants no jail time. I'm not sure I would have asked for jail time anyway, because according to your report he seemed to be more of a bystander in the whole deal."

"Yeah, all he really did was drag the elk down the hill and drive the two Collins men to the mountains. Still, he knew what they were doing was wrong and didn't have to be there. And, if I remember his record right, he's been arrested before, so he's no angel."

"Okay, well, let's meet with him. And without making too many promises, let's see what he can offer up. I'm okay with telling him no jail time. What do you think about his truck and rifle?"

"That's your call. Or a judge's call. I'm okay with it if you can work it out. Again, let's see what he has to offer."

With that, the two men headed into the conference room where a very scared-looking Joe Walker sat with Adriene Molina, an attractive, thirty-something public defender.

"I assume you had a chance to talk to Officer McCain," Molina said. The attorney was wearing a dark gray business suit, white blouse, and a black-and-gray silk scarf around her neck. She wore her dark brown hair pulled back and was wearing just a hint of makeup. An almost cartoonishly large pair of glasses with heavy black frames was perched on her nose.

"Yes, I did," said Franks. "And we are willing to consider some of your client's requests, if – and that's a big if – the information he provides is valuable."

"We certainly think it is," Molina said. "Shall we proceed?"

The two attorneys went back and forth on what the county was willing to give up before Walker would tell what he knew. When they finally settled on no jail time and his truck being returned, they asked Walker to proceed.

"You mean I don't get my daddy's rifle back?" he asked.

"We'll see about that, Mr. Walker," Franks said. "Let's hear what you have to say first."

"What do you wanna know?" Walker asked.

"You said you had some information on some other poaching that is going on. Officer McCain here would be very interested in hearing about that."

"Okay, well, the two guys I was with are part of a larger gang that regularly kills deer and elk and bears out of season. I haven't been with them on any of their hunts, but I've heard them talking, and they don't care about seasons or whether it is day or night. They just like killing animals."

With that, McCain sat up and started taking notes. He'd heard rumors of a poaching ring on the west side of the Cascades, but so far none of his fellow WDFW officers had been able to verify the chatter. They had found some dead elk in pastures around Packwood and Randle with their heads cut off, but they hadn't found the perpetrators.

"It's mostly members of one big family," Walker said. "Old Man Collins is kind of the ringleader, and he has his son Jase and a few nephews and a couple nieces' husbands who are all in on the deal. They sell the horns and some of the meat, but sometimes they just cut off the heads of the bulls and bucks."

"So how did you get tied up with them on the elk they shot the other day?" McCain asked.

"They needed my truck. None of their trucks was in working order enough to drive over the pass. They'd heard of a big bull up above Rimrock Lake, and they really wanted to go get it. They know a rich guy down in Nevada that was willing to pay big bucks for a trophy elk, and they figured if they could get it, they'd be in for a big payday."

"So, you've never been with them on any of their other kills?" Franks asked.

"No, this was the first time. I really didn't want to go this time, but I borrowed some money from them a couple months ago, and they told me if I drove them over here, they'd call it all square."

"Can we get a list of the names in the gang, and any other information you might have on dates when they killed other animals?" McCain asked.

"I can get you the names, but I don't know the dates. I can try to find that out."

"Okay, that would be great," Franks said. "Now what about the information you have on some drug stuff going on?"

"Well, I don't know if you'd call it drugs," Walker said. "It's actually just marijuana. My girlfriend is from Mexico, and she has a brother and a nephew who work for an outfit growing marijuana up there in the mountains somewhere. He told her about how much money he's making and what a good job it is."

"Can we get the name of her brother and nephew?" Franks asked.

"Sure. It's Juan Delgado. And his son is Juan Delgado Jr. They just call him Junior."

"Any idea how we might reach these gentlemen?" Franks asked.

"I'm not sure. My girlfriend says they spend a bunch of time in the mountains growing the pot, but sometimes they are in Yakima."

As Walker spoke, McCain was thinking about the killings in the pot fields in Kittitas and Yakima Counties. He couldn't quite remember, but he was sure he had heard the name Juan Delgado sometime in the last couple weeks.

"Okay, this helps a great deal," Franks said. "Do you have any other questions for Mr. Walker, Officer McCain?"

"As long as I get the names of those poachers, I think I have what I need," McCain said. "And I'm fine with letting Mr. Walker have his father's rifle back. But just know, if I ever hear of you involved in anything like this again, I'm going to bring the full extent of the law down on you. Losing your daddy's rifle will be the least of your concerns."

"Do you understand that Mr. Walker?" Franks asked.

"Yes, sir. I'm done with those guys for good."

"Ms. Molina, if we can get the contact information on Mr. Delgado, I am sure the sheriff's department would appreciate that as well."

"I'll make sure we get that to you ASAP. Thank you, gentlemen."

The public defender and her client both stood and hurried out of the room.

After they were gone, Franks turned to McCain and said, "So, did you get what you need?"

"I think so. When you get those names, I'll pass them on to the officers who work over in Cowlitz and Lewis Counties. That will give them an idea about who to keep an eye on. Maybe they can get one of the guys to flip. If so, they should be able to put a good case together."

McCain paused for a second and thought about the name Juan Delgado.

"Did the name Juan Delgado mean anything to you?" he asked.

"No, not that I know of," Franks said. "But I haven't been involved in prosecuting any of the drug cases around here."

"I know I've heard it recently, but I'm not sure where," McCain said.

After thanking McCain for his help, Franks headed out. McCain took his time walking back to his truck. Where had he heard the name Juan Delgado?

When he got to his truck, he checked the time on his phone. The screen read 3:27. He decided he'd run back to the office and grab a couple of the new trail cameras that had been purchased for surveillance purposes. He figured he'd get the cameras, then take them and the all-important operating manuals home with him. If he could decipher how they worked, he would run them up to the Little Naches in the morning.

When he got home, he saw that Jack was over at the neighbor's house, playing in the front yard with Austin Meyers and his Lab, Bear. Austin was the fourteen-year-old son of Jessie Meyers, and he was a big fan of Jack. McCain had been working with Austin on training Bear to follow commands. The dog was just over a year and a half old, and already he was taking hand signals on retrieves and turning into a great dog.

"Hey, Luke," Austin said when he saw McCain pull into the driveway. "I grabbed Jack. We're working on our commands with Bear."

McCain had told Austin that anytime he wanted to get Jack out of the back yard to play, he was more than welcome to do so. Jack often stayed with the Meyers family when McCain was out of town at meetings or other business around the state.

"That's great. How's Bear doing?"

Like Jack, Bear was a yellow Labrador retriever. He wasn't quite as big as Jack, but he had a strong, athletic body. It took almost a year for the dog to gain the coordination to go with his body, but now he was starting to shine.

"He's really starting to get the hand signals. I'd like to work him down at the river tonight. Do you think you and Jack would want to go with us?"

McCain thought about the homework he had to do with the trail cameras, but looking at Austin and then at Bear, and thinking about how the young man had no father around to help him with such things, he said, "Sure, let's head that way after dinner."

"Great! We'll come get you," Austin said.

"Come on, Jack," McCain said. "Time for dinner."

That's all the big yellow dog needed to hear. He flew past McCain, jumped onto the porch in one big leap, and sat at the front door, waiting to be let in.

"You're not a Labrador retriever, you're a chow hound," McCain said as they headed into the house.

CHAPTER 12

That evening, McCain threw a couple burgers on the grill, Sinclair mixed up a salad, and the two sat down for a quick dinner.

"How did it go with the ADA?" she asked.

"Pretty good. We got some good stuff on a poaching ring over by Morton, and the guy has a girlfriend who is related to a couple men who grow pot in the mountains."

"Not one of the men you found dead?"

"No, but the name he gave us sounded familiar to me. I couldn't remember from where though."

"What's the name?"

"Juan Delgado. I know I've heard it recently."

"He's the man who was shot in a drive-by down by the fairgrounds a few nights ago. YPD thinks it's gang related."

McCain thought for a minute and said, "What if he was killed by the same guy who is taking out the pot growers in the mountains? If Delgado worked up there for the cartel, it's a possibility."

"The cops identified Delgado almost immediately, but I don't think they knew he was connected to the cartel or they would have passed that on to me."

"Worth checking out in the morning," McCain said. "It would be interesting to see what caliber of rifle he was killed with."

They were just finishing dinner when McCain heard a knock on the door.

"That'll be Austin. We're going to take the dogs down to the river. Leave the dishes, and I'll do them later. It's my night."

"Naw, I'll get them. Then you can do them the next three nights," Sinclair said with a smile.

McCain opened the door and told Austin that he and Jack would meet him and Bear at the back gate. When he opened the gate, the two yellow dogs took off like a shot, down the dirt road toward the Naches River.

Being so close to the river was one of the reasons McCain liked living where he did. He would often grab his fishing rod and go down during summer and early fall evenings to fish for trout. And he liked taking Jack down there for a run and for training.

Duck hunting season was just a week away, and McCain had been working with Austin and the dogs on marking and making water retrieves. The sessions were old hat to Jack, who was oftentimes asked to sit and watch as the younger Bear was put through the paces of sitting and marking the dummies being thrown, and then being sent for the retrieves. Jack was trained to sit, even when the shotgun went off. He wouldn't break for the retrieve until McCain said the dog's name. Bear was still learning that lesson.

"Why won't he stay like Jack," Austin asked after Bear took off when McCain fired the training pistol.

"He will, but he's so enthusiastic about retrieving the dummy it's hard for him to sit there," McCain explained. "He'll figure it out. It took Jack a while to learn it too."

McCain was not one of those who believed in hard-handed training. Jack was smart enough that all McCain had to do was talk to him in a scolding voice, and the dog knew he had done wrong. Bear was smart too, and all it would take is some stern words and keeping him on a leash to make him sit until he was asked to go for the retrieve a few times. McCain was confident he'd get it.

The last time they had trained, McCain had obtained some feral pigeons so that Bear would know the feel of a live bird in his mouth. But today, they were back to using training dummies. They ran the dogs through several retrieves on land and in the water, training for both multiple retrieves and blind retrieves where the dog has no idea where the dummy fell. Afterwards, McCain let the dogs rest. He and Austin found their favorite downed log and grabbed a seat.

"So, how's school going?" McCain asked.

"Good. Most of my teachers are okay. And football has been fun."

Austin was the quarterback on the JV team, and his team was undefeated through six weeks.

"Your mom said you threw a couple touchdown passes last game. Sara and I are going to try to make it to your next home game."

"That'd be great. We play next Thursday at the high school at six o'clock. Should be a good game. We play Highland, and they're always good."

"Looking forward to it."

"Hey, Luke. Did you ever go to your high school dances?"

"Sure did. They were fun. You have one coming up?"

"Yeah, it's homecoming in two weeks, and there is this girl I'd like to ask to the dance, but I don't know if she even knows I exist."

About that time, Jack and Bear went tearing out after something. Austin stood up and watched.

"Just a cottontail," Austin said. "They'll never catch it."

"It's my guess the girl knows exactly who you are, and if she hasn't been asked by anyone yet, I'm betting she would love to go with you. I remember how much courage I had to muster to ask a girl to the dance the first time. I was so worried she'd say no. But you know what? She was hoping I would ask her."

"Really?" Austin said. "I did see her looking at me once. And she smiled at me yesterday at lunch. Or maybe she was laughing at me. I tripped over a garbage can on the way to sit with my buddies."

"You know, maybe you should talk to Sara about all of this, to get the female perspective. But it's my guess you're going to be at the dance with this young lady in two weeks. That is if you ask her."

Just then, Jack and Bear came back with their tongues hanging out. Between all the retrieving drills and chasing the rabbit up and down the river, they were pooped.

"Let's head for home. You can talk to Sara when we get there if you want."

When they got back to the house, McCain took extra time tidying things outside so Sara and Austin could talk in private. McCain needed to clean a few items out of his personal truck and start preparing for the upcoming big game hunting seasons. He was planning on taking some time off when the deer season opened, so he grabbed his hunting pack and worked on it on the back deck.

The whole time, Jack was sitting close and sticking his nose into everything that McCain brought out of the pack. He was especially interested in a couple energy bars that were still in the pack from the previous year.

"You don't need any extra energy," McCain said to the dog.

Jack looked at him quizzically, tipping his head to one side, like he was really trying to figure out why McCain wasn't giving him a bite of the bar.

When he finally heard the front door open and then close, McCain went in through the back door. Sinclair was just coming into the kitchen.

"Did you give him the courage to ask the young lady to the dance?" he asked.

"Let's just say we had a good talk. I forgot how shy and nervous boys can be at that age."

"Well, I hope he asks someone, and they go and have a good time. Those are some of my fondest memories from high school," McCain said. "Of course, I didn't have to ask any girls. They were lining up to ask me to the dances."

"Pfft," erupted Sinclair, spitting out the drink of water she'd just taken in laughter. "It went out my nose too," she complained.

"I don't see why you think that's so funny," he said with a hurt look on his face. "It could have happened like that."

"I might have asked you," she said. "But I wasn't into the jocks and big-man-on-campus guys. I would have definitely gone with a kid like Austin."

"Well, that makes me feel better. Maybe if he can't find a date for homecoming, you can go with him."

"I'd be honored," she said. "Now, what if I ask you to come join me in bed? Would that smooth those ruffled feathers?"

"I'm not sure, but it's definitely worth a try."

* * *

McCain was up early the next morning. He wanted to study up on the trail cameras and run them to the Little Naches where the four-wheelers were crossing the river. He was reading the instruction manuals at the kitchen table when Sinclair walked in.

"I'm starving," she said as she opened the refrigerator. "Want some bacon and eggs?"

"Hmmm, must have been that good workout last night," he teased.

"Breakfast or not?" she asked again, ignoring his comment as she pulled the fixings out of the refrigerator.

"Actually, I already ate," he said. "And I want to get going shortly."

He finished reading the manuals as Sinclair fixed what, for her, was a pretty substantial breakfast.

"I'm headed up to the Little Naches with these cameras this morning. But if you find out anything on the caliber of rifle that killed Delgado, let me know."

"Will do," she said.

"If I can make these things work, I might stop by Mr. Ashford's place and put one or two there to see what's going on with the late-night trucking activity."

"Good idea. Might save you a late-night stake out or two."

McCain gathered up the cameras and manuals, kissed Sara goodbye, and called Jack. When he turned around to close the door, he could see Sinclair rinsing her hands in the sink. He definitely would have asked her out to the dance if he'd known her, even though she was probably way out of his league back then. That made him even more thankful she was in his life now.

CHAPTER 13

As he and Jack took State Route 12 through Naches and to the Y where 12 and SR 410 split, McCain thought about the man killed in the drive-by. If he remembered correctly from the newspaper story, Delgado had been shot while sitting with a few other people on his back patio. How do you shoot a person in the back of the house from the road, he wondered. And why weren't any of the other men shot? He made a mental note to talk to Sinclair about that when he returned home that night.

When he arrived at the spot where the ATVs were crossing the river, he let Jack out, and the two started walking. As they neared the river, McCain heard the engine of a four-wheeler coming from the hill on the other side of the water. McCain told Jack to heel. They stepped into the brush and waited. As McCain listened to the ATV getting closer, he realized there wasn't one but two vehicles coming his way.

A minute later, two red Honda four-wheelers crested the hill on the other side of the river, roared down the hill and splashed through the river on their way up to the main road. The ATVs were driven by two drivers wearing helmets with shaded visors.

As soon as they got through the river, McCain stepped out to where they could see him, put his hand up, and yelled "STOP!"

The riders never skipped a beat. They blew right by McCain and headed down the main road toward 410.

"Crap," McCain said as he started running to his truck. "C'mon, Jack."

He didn't really have to tell Jack to come. The yellow dog was running right beside him. McCain opened the driver's door, and Jack flew into the passenger seat. With a quick jump, McCain was behind the wheel and hitting the ignition.

As he tore out after the ATVs, McCain got on the radio. "Wildlife 148 in pursuit of two red ATVs heading south on the Little Naches Road. Request assistance."

"Copy, Wildlife 148," said the county dispatch.

It hadn't rained in this part of the world in over a month, so even though the road was paved, a plume of dust still trailed the four-wheelers. McCain couldn't maneuver as fast as the ATVs, but he could keep track of them by the small dust clouds rising above the trees ahead.

"Wildlife 148, state unit 343 and county in route. County's ETA is fifteen," the dispatch said.

"Copy," McCain said into the mic.

He was trying to watch the dirt plumes and the road at the same time, hoping nobody was coming up the road. McCain couldn't tell for sure, but he felt like he was losing ground on the four-wheelers.

"Wildlife 148, State 343 on the Little Naches Road. I've blocked it about two miles up from SR 410. I see some dust coming up. I believe your ATVs are coming my way, and fast."

"Copy, State 343, thanks. I'm guessing we'll all be there shortly."

About twenty seconds later, McCain saw a much larger plume of dust coming up, and then there was none.

"Wildlife 148, State 343. I have the riders. Requesting an ambulance to the Little Naches Road, two miles up from SR 410."

"Received," crackled the voice of the dispatcher.

When McCain rounded the corner, the dust was still settling. A white Washington State Patrol SUV was sitting sideways, blue lights flashing, blocking the road. A gray-uniformed trooper was bent over, tending to a man lying in the bar ditch next to the road. A red four-wheeler was turned on its side against a dirt bank, wheels still turning. A second man, still in a helmet, was standing next to another red Honda four-wheeler, watching as the trooper provided aid to the man on the ground.

McCain pulled up next to the ATV, hopped out, and went over to the standing man.

"We'll get all this worked out in a little bit," McCain said to the man. "But for right now, give me the keys to your ATV. I want you staying here."

"Yes, sir," the guy said in a shaky voice as he handed McCain the keys.

McCain walked over to the trooper and the downed man. The rider, who was still wearing his helmet, was rolling around and moaning. He was definitely injured, with at least a broken wrist from what McCain could see.

"How's he doing?" McCain asked.

"He took a pretty good spill," the trooper said. "The way he hit the side of the ditch here, he could have internal injuries, and probably some broken ribs. He's lucky he was wearing a helmet."

"The ambulance in on the way," McCain said to the downed man. "They're getting here as fast as they can."

The trooper was doing all the things law enforcement officers are trained to do in a situation like this. He was checking the man's eyes and watching for signs of internal bleeding and possible shock.

McCain turned back to the standing man and asked him to take off his helmet.

"What's your name, and how old are you?"

"Tyler Healy. I'm 17," the kid said.

"Well, Mr. Healy, you and your buddy are in a whole bunch of trouble."

"Yes, sir," the kid said again.

"What's your friend's name, and how old is he?"

"Travis Cobb. He's 17 too."

"Okay, so tell me why you were running up through the river and over the hill. You know it's illegal to run through the river and off the open roads, right?"

"Yes, sir."

"And, you also know it is illegal to elude the police?"

"Yes, sir."

"So, why were you doing it?"

"We didn't want to get caught with . . ."

There was a long hesitation.

"With what?" McCain asked.

"With the pot."

With some coaxing, Healy told McCain that he and Cobb had been hunting up this way during the early archery elk season and stumbled into a marijuana field off the river a mile or so. As soon as they saw it, Healy said they knew exactly what it was. So, they devised a plan to come back after the season, sneak into the field, and harvest a few plants for themselves and some of their friends.

"We rode our four-wheelers in a ways and then walked the rest of the way, in case anyone was around guarding the field," Healy said.

"And did you see anyone?" McCain asked.

"No, but we heard some guys talking in Spanish. We grabbed a couple of the closest plants and got outta there."

"And you were back up for more this afternoon?"

"Yes, sir. This time we just grabbed some buds and put them in a big baggy. It's under the seat of Travis's four-wheeler."

Travis Cobb was still writhing in pain when the ambulance arrived. The medics did a quick check of his vitals, loaded him on a gurney, wheeled him to the back of the ambulance, and headed back to Yakima, lights flashing and siren blaring.

"Is he going to be alright?" Healy asked.

"Your friend should be fine," the trooper said. "He's pretty banged up. They just want to check him out at the hospital to make sure he's okay."

McCain had talked to the trooper and told him what Healy had said about the marijuana field. With Cobb on his way to the hospital, they tipped the ATV back onto its tires and checked in the compartment under the seat. They found the big bag of pot.

About that time, YSO Deputy Paul Garcia rolled up.

"I got here as quick as I could. Was the guy okay?"

"Yeah, he should be fine," the trooper said. "I'll let Officer McCain tell you all about it. I need to get down to the hospital to do the paperwork on Mr. Cobb."

The trooper loaded up and headed out, and McCain gave Garcia the ten-cent version of what had taken place.

"I need to deal with Mr. Healy here," McCain said. "Maybe you can go and check out the pot field?"

"Maybe Mr. Healy can run me up there," Garcia said.

"Not a good idea," McCain said. "That's why we're here in the first place. Whoever goes is going on foot."

Garcia, who was about five-foot-eight, and was pushing two hundred and thirty pounds, hated hiking anywhere.

"Tell you what," Garcia said to McCain. "I'll deal with the ATV rider, and you and Jack can walk into the pot field. You're going to have to take your FBI agent in there anyway, right?"

"Okay, but I'll need your report as quickly as I can so I can get it to the biologist in our office. She's been after me to catch these guys. She won't give a damn about the illegal pot fields, only about catching the riders running through the river."

"Copy that," Garcia said. "Come on, Mr. Healy. Let's get this all figured out."

During all this, Jack had been dutifully sitting in the passenger seat of McCain's truck. When McCain opened the door, Jack flew out, ran over to a tree, and lifted his leg.

"Dang. Sorry, boy," McCain said to the dog, waiting for him to come back and jump in the truck.

Back at the river crossing, McCain jumped from rock to rock to avoid disturbing any possible spawning habitat, although the ATV tires had done a pretty good job of that. Jack ran through the water without a care of any kind.

As they followed the ATV tracks back up the hill, McCain wondered what they might find at the pot field. There had been dead bodies at the last two. He hoped he wasn't walking into the trifecta.

When he'd gotten up the hill about a mile from where the ATV tire tracks stopped, McCain whistled for Jack and told him to heel. He didn't want the dog making a bunch of noise running around the woods. And he wanted him close in case they ran into the field workers – or possibly a killer.

McCain found the lower end of the pot field with no problem. He stopped and listened before moving around the eastern edge of the field. A small spring-fed creek ran down a little draw on that side of the pot field, and McCain figured that was where the growers were getting their irrigation water. Thinking back to the Kittitas pot field, McCain remembered the growers' camp was on the creek-side of the field and reasoned that's where one would be on this field, if there was one at all.

McCain, with Jack by his side, slowly worked his way up along the edge of the pot field. Suddenly, Jack froze, and his ears went up. He'd either seen something or, more likely, heard something. McCain stopped, too, and listened.

A second later, McCain could hear the voices of two men talking in Spanish. They were still about two hundred yards away according to McCain's calculations, and the men seemed to be having a normal conversation. McCain knew some Spanish, but when two native Spanish speakers were talking to one another he could never keep up.

As McCain took one quiet step after another, the voices became louder. Keeping trees and the hill's incline between him and the voices, McCain crept closer. Finally, he saw the top of a camouflaged tent and stopped. The men were moving around, he could tell, but he still couldn't see how many there were. He had heard two distinct voices but wasn't discounting the fact that there might be another person or two in the camp.

He inched closer and finally was able to peek around a big Douglas fir tree and see what was happening. There were two men, and they looked to be packing up stuff. McCain watched for several minutes and was confident the two men were the only ones in the camp. He watched and waited.

Finally, both men went into the tent. McCain made his move. He quickly and quietly made his way down to the edge of the camp. Jack was still right by his side.

About the time he got to the little opening where the tent and growing supplies were placed, one of the men came out of the tent. He saw McCain and started telling something to the other man that McCain didn't get.

"FREEZE!" McCain yelled as he pulled his service pistol and pointed it at the man. "La Parada! Manos arriba!"

The man standing outside the tent complied, stopping and raising his hands in the air. But he wasn't the one McCain was worried about. If the guy in the tent had a gun, well, that could be an issue.

"Salire las manos primero," McCain said to the man in the tent, wanting him to come out hands first.

"Habla ingles?" McCain asked the man outside the tent.

"Sí," the man said.

"Good, please step over this way and ask your friend to come out of the tent, hands first."

The man started walking toward McCain and said something in quick Spanish. McCain asked the man to turn around and put his hands behind his back. He complied, and McCain moved in to put his handcuffs on the man. As he was doing that, McCain could hear rustling in the tent, but the second man never appeared.

"Sit here," McCain said to the handcuffed man. "My dog's going to watch you. He's trained to attack if you try to run. Understand?"

The man looked at Jack with deep concern and nodded his head.

"Sit and stay," McCain said to Jack. Then he said, "Guard!"

If the handcuffed man had been perceptive, he would have seen Jack tilt his head when McCain told him to guard. That was not in the dog's vocabulary, and Jack had no idea what it meant. But the man didn't know that.

Jack sat and looked at the handcuffed man as McCain moved slowly to the tent. Again, he told the man to come out, hands-first, in Spanish. There was no reply. In fact, McCain now was hearing nothing. It was the perfect spot for an ambush, McCain thought as he sorted out what to do. Finally, he backed up to the handcuffed man, told him to stand up, and walked him slowly to the front door of the tent.

"Tell him you are coming in," McCain said.

The man spoke in Spanish, and from what McCain could translate quickly in his mind, it sounded like the man said what McCain had asked him to say. They walked slowly to the tent door. McCain started pulling the flap away so that he could see in. When it was open enough for him to see the whole inside of the tent, McCain was amazed. There was no one there. It was like the man had vanished into thin air.

On closer inspection of the tent, it had a slit in the back wall, just big enough for a person to duck through and get away. McCain ran out of the tent and around the back but couldn't see the guy. He could be hiding in the brush or he could be running up the creek.

Now McCain was at a stalemate. He really wanted to pursue the man who had slipped out the back, but he couldn't leave the man he already had in cuffs. He decided one in the hand was better than, well, another in the brush.

But what if the guy who escaped had a rifle, McCain thought. They'd be sitting ducks. He stayed low as he went back around the tent. Jack still sat in front of the man, who was looking at the dog with a little fear in his eyes.

"Looks like your buddy slipped away," McCain said as he snuck over to the man. "That's okay. You're going to be in the hot seat."

The man gave McCain a perplexed look and then went back to watching Jack.

"Come on, boy," McCain said to Jack. "Let's get our friend here down to the county jail. Sara can deal with him from there."

With that, McCain grabbed the pot grower by the elbow. He, Jack, and the man hurriedly walked down the hill, back toward the river where the truck was parked. As they walked, McCain kept checking the area around them to make sure they weren't being followed.

They weren't, but McCain had an eerie feeling that someone was watching them.

CHAPTER 14

The following day, McCain decided that since the trail cameras weren't needed any longer at the illegal river crossing, he'd run them up to Walt Ashford's place and put them there. If nothing else, it would save him from spending the night waiting and watching for the trucks the old gentlemen had been seeing. After breakfast, he and Jack loaded up and headed for the Nile.

When he found Walt Ashford's address on Nile Road, he pulled into the driveway. A split-rail fence surrounded the property and followed the gravel driveway to a large log house with a blue metal roof. Shrubs lined the driveway, and as he drove in, McCain noticed a plot of dirt that had obviously been the summer garden. Now it was just dirt, and there was a pile of shriveled plants, branches, and leaves with a few yellow squash mounded up at one end. McCain was impressed. Ashford definitely stayed active, keeping this place looking as nice as it did.

The old gentleman was stepping onto his covered porch as McCain got out of his truck.

"Officer McCain," Ashford said. "What a nice surprise."

"Hi Walt," McCain said, remembering the gentleman had requested he call him by his first name. "I've been thinking about our discussion the other day and was wondering if I could put a couple trail cameras out by the road to see if we can get a glimpse of those trucks you've been seeing."

"Of course," Ashford said. "Come on in. And bring that yellow dog I see in the truck. I'd like to meet him."

With that, McCain opened the back door of his F-150, and Jack came rolling out. He ran immediately over to Ashford, who gave him some pats on the side.

"So, this is the famous dog that tracks down serial killers," he said, scratching Jack's ears. "What a real pleasure to meet you."

Jack wagged his tail rapidly at the attention.

Ashford was wearing tan slacks with a light-blue, button-up dress shirt under a brown corduroy vest. There was no bolo tie today, McCain noticed.

"Let's go inside and sit down," Ashford said.

McCain and Jack followed him through the front door into a massive living room that had vaulted ceilings with a huge wooden beam running down the middle. The large couch and chair were dark brown leather.

McCain sat down and had Jack sit next to him on the hardwood floor.

"Would you like something to drink?" Ashford asked. "I have some lemonade or sweet tea. And I have water, of course."

"I'd love a glass of lemonade," McCain said.

As Ashford went into the kitchen, McCain looked around the room. There were photos everywhere, mostly of Ashford and his wife and their kids and grandkids. Some of the photos were of Ashford with a big fish he'd caught here or there, or of a bull elk or a buck deer he'd bagged.

McCain was intently looking at one of the photos when Ashford came in with two glasses of lemonade and a small plate of cookies.

"That's my Catherine," Ashford said. "I was a lucky man. We spent sixty-eight years together. Do you have a wife?"

"No, not yet," McCain said. "But I have a girlfriend who is pretty special. She even likes this spoiled Lab."

Walt Ashford chuckled and offered Jack a bite of cookie. The dog gingerly took it from the old man's hand and crunched it up.

"Well, that should tell you something. A woman who loves your dog as much as you do is pretty special. She sounds like a keeper."

"Well, she is an FBI agent, so I really need to mind my Ps and Qs around her or she might just arrest me."

Ashford chuckled again and slipped another bite of cookie to Jack.

"So, tell me about these cameras you have. I've read a little about them in my hunting magazines, but all that new technology has passed me by."

McCain described how the cameras worked and that they even took decent photos at night. He told him that if they could get a good angle on the road, they should be able to identify the trucks.

"Well, that would be better than sitting out here hoping they'd come by at some point," Ashford said.

"Yes, I definitely think it's worth a try. If it doesn't work well, then I'll need to come out and spend a couple nights – hopefully not more than that – watching and taking photos. Let's see how this works first."

The two men chatted a bit more, and Ashford asked McCain to tell the story of tracking down the Cascade Killer. He listened intently with a twinkle in his eye as McCain went through the story.

"My goodness, how lucky it was you showed up when you did."

"I think it's the only reason she's still with me. She feels indebted," McCain said with a chuckle. "And she does like Jack. Well, let's go try to find a couple spots to place these cameras."

The two men walked slowly down the driveway toward Nile Road. Jack stayed with the men, walking next to Ashford. McCain looked up and down the fence along the road and found a couple places that looked like they would give a good view of the road.

"The only problem I see with this plan is we'll have to sift through about five thousand photos of rigs going up and down the road," McCain said.

"I could turn them off in the morning and back on again at night if that would help?"

"That would help, but don't feel obligated. Maybe turn them on tonight and tomorrow night, and let's see what we get."

McCain showed Ashford how to turn the cameras on and off and then went and placed one on either side of his driveway, one facing up the road and the other facing down. Jack sat next to Ashford as he stood in the driveway and watched McCain place the cameras on fence posts.

When they were done, Ashford, McCain and Jack ambled back to the house. Again, Jack walked close to the old man who had his hand on the dog's head as he walked.

CHAPTER 15

The loss of Juan Delgado was a hit to the cartel. He'd been a good worker, an even better manager, and he was especially adept at growing marijuana. He knew the best fertilizing and watering schedule to get the highest yields from the crops grown in the Cascades. His absence created serious issues when it came to harvesting and transporting the marijuana out of the mountains.

Fortunately, Juan Delgado Jr. had spent time working alongside his father and watching how he did things. He'd learned a great deal from the man, and when his father had been murdered, Junior was asked to step in and fill his shoes. He missed his father immensely and wanted to make him proud, so he gladly took the job when it was offered to him.

It had been a week since his father had been killed in what the cops were calling a gang shooting, but Junior Delgado knew otherwise. His father hadn't been in a gang, ever. He had come to the United States to make a better life for himself and his family. He didn't have time for gangs. He'd been working hard, practically from the day he arrived.

Junior wondered who might have killed his father. He believed it was the same person who had killed the workers at the pot field near Ellensburg and the other worker in the mountains west of Yakima. Junior was going to find out, and he'd get his revenge.

The problem was, with his father gone and some of the other workers out of the picture, he had to pay extra attention to the other grow sites. They needed to be harvested on time and moved out of the mountains quickly. Being short-handed meant he was working sunrise to sunset. Luckily, he'd been able to recruit a couple new workers who helped a great deal. They, and the workers who were tending to the other fields, had developed a plan to move from one field to the next until they were all harvested.

At the end of a particularly long day, after finishing up the first of the remaining six fields, Junior Delgado was driving down SR 12 on his way back to Yakima. He was pleased with the field's yield and how smoothly the harvest had gone. He was thinking of the next day's tasks as he rounded a big sweeping corner when *"whap"* – a hole appeared in the windshield of his Dodge Ram truck. A millisecond later, he felt a pain in his chest. He couldn't breathe. What was happening, he thought to himself. A second later, the truck careened off the highway, sideswiped a pine tree, and ended up on its top in the Tieton River. Water quickly engulfed the cab of the truck, but it was of no concern to Junior Delgado. He was dead before the truck left the roadway.

A few minutes later, a white Chevy pickup came around the corner. The rig slowed, and as it went by, the driver took a good long look at the taillights of the upside-down pickup in the river.

* * *

Sinclair had done some checking with the Yakima PD investigators on the shooting of Juan Delgado Sr. They still were of the belief the shooting was gang-related, and although it wasn't technically a drive-by, Delgado had definitely been targeted and there was most likely a reason for that.

Sinclair had requested the police report and the autopsy information. When she inspected them, Sinclair noticed something interesting. According to the report's photos, the bullet had entered Delgado's neck just below his chin. But it had excited about four inches lower, in the back of his neck. Investigators had found the bullet stuck in the wood siding almost at grass level at one end of the house. They determined the bullet to be from a .30-06 caliber rifle, but that was about all they had from the mangled piece of lead.

"That tells me he was shot from someplace higher in elevation," Sinclair said to McCain as they discussed it that night at dinner. "I'd think it would have to be from a sniper."

"That's what I thought. What did the YPD detectives say about that?"

"They thought his head might have been leaning forward, that he must have been looking down at something when he was shot."

"I guess it could have happened like that, but it doesn't seem likely. I agree with you. Someone sniped him from a rooftop. And if the shooter was good, it could have been from quite a ways away."

"The other thing to remember is no one reported hearing any gunshot," Sinclair said. "That tells me the shooter might have had a silencer."

"Since we know from Joe Walker that Juan Delgado was working in the pot fields, this feels like it's related to the other killings. More and more it feels like there's a vigilante taking out the people working in the fields."

"I agree," said Sinclair. "I'll talk to YPD tomorrow, but I'm now of the opinion that this is definitely related to the other killings at the pot fields."

The next morning, as McCain was in his office getting ready to head into a meeting, his desk phone rang.

"Guess who the State Patrol just pulled out of the Tieton River?" Sinclair said to McCain as he answered his phone. She didn't let him guess. "Juan Delgado Jr. He was shot in the chest as he was driving down SR 12."

"Oh, man. That's not good," McCain said. "Joe Walker, the elk poacher, said he was working in the pot fields too."

"It looks like he was hit while he was driving. If he was doing fifty-five or sixty, that would take some fancy shooting."

"If I worked in one of the pot fields, I'd be feeling a little nervous right about now. In fact, I'd be considering calling in sick."

"That's probably what the shooter wants. But how is he, if it is a he, getting the information on who's working the fields? I can see finding a field and staking it out and shooting the workers if you have a vendetta. But these last two weren't close to the fields."

"I don't know," said McCain. "This whole thing has me perplexed."

"Well, I need to figure it out here pretty quickly," Sinclair said. "The body count is adding up."

With that, she said goodbye and hung up. McCain sat and considered everything his FBI agent girlfriend had just told him. He silently wished her luck.

After his meeting, McCain ran home, grabbed Jack, and headed up to see what he might find on the trail cameras he'd placed at Walt Ashford's place. On his way through Naches, he stopped to grab some chicken strips to-go from the drive-in next to the highway. He got his chicken strips and was sitting in his truck eating, with a yellow dog watching each bite with high anticipation, when a man in a red Ford F-150 pulled up next to him. McCain recognized him as one of the guys from the ATVs who had reported the shooting on the Little Naches.

When he pulled up, McCain rolled down his window.

"Hi, Officer McCain," the man said. "Art Duncan from up on the Little Naches."

"Sure," McCain said. "How are you, Mr. Duncan?"

"I'm just fine. I ended up getting a spike bull with my muzzleloader, so I have some good meat in the freezer. Don't know if I will even go deer hunting since I don't really need any more venison."

"Congratulations," McCain said. "How about your buddy? Mr. Clark was it?"

"That's right. He didn't have any luck, so he will be hunting for deer. I haven't seen anything in the news about the shooting of that man in the pot field. Have they found the shooter?"

"No, not that I've heard of."

"How about those people driving through the Little Naches River? I really hope you catch them. I hate law-breakers. They give us all a bad name."

"Yeah, we got them. Just a couple of kids. One of them crashed his ATV as he ran from police and got kind of busted up. I think they learned their lesson."

"I hope so. We'll still keep a watch on stuff up there. If we see anything else that's out-of-line, okay if we call you?"

"That would be great, thanks."

Duncan rolled up his window, pulled back onto the highway and headed east toward Yakima.

Nice guy, McCain thought. It was people like Duncan who kept their eyes and ears open that helped solve many wildlife crimes. The hard-working wildlife police officers were spread very thin, and if it wasn't for people reporting violations, there would be way more unsolved cases out there.

As he ate half of his last chicken strip, he wondered if someone who knew more about the pot field worker killings might step forward with information. His thoughts were interrupted by a loud bark. Jack had watched McCain eat almost all the strips, and he was not going to let the last half get eaten without objection.

"Sorry, boy," McCain said as he handed the last bite to Jack. "Good thing you said something."

Jack swallowed the meat, wagged his tail, and then started snarfing around the seat for crumbs.

McCain was just getting ready to head up the highway to check the trail cameras at Mr. Ashford's place when he got a call on the radio.

"Wildlife 148, you have a copy?" the dispatch voice asked.

"This is 148. Go ahead."

"I have a call from a citizen who is reporting a pack of dogs chasing and killing deer up in the Wenas. Can you check it out?"

"Copy. I'll head that way now. Text me the information on the reporting party, and I'll make contact."

McCain drove through Naches, up the grade to North Wenas Road, and headed west as his phone buzzed. It was a text with the information he needed to contact the caller. The woman's name was Sheila Lewis. She lived off North Wenas Road, two miles above Wenas Lake. McCain pulled over for a minute, got the woman's phone number and dialed.

When the woman answered, McCain said, "Ms. Lewis, this is Officer McCain with the Department of Fish and Wildlife. I'm on my way to your place, but could you briefly tell me what's going on?"

"It's my neighbors' dogs," she said. "As soon as they leave for work, the dogs go on the prowl. I think some dogs from other neighbors join in, and for the last few days I've seen them chasing deer. I figured the deer could get away, but today I saw them drag one down and kill it."

"Okay, is the dead deer on your property or the neighbors?"

"It's actually on state land on the other side of the creek.

They shouldn't be doing that anyplace."

"I agree," McCain said. "I'll be there in ten minutes."

When McCain arrived at Sheila Lewis's house, the woman was standing in the driveway. She had a worried look on her face and spoke frantically.

"They're doing it again. I just saw them. They ran across over there chasing another deer."

Washington State laws allow for police officers to use deadly force if necessary on dogs pursuing wildlife. So McCain grabbed his .223 rifle just in case that was necessary. He had Jack stay at heel, and they headed to where Lewis had last seen the dogs. As they got close to the spot, Jack's ears went up, and a low growl rumbled in his throat.

"Easy, boy," McCain whispered to the Lab.

As they approached the creek, McCain saw four dogs tearing into a deer. He raised his rifle and shot, killing the most aggressive dog. He thought the other dogs would turn and run at the shot, but instead they turned and started toward him and Jack. McCain quickly raised his semi-automatic rifle and shot again, taking down the largest of the three remaining dogs. The other two kept coming.

"Stay, Jack!" McCain hissed.

He knew Jack would jump into the middle of the action if they kept coming. Both dogs looked like they were nothing to mess with, and the last thing he needed was for Jack to get torn up in a dogfight.

The two remaining dogs kept coming. McCain shot again, killing the nearest dog with a bullet to the head. The final dog decided to head for safer ground. McCain watched the dog run up the hill, across the road, and up onto the porch of a double-wide manufactured home. Unfortunately, the deer was still alive, so McCain put it down with a shot from his rifle. Then he and Jack walked back to where Lewis was standing in the driveway.

"Well, that was something," Lewis said. "Weren't you afraid when those dogs came at you?"

"Not really, but it was getting kind of hairy there for a minute," McCain answered. "I need you to do something for me, if you would. First, please call 911 and ask for a sheriff's deputy to come out here. Then, please write down everything you just witnessed, starting with your call to our office and my discussions with you on the phone earlier and here in the driveway before I went to look for the dogs."

"Okay," she said. "We've told the neighbors that their dogs are running deer when they aren't home, but they didn't believe it. They say they're always on the porch when they're home."

"Put that in your statement, too, if you would. I need to go gather up the dead deer and figure out what to do with the dogs."

McCain and Jack headed back to the creek. He knew where the second deer was, but he needed to find the first deer. When they were close to where Lewis had said the first deer was killed, McCain sent Jack out.

"Go find it, boy."

Jack trotted out and started casting back and forth, just as he would if he were covering a field looking for pheasants. It didn't take him long to find the deer. When he did, he stopped and stood by it, looking back at McCain.

"Good boy," McCain said when he got to Jack, rewarding him with pats on the sides.

The deer was a yearling buck with two buttons on the top of his head that would have been antlers the following year. The buck wasn't damaged too much, so McCain pulled out his knife and field dressed it. No need for the meat to go to waste. Once he had removed the entrails, he grabbed the deer by the back legs and dragged it to where he'd put down the other deer. He did the same thing with the young doe, dressing it so that the meat would cool. He was just finishing up when the voice of YSO Deputy

Williams interrupted the peace and quiet.

"Hey, Rifleman. Where are you?"

"Over here," McCain hollered.

He had asked Williams to stop calling him Rifleman over and over, but to no avail. Shooting this pack of dogs wasn't going to help. As Williams arrived, Jack went over to greet him.

"Hey, Jack," Williams said, rubbing the dog's ears. "Dang, the dog owners aren't going to be pleased about this. Glad it was you and not me. I probably would have missed."

"Yeah, well, we need to figure out what to do with the dogs," McCain said. "We need to ID the owners and try to reach them. Maybe Ms. Lewis back there can assist on that. The last dog from the pack ran to that green double-wide on the hill. It's sitting on the porch. You might be careful when you go knock on the door."

"That won't be happening. I'm not walking up to that door. I'll figure out another way to contact the owners."

"Whatever," McCain said. "The dog will need to be put down is my guess, or they'll have to figure out a way to guarantee that it will stay home."

When McCain and Jack got back to the truck in the Lewis driveway, dragging the second deer behind them, Williams was on the phone talking to someone. Williams clearly was not happy.

"Yes, they're both dead, Mr. Lindsay." There was a long pause while Williams listened. "Well, you should have kept them at home." Another long pause as a fast-talking voice rattled in the phone. "You do what you think is right, but we have witnesses that watched your dogs take down two deer, and then they turned on the officer. By allowing your dogs to run free and create this situation, there have been several violations." More fast-talking on the other end of the line. "Yes, you will be receiving citations." Another pause. "Well, that's your prerogative." Click.

"He didn't sound very happy," McCain said.

"He should keep his dogs at home," Williams said. "He said

he's not paying any fines and that he'll be suing everyone up to and including the governor. According to him, his two dogs are pussycats and wouldn't hurt a thing."

"Well, they're dead pussycats now," Sheila Lewis said.

"We'll need to take the dogs to have them tested for rabies," Williams said. "So, if you can give me a hand rounding them up, I'll take them to town."

"What about the other dog's owner?" McCain asked.

"I haven't gotten any contact information on them. I have the address, so I'll look them up. Ms. Lewis said they go to work early and are usually home by three o'clock."

"What are you going to do with the deer?" Lewis asked.

"I'm going to run them to the butcher so the meat can be processed and donated to the Mission."

"At least their killing wasn't a total waste," Lewis said. "Thank you so much for coming. I hope the neighbors don't hate me for getting their dogs shot."

"You did the right thing," Williams said. "If they give you any trouble, give me a call. It is against the law to let dogs run free like that, and all this is their fault."

Williams gave the lady his card with his contact information, and both he and McCain headed back to the creek to get the dogs.

CHAPTER 16

McCain was driving the deer carcasses to a butcher in Wapato when his phone lit up. He looked at the screen and saw that it was Sinclair calling.

"Hey," he said after pushing the Bluetooth button on his steering wheel. "What's up?"

"We have some more information on the Delgado kid killed in the truck that went into the Tieton River," Sinclair said.

"Let me guess. He was shot with a thirty-caliber rifle."

"That's what the coroner thinks. And I'm thinking this vigilante thing might have legs."

"It sure sounds like it."

"The problem is no one has seen anything."

"Well, except the guys on the ATVs," McCain said. "They may have actually seen the shooter. But not good enough to get a decent description."

"We're going to start looking at all the known overdoses in the county for the past year. Maybe some irate father of a child who OD'd is pissed that his kid started smoking pot, and the next thing you know, he's doing meth and fentanyl, gets some bad stuff, and dies."

"That's a bit of a stretch, but I guess you could make a case for that."

"Stranger things have happened."

"Yeah, but I think I'd keep looking at the competition," said McCain. "Maybe some pot shop owners have had enough with the illegal stuff hitting the streets and have brought in someone to eliminate the illegal competition. It's gotta be cutting into their sales."

"Could be," said Sinclair. "Definitely worth checking. It sounds at least as plausible as the crazed-father deal. What are you up to?"

He went into the story about getting the call on the pack of dogs and what had transpired.

"I'm taking the deer to the butcher's now."

"Is Jack okay?" Sinclair asked.

At the sound of his name coming over the Bluetooth speakers, Jack stood up in the back seat and started wagging his tail.

"Yes, Jack is fine. Oh, and by the way, I'm okay too if you're concerned."

"I'm always concerned about you, but since you are talking to me, I assumed you are fine. I can't see Jack, so I had to ask."

"Good comeback, counselor," McCain said. "We'll be home by dinner."

He clicked off and said to Jack, "I'm not sure how you rate, but you do."

Jack wagged his tail, turned a couple circles in the back seat, and settled in for a nap.

Sinclair had studied law at the University of Oregon, but her career path had taken her into the FBI. She had come to the Yakima office a couple years earlier to help with the growing number of missing and murdered Native American women from the Yakama Nation. McCain and Sinclair rarely argued, but when they did, she always won. Sinclair was smart, quick, and would have made an excellent courtroom attorney, McCain thought. That was one of the things he loved about her.

After he dropped off the deer carcasses at the butcher, he decided he still had time to run up to Walt Ashford's place. It had been a couple days since he placed the cameras on the fence next to the road, and he took a chance that there had been some activity.

When McCain arrived, Walt was just walking up the driveway. The man had on a heavy sweater and khakis, and he was carrying the same walking stick he'd had at the WDFW offices in Yakima.

"Hi, Walt," McCain said as he let Jack out of the truck. Jack immediately ran over to the old gentleman but slowed before he got there. It was like Jack knew that the old man was a bit fragile and unsteady and didn't want to knock him off-balance. "Nice afternoon for a walk."

"I'm just heading to get the mail," Ashford said. "Every day at four o'clock. And I walk to get the paper every morning at seven."

Ashford's gravel driveway was about four hundred yards long, so it was a bit of a walk.

"I've been doing that every day for the last thirty years," he said. "Come to check on the cameras?"

"Yes, sir."

"Well, you should have something. When I got up to pee at four this morning, I saw one of the trucks coming down the hill. It passed right by on the road. Hope you can get a license plate."

"Let's just see what we can see," McCain said.

He downloaded the photos from the first camera to his handheld reader and then walked to the second camera and did the same thing. When he had all the photos from both cameras on the device, he walked back to where Ashford was standing, Jack by his side.

"Could we go to your house to review these?" McCain asked. "It might take a few minutes."

"Sure," Ashford said. "I have some lemonade made up. And

I might have another cookie for Jack."

Jack wagged his tail and nuzzled against Ashford's leg.

When they were inside, McCain sat down at the kitchen table and started swiping through the photos. The first group of photos was taken from the camera down the road. Virtually every photo was of a vehicle, but many were just blurs. Toward the end of the shots from that camera, McCain found some of a large, light-colored commercial truck. Because they were night shots, McCain couldn't tell the exact color of the truck, nor get a read on the license plates. He wasn't sure if the photo quality was poor because of the truck's speed or if the plates were just dirty.

Ashford came over with glasses of lemonade and a small plate of cookies.

"Find anything?" he asked.

"Well, I have found the truck you saw last night. The time stamp matches, but take a look and see if they are the ones you've been seeing."

"Yes, that's one of the trucks. But my old eyes aren't able to focus on the license plate."

"It's not your eyes, Walt. The photos are blurry. I think they've covered the plate with mud or dirt."

"That happens up here on these dusty roads," Ashford said as he slipped a bite of cookie to Jack, who had put his head on the man's knee.

McCain kept swiping and found the photos from the camera pointing up the road. He moved through the photos, watching the time stamp. When he hit four o'clock, he slowed down. He swiped through a couple more photos, and up came the big truck. McCain could tell it was a GMC truck with a big van behind the cab. Otherwise, he could see nothing else that might distinguish the truck other than the make and size. He thought a couple letters and numbers on the front license plate might be readable on a larger screen, but he'd have to wait on that.

"Well, I'm not seeing much in these," McCain said. "Maybe we can get something on a bigger computer screen. One thing I don't see on the truck is refrigeration. If they were taking big game and hauling out carcasses, they'd definitely want to keep the meat cool."

"Maybe they're totally legitimate," Ashford said. "I just thought it was strange that they always come out of the mountains in the cover of darkness."

"Something's going on," McCain said after he took a big drink of lemonade. "Let's see what the photos tell us. I still might need to be up here in person to check it out. I'll let you know."

McCain stood up to tell Ashford thanks and so long. Jack remained next to the old gentleman.

"Okay, one more bite of cookie before you go," Ashford said to Jack, breaking off another piece for him.

"Come on, Jack," McCain said. "The last thing Walt needs around here is a big oafy dog constantly begging for treats."

"Oh, I very much enjoy it," Ashford said as he patted Jack on the back of the head.

When they got back to the truck, McCain looked at the time. There was still about an hour of daylight left, so he decided he'd run up Nile Road and see if he could locate where the trucks might be coming out of the mountains.

As he drove, he called Sinclair on the Bluetooth. Her phone rang several times and then went to voicemail.

"Hey, just me," McCain said. "I'm up in the Nile, visiting with Walt Ashford. Since I'm here, I'm going to take a look around the mountain while there's still some daylight. I won't be home until about seven. Eat without me if you're hungry."

McCain pressed "end call" on his steering wheel and headed west on Nile Road. He turned south on the road that followed Nile Creek and eventually led to Little Bald Mountain. He didn't have time to go all the way to the top now, but he drove along and looked for any clues that the trucks had been on that road.

Seeing nothing of interest, he decided to stop by a campsite that had a fire going in a rock ring near a couple truck campers and a travel trailer. Three older men were sitting around the ring in folding chairs, poking at the fire with sticks.

McCain rolled down his window, took in the welcoming smell of burning tamarack, and said, "Gentlemen, how are you doing this evening?"

The three men all looked to be in their late sixties or early seventies.

"Finer than frog's hair," a man in sweatpants and a camo jacket said. He was wearing a hunter orange ball cap. "How can it get any better? There's just something about poking a campfire with a stick that calms a fella down."

The other two men nodded their heads in agreement.

"You guys up to hunt deer?" McCain asked.

"We don't hunt anymore," a second man said. He was wearing blue overalls, a flannel shirt and a green John Deere tractor hat. "We just come up to hold the family camp for our boys. They'll be here before elk season opens."

"I see," McCain said. "I've received reports of some big tan trucks driving up and down this road in the middle of the night. You guys see anything like that last night?"

"You know, I got up to pee at 3:30 or so, and just when I was about to fall back asleep, I did hear a big truck moving down the road," the man in the John Deere hat said. "But I didn't look to see what kind it was."

"Something else kind of weird happened today," said the third man, who was wearing a pair of gray jeans, a blue Carhartt shirt, a brown Carhartt jacket and a bright red MAGA hat. "Some guy pulled in here earlier asking if we'd ever run into any pot fields up in the mountains. I wouldn't know a pot plant from a petunia and told him so."

"That is weird," McCain said. "What did he look like?"

The men gave a similar description of the man who'd been talking to hunters up the Little Naches. They also said he was driving a white Chevy pickup.

"Anyone happen to take down a license plate number or a photo of the truck on their phone?"

"My phone is a phone, nothing more," said MAGA-hat man. The two other men nodded. "And we didn't think about the tag numbers. If we see him again, we'll try to get them."

"Okay, well, thanks. And keep poking that campfire," McCain said.

"Oh, you can count on that," the man in the orange hat said. "There's nothing better."

McCain had asked Sinclair to check with the DEA on the thin, fit man with the short, brown hair to see if he was one of their agents. They told her they had nobody working in the Central Washington region that fit that description. And if it had been one of theirs, he would have identified himself as a federal agent and shown credentials.

Who was this mysterious man, McCain wondered as he drove back to Lower Naches. And was he the guy taking out the illegal pot growers?

CHAPTER 17

"Are you hungry?" Sinclair asked as McCain and Jack walked through the front door.

"Are you asking me or Jack?" McCain asked teasingly. "Seeing how concerned you are about him."

"I was asking both of you, although I know Jack's answer."

"Something sure smells good," McCain said, sniffing the air as he went to retrieve Jack's dish while the yellow dog jumped up and down next to him.

"I decided to make spaghetti."

"Well, if it tastes half as good as it smells, it's going to be delicious. And, by the way, I'm starving."

"Sounds like you had an interesting day."

"Yeah, people really need to keep their dogs at home. Especially in the country where there's wildlife," McCain said. "That's pretty weird about the Delgado kid being shot with a thirty-caliber rifle. Have you folded that into your investigation of the other pot workers' deaths?"

"Yes, I talked with the sheriff and the YPD today. After laying out the evidence on who we think the Delgados were and what they were doing, they turned the files over to us."

"That guy I told you about is still bugging hunters about illegal pot fields in the mountains. I talked to some old boys up by the Nile this evening who said he came into their camp today, asking them if they'd seen any illegal pot fields."

"Depending on how old they are, they probably have no idea what a pot plant looks like."

"That's what they said. Although they had to be young men in the 1960s. Lots of pot was being smoked in those days. You know, peace, love and all that."

"That's true," Sinclair said. "Dinner will be ready in ten minutes."

"Just enough time to feed a starving dog."

Jack barked. He'd had enough talking. He was ready for his dinner. Now!

The spaghetti was as good as it smelled. McCain ate a second helping, as did Sinclair. After dinner they sat and talked a bit more about the pot field killings.

"I feel like we're kind of spinning our wheels on this deal," Sinclair said. "We have an idea why the men might have been killed, but not about who could have done it."

"Any more thoughts on why the hunter might have been killed at the same time as the workers near the field in Kittitas County? I'd have thought it was the same person doing the shooting, but it makes no sense that the person would use two different rifles."

"No clue," Sinclair said. "I'm still thinking the poor guy was in the wrong spot at the wrong time."

"I'd like to talk to this guy who's asking all the hunters if they've seen any illegal pot fields around," McCain said. "What's his story?"

"Again, no clue. But it would be good to find out who he is."

"Well, maybe I'll run into him," he said. "It seems like I've been all around him but just haven't been in the same spot at the same time."

"What's going on with the trucks up by Mr. Ashford in the Nile?"

"Now I'll say it – no clue. My initial thought was they were poachers moving carcasses out of the hills at night. But from the trail camera photos I saw today, the truck didn't have a refrigeration unit on the box. Plus, there aren't enough animals around to be able to kill so many that you'd need such a big truck to haul them out. I'm thinking it's something else. Maybe illegal timber cutting, or it might be more marijuana growers. I think I'll head up there again tomorrow and really look around."

"Doesn't deer season open tomorrow?" Sinclair asked. "You'll have your hands full just dealing with that."

"Probably, but still, I'll see what I can see. There are lots of eyes in the woods during deer season. I'll ask a bunch of questions."

"Good idea. I'm going to go take a hot shower and read for a bit. It's your night for the dishes, I believe. I tried to not make too big of a mess."

McCain looked over at the sink and the counters on either side. Pots were stacked on pots.

"I should be done by breakfast."

He looked over at Jack who was sprawled out, dead asleep in front of the couch.

"A lot of help you are," McCain said to the dog. But Jack was in the middle of a dream, whimpering and moving his legs like he was trying to catch something. Probably a squirrel he couldn't quite reach, McCain thought.

* * *

McCain was awake when his alarm went off at 4:30 the next morning. When he was a kid, he loved the opening of deer season. He would go with his dad and brother to the mountains west of Yakima, and they would hunt all day. They weren't always successful, but he loved being in the mountains, learning about the animals.

When he was old enough to drive, McCain and some buddies would go up and spend the night in the mountains and hunt both days of the opening weekend. They'd have to come home on Sunday night to go to school on Monday, but as soon as the bell rang each afternoon, they'd hustle up into the hills and hunt until dark. He learned a great deal during those formative years, and it put him on the path to the career he now enjoyed.

This opening day was different from the ones of his youth. He was on the clock today and would be busy contacting hunters to ensure they adhered to the hunting laws of Washington State. Even though he wasn't hunting, he was anxious to see what the day would bring.

Jack heard McCain stirring in the kitchen and soon wandered in to see what was going on.

"You ready for a fun day?" McCain asked the dog.

Jack lay down on the tile floor and immediately went back to sleep.

"I guess that answers that."

McCain went in and kissed Sara goodbye. When he returned to the kitchen, he said, "Come on you lazy mutt, let's go earn our keep."

He and fellow WDFW officer Stan Hargraves had met the day before and coordinated where they were going to be patrolling. Hargraves was going to work in the mountains west of Yakima, and McCain was going to be working in the hills west of Ellensburg in Kittitas County.

Because it was early, McCain ran through the twenty-four-hour drive-thru at McDonald's just off the highway and grabbed a couple of bacon, egg and cheese biscuits. Jack poked his nose through the space between the two front seats as soon as he smelled the breakfast sandwiches.

"Okay, just hold your horses. I'll get you a bite. Let me get the thing unwrapped."

McCain could hear the dog's tail whacking the back of the passenger seat. He should have just given Jack one of the sandwiches straight away, because that's pretty much what the dog ended up eating between the bites McCain tried taking.

It was just becoming daylight as McCain drove up the Forest Service road to Manastash Lake. He was driving slowly around a gradual turn in the road when he saw red taillights through a cloud of dust ahead. Suddenly, both the driver's door and the passenger-side door flew open. Out of the jacked-up, red Chevy 4X4 pickup came two men, rifles in their hands. They left the doors wide open as they ran up the hill into the woods.

McCain watched them for a minute until they disappeared over a small hill and then noticed their truck was still gradually moving forward. He looked to see if there was someone in the truck. Seeing no one, he drove toward the rolling truck as quickly as he could. Unfortunately, the road was falling away, gradually getting steeper, and the driverless truck was starting to gain speed. McCain thought about jumping out and running down to get into the pickup, but valor gave way to a cooler head. The truck was moving faster now, and there was no way to get to it before it left the road at another bend. McCain watched as the red truck careened off a big pine tree, smashing the passenger door closed before disappearing over the edge of a steep side hill.

McCain parked carefully, applied his emergency brake, told Jack to stay, and went down to see where the truck had ended up. He was walking down the hill to the spot where the truck left the road when he heard a rifle shot up the hill, and then another. Then there was a holler.

"Whoooo-hoooo!" yelled a man up the hill.

McCain took it to mean one of the two men who had bailed

out of the truck had killed a deer. Unfortunately, their joy over bagging a buck would be dampened when they got back to the road. Their red Chevy had obviously rolled at least once after it had left the road, and there wasn't a straight piece of metal on the thing.

Since it might be a while before the men made it back down to the road, McCain decided to hike up and break the bad news. Before he started the climb, he radioed dispatch and made a report of the pickup off the road.

"Hold off on sending a tow truck until I talk to the owner," McCain said. "But he's going to need it."

"Received," said the dispatcher.

"Come on, Jack," McCain said as he opened the back door. Jack flew out, ready to go someplace, anyplace.

"Wow, you're in a hurry this morning."

Then it occurred to McCain that Mother Nature was calling, and the dog was desperate. After Jack had done his business, they headed up the hill to where McCain had heard the shot. When they got close, Jack's ears went up. McCain knew the dog could hear voices.

"Go find them," McCain said.

Jack led him right to the two men.

"Hi, fellas," McCain said as he spotted them working on field dressing the deer. "Looks like you had some success?"

"Yes, sir," one of the men said. He was in his early 20s, McCain thought, wearing blue jeans, a bright orange sweatshirt and a camo Cabela's hat. "This is Justin's first deer."

Justin, another young man, was smiling ear-to-ear. The buck was legal, with three points on each antler. The men had already notched a deer tag and affixed it to one of the horns.

"Well, congratulations, Justin," McCain said. "Looks like a nice one."

"We spotted him from the road," Justin said. He wore a black sweatshirt under a hunter orange vest and had the same cap and jeans as his buddy. "He ran up the hill, but we got here in time to get a good shot. I missed the first time but dropped him with the second shot."

"You did the right thing not shooting from the truck and getting off the road," McCain said. "And about the truck . . ."

The owner of the truck, a twenty-something named Tom Haney, couldn't believe it when McCain told him what happened.

"My wife is going to kill me," Haney said. "I just put about a thousand bucks into that truck against her wishes. She's going to be pissed."

"Yeah, well, if you have it insured, you should be alright," McCain said. "I can help Justin get the buck down the hill to the road if you want to go start figuring out what you want to do. I reported it to the sheriff's office but didn't have them send a wrecker yet. I wanted to talk to you first."

"Aw, geez," Haney said. "I think I'll just go down there and move into the thing. I really don't want to go home. Jennifer is going to be royally pissed."

McCain looked at Justin. He was still smiling and looked like he was about to burst out laughing. He obviously felt for his buddy, but he seemed more happy about tagging his first buck. Haney wandered down the hill while McCain grabbed an antler to help drag the buck down to the road.

"Jennifer is definitely going to be pissed," Justin said. "Frankly, she's pissed at everything Tommy does. She's a first-rate, absolute, A-number one bitch! Poor guy had to beg and beg just to go hunting this morning, and now this happens. He might lose a testicle over this one."

McCain couldn't help but chuckle.

"Yeah, some women are like that," he said to Justin. "Never quite figured out why."

CHAPTER 18

After making sure the two men from the wrecked Chevy had tow-truck assistance and a ride home, McCain checked two other hunters with legal bucks and several others who were still out hunting. Everyone was licensed correctly and wearing the right amount of hunter orange.

Just before one o'clock, McCain decided he'd run into Ellensburg and grab a hamburger. He was heading that way when he got a call on the radio.

"Wildlife 148, I have a call from a hunter who has mistakenly killed an illegal buck. He wants to see an enforcement officer."

"Received," said McCain. "Get me the location, and I'll go talk to him."

The dispatcher told McCain that the man was in a campground about eight miles up the Taneum Road, which was convenient because McCain was driving down that very road and was only a few miles from the location.

When he pulled into the campground, he spotted a guy in a blaze orange jacket waving at him. McCain drove over to the man who was standing next to a Dodge Ram pickup. On the tailgate was a huge deer. The thing, McCain thought, looked like an elk.

"Thanks for coming, officer," the man said.

"Sure," McCain said. "Thanks for calling it in."

McCain got out of the truck and looked at the buck. Again, he couldn't believe the size of the animal. The buck was old, with a scarred-up Roman nose and ears that were tattered from fighting. The antlers were big too. They were close to thirty inches wide – dark, heavy and tall. The only problem was there were no eye guards, just two points on each antler. It was a giant forked-horn.

The man who shot the deer was Rod Hudson and, as he told his story, McCain started to understand how the man had made the mistake of shooting the big buck. Washington regulations for mule deer are that only bucks with at least three points on one antler are legal to shoot.

"I jumped him out of some aspens, and as soon as I saw him, I knew he was big. I looked through my binoculars and was positive he had at least three on one side. I mean, a deer that old and that big is usually a four-point. It must have been the angle, and I was catching the tip of the opposite antler as a third point as I looked at him. Anyway, I shot. He humped up, turned downhill, and piled up in a tangle of junipers. I was ecstatic until I walked up and saw this," Hudson said as he pointed to the antlers.

There were times when McCain hated some of the rules he had to enforce. This was one of them. Every biologist in the department would want this old buck with the abnormal rack out of the gene pool. The man had actually done everyone a favor. But rules were rules.

"First of all, I totally understand how this happened," McCain said. "Frankly, I've never seen a bigger, older buck with a set of antlers like this. And I really appreciate you turning yourself in."

Hudson smiled a kind of sickened smile.

"So, here's what I'm going to do. Normally, I would confiscate the deer and write you a citation for shooting an illegal animal. But today is your lucky day. I'm going to write you a warning and send you on your way."

"Gee, really?" Hudson asked. "That's very nice of you."

"Well, this is a very rare exception. Kind of a once-in-a-lifetime deal, so just know there is no get-out-of-jail card if it happens again."

"No, sir. Thank you."

McCain could see the man thinking.

"You know what?" Hudson said. "Since you've been so lenient on this, I might have some information you'd be interested in."

"Okay," McCain said. "Whatcha got?"

"You know those mountain goats they transplanted out of Olympic National Park a while back?"

"Yes, I'm familiar with the operation," McCain said.

Back in the early 1900s a few mountain goats were transplanted into the Olympic Mountains in Northwestern Washington. A few years later, the mountains and surrounding area were designated a national park. The designation meant no more hunting of the goats or any game animals within the boundaries of the park. With no hunting for decades and very few natural predators around, the non-native mountain goats had become overpopulated and were having a seriously negative effect on the ecosystems in the park. In recent years there even had been a few altercations between the sometimes-ornery goats and people who enjoyed hiking the many trails around the park.

So, state and federal officials developed a three-year plan to dart and translocate as many of the 725 goats living in the park as they could, moving them via helicopter to the rugged wilderness areas of the Cascades. The native goats in the Cascades needed a boost, so it was a win-win operation. And, when all the dust settled, there'd be more chances for hunters to draw one of the once-in-a-lifetime goat permits from the state.

"My brother-in-law is kind of the black sheep of the family," Hudson started to explain. "He seems to always have his hand in something just a little bit shady."

"I know a few guys like that," McCain said.

"So, somehow he knows a guy who knows one of the helicopter pilots who took a bunch of those goats into an area up by Snoqualmie Pass. He figures out where the goats are, and all of a sudden he's a goat hunting guide. It's all under the table, mind you, but he's advertising somewhere on the internet that he'll take hunters and put them on a goat for ten thousand dollars a head, including license, tag, taxes and what have you. I'm not supposed to know about it, but my wife's sister is married to this genius. She told my wife, and my wife told me. If she knew I was telling you, I'd probably be served divorce papers with breakfast on Sunday morning, but I just don't think it's right."

"Well, thank you for telling me, Mr. Hudson," McCain said. "Any chance you could get a line on the advertisement your brother-in-law is putting on the internet?"

"I don't know. Seriously, if my wife finds out I ratted on the idiot, I'll be out on my ear."

"Okay, well, don't push it. I think one of our tech guys can figure out where he's selling his guided goat hunting trips."

McCain got the name and address of the brother-in-law, thanked Hudson again, who in turn thanked McCain again, and they went their separate ways.

When McCain got back into his truck, Jack was eagerly awaiting him.

"See there, boy," McCain said to the dog. "No good deed goes unrewarded, or whatever the saying is."

Jack licked McCain's cheek and pounded a steady beat on the back seat with his tail.

"Okay, boy. Let's go get some lunch."

After lunch, McCain drove into the Colockum area northeast of Ellensburg and checked several more deer hunters. Again, only two hunters had been successful, one of them a twelve-year-old boy deer hunting for the first time. The boy, who was hunting with his grandpa, made an amazing shot on a nice three-by-four buck, or so the story went. The kid was very proud and happy, as was his granddad.

"Good for you," McCain said after he checked the boy's license and tag. "Congratulations!"

As McCain drove back to Yakima, he thought about the boy hunting with his grandfather. It took him back to many of the hunts he had enjoyed with his dad and grandpa when he was growing up. He was still reminiscing when Hargraves called to check in on how the day had gone. McCain told him about watching the red truck go off the road, and the illegal goat hunting operation that he'd learned of from Rod Hudson.

"We'll need to get one of the tech guys looking into it on Monday to see if we can get a line on this guy," Hargraves said. "Then one of us might just be going on a goat hunt."

Wildlife officers often go undercover as hunters and book a hunting or fishing trip with someone who's reportedly breaking the law. It's sometimes the only way to catch them in the act.

"And I think I know who it will be," McCain said. "You're not in good enough shape to be hiking around those mountains."

"Hey," Hargraves said, sounding like his feelings were hurt. There was a pause and then he said, "But yeah, you're probably right."

After discussing more of the contacts they'd made during the day, including a guy Hargraves caught hiding an illegal buck under his pickup in the bracket that should hold a spare tire, they agreed to meet first thing Monday morning and discuss a plan to catch the goat poacher.

"So, how'd you figure out the guy was hiding a deer under his truck?" McCain asked.

"I was following him down the road out of the Wenas, and I could see this thing dragging along the road. As I looked closer, I could see it was a deer leg. He might have gotten away with it if he'd tied the legs up tighter."

As McCain drove the rest of the way home, he listened to Jack snoring in the back seat and thought about the day and everything that had happened. It was one of those days when he really loved his job.

Chapter 19

Jerome Dirksen had been a decent student and a pretty good athlete in high school, but he also liked to have a little fun. Like many of the other kids in his school, he'd gone to a few keggers and smoked pot now and again. No big deal. Everyone did it.

But after he graduated, life started to take a turn. Several of his friends had gone off to college and a couple went into the military. He was a bit lost, and out of boredom and self pity, he started drinking more and playing around with other drugs. He excused his substance abuse, telling his buddies it helped him get over the fact he'd had "a shitty life."

His parents had divorced when he was twelve. His dad had immediately remarried, and for whatever reason the new wife didn't take a liking to Jerome. She started popping out kids, and from the arrival of the first half-brother, his father had very little time for Jerome or his sister. On top of that, his mom had mowed through a string of boyfriends. Each, in Dirksen's opinion, was a bigger jerk than the last. So, as soon as he turned eighteen and could legally be on his own, he was out of there.

After high school, Dirksen went to work at one of the big

box home stores that sold hardware and appliances. But after a while, making only minimum wage just wasn't cutting it. He needed something else to help cover his monthly bills. So, after a friend had hooked him up with some cocaine one day, Dirksen inquired about becoming a seller too. One thing led to another, and pretty soon Dirksen had quit his job at the home store and was making some serious cash providing pot, cocaine, and a few other goodies to a robust list of clients.

He had just made a late-night delivery to a doctor's wife in West Valley and was walking back to his car when a bullet hit him in the center of his chest. The residents in the affluent neighborhood had not heard the shot, so unfortunately for Dirksen, no help was coming. Not that it would have done any good. Within ninety seconds, he had lost a significant amount of blood, and in another thirty seconds his "shitty life" was over.

* * *

It had taken a while, but the crime reporter at the *Yakima Herald-Republic* started putting together the possibility that the pot fields killings and the murder of Jerome Dirksen, a known drug dealer, might be connected.

Sinclair had already made that connection when she learned that Dirksen had been killed by a bullet from a high-powered rifle, most likely a thirty-caliber of some kind. As with the shot that killed the elder Delgado down by the fairgrounds, the bullet had entered Dirksen's body higher than where it exited, meaning the shot came from higher ground. Typical of a sniper shot.

After some discussion with the folks at the sheriff's office, it was agreed that they would hand over the Dirksen murder to the FBI. Sinclair added it to her growing file of men with ties to the illegal drug industry who had been killed in Yakima and Kittitas Counties.

When the reporter called YPD and then the sheriff's office to talk about the killings, both agencies sent her to Sinclair. The reporter's name was Theresa Wallens and, after she thanked Sinclair for talking with her, she asked if the FBI thought some kind of vigilante killer could be on the loose, targeting workers in the illegal drug industry. Wallens didn't know about the two Delgados, who Sinclair believed had also been killed by the same shooter.

"We've considered that as one possibility," Sinclair told her without mentioning the Delgados. "But we are looking at several other motives as well. These men are all working with and around bad people, so who knows the reasons for their tragic deaths."

"But," Wallens pressed. "You do think these could be revenge killings?"

"We just don't know. It could be, but it could be just a coincidence too."

Wallens asked several other questions, most of which Sinclair said she couldn't answer due to the ongoing investigation. When she finally hung up the call, Sinclair wondered what might appear in the paper the next morning.

When the first story hit the paper, it sent the news directors at local TV stations into overdrive. Sinclair was hounded for interviews by a bunch of twenty-two-year-old rookie reporters who, as usual, asked a bunch of stupid questions.

All the killings had occurred over a three-week period, but other than the fact that they had all involved people working to produce or sell illegal drugs, there was no rhyme or reason to the shootings, nor any clue when or where the next one, if there was a next one, might occur.

The worker McCain had collared at the pot field after catching the ATV-riding kids had provided very little useful information during Sinclair's interview with him. The man, a Mexican national named Carlos Martinez, was in the United

States illegally. He claimed he was hired to do the pot farming by a man named Raul and said he was paid in cash at the end of each week.

"Good pay too," Martinez said. "Seven hundred dollars a week."

Martinez said Raul provided him a cell phone, and he would contact him weekly to see if he or the other worker needed any growing or living supplies. A man, who Martinez didn't think was Raul, would show up, usually on Sundays, with food, drinks, and other provisions for the week. Sinclair asked if he was aware that some men working in other pot fields in the area had been murdered. He told her he hadn't heard that, but if he thought someone was killing the workers, then he would have left.

"Even seven hundred dollars a week isn't worth dying over," Martinez said in broken English.

He told Sinclair he didn't really know the man he was working with who had escaped through the slit in the back of the tent. His first name was Eduardo, Martinez said, but he didn't know his last name and had no idea where he was from or where he might have gone.

Sinclair believed him and, after pushing him a bit but getting no more usable information, she turned him over to United States Immigration and Customs Enforcement agents, better known as ICE. They would be providing Martinez a flight back to Mexico.

Most couples try not to bring their work home and bore their partner with the minutia of their day-to-day activities, but McCain and Sinclair often discussed nothing else over dinner and before bed. Both seemed to always be thinking about work, and since each had some involvement in the pot farmer killings, their discussions would inevitably turn to the subject.

In addition to working the mountains, mostly contacting deer hunters over the past several days, McCain was trying to figure out what the deal was with the trucks coming out of the mountains at night in the Nile. He'd checked the trail cameras at Walt Ashford's place twice, and while they showed more truck activity in the photos, the quality was not very good, and the license plates were covered in dust and mud.

"I guess I'm just going to have to go up there and spend a couple nights watching for them," McCain said to Sara as he finished washing the dinner dishes. "You know, it could be a good thing," he continued. "It might just spur someone into helping you with a name or something."

"Yeah, maybe," she said. "I know one thing it will do. I'll have Simon Erickson in my office before lunch tomorrow."

Erickson was the go-get-'em reporter for one of the local TV stations. The young reporter had a bit of a speech impediment, frequently starting "th" words with a "d." If a story was breaking, he would be front and center on the six o'clock news, doing a live report from someplace in the region.

"You can bet on it," McCain said. "I've told you before, ol' Simon has a bit of a crush on you, I think."

Right about then, Jack stood up and looked at the front door. If the yellow dog wasn't totally sound asleep, he'd oftentimes hear someone walking up the steps to the front door and would give Luke and Sara a little heads up.

Ten seconds later, the expected knock came, and McCain went to the door. It was Austin Meyers. He had a small bouquet of flowers in his hand.

"Hey Austin," McCain said. "What's up?"

"Is Sara here?"

"She sure is. Come on in."

McCain walked into the kitchen and whispered to Sara, "Austin is here, and he has a little gift for you. You want me to take Jack for a walk so you can have some alone time with him?"

She slapped his upper arm and gave him a stern look but didn't say anything.

"I'm being serious," he said.

When Sara walked into the living room, Austin was kneeling and petting Jack. He stood up and handed her the flowers.

"I just wanted to say thanks for helping me work up the courage to ask Ashlee to homecoming. She was happy I asked her, and we had a great time, other than the fact that her dad had to drive us to dinner and then to the dance."

"What a gentleman," Sinclair said. "Isn't he a gentleman, Luke? It's been like almost a year since anyone has given me flowers. I love flowers. Thank you so much."

"Very subtle," McCain said to Sinclair before turning back to Austin. "So, the dance was fun, huh?"

Austin went on to tell them about the dance. He said that he and Ashlee had been hanging out at school some since then, and his mom was even going to let her come over to his house to work on a biology project, if her mom would let her.

"Hey, I wanted to ask you," McCain said. "Duck season opened last week. You think you and Bear would like to join Jack and me on a little hunt on Sunday?"

"Would we ever! I need to check with my mom, but I'd love to get Bear out on his first real hunt."

"Okay then, ask your mom and let's plan on it. We'll figure out a time on Saturday for Sunday morning."

"I can't wait," Austin said as he headed to the door. "And thanks again, Sara. You're the best!"

When Austin was gone, Sara turned to McCain and said, "So, who do you think he likes better – you or me?"

"I didn't know it was a contest, but if this deal goes much further with Ashlee, it will be you, hands down, no matter how many ducks we shoot."

Sinclair laughed and went back into the kitchen to finish scooping a dish of mint chocolate chip ice cream for dessert.

CHAPTER 20

The next morning, a more in-depth article about the killings and investigation appeared in the paper. The headline in the *Yakima Herald-Republic* read, "FBI INVESTIGATING POSSIBLE VIGILANTE KILLER TAKING OUT ILLEGAL DRUG WORKERS IN THE AREA."

The story went on to tell about the three workers killed in the illegal marijuana fields and the most recent killing of the drug dealer, Jerome Dirksen. It also mentioned the murdered hunter, Shane Wallace, whose body was found buried in the pot field in Kittitas County. There was still some question as to how Wallace's death related to the other killings, according to the report. Kittitas County Sheriff Mark Anderson was quoted saying he hadn't considered the possibility of a vigilante killer. Once the other body was found in the marijuana field in Yakima County, he had turned the investigation over to the FBI. Sinclair was quoted as saying the vigilante angle was a possibility, but they were looking at it from all sides.

The story alluded to the reason Dirksen was out in a gated community in West Valley, which raised some questions from homeowners in the development. Wallen had even interviewed a Jill Carruth who owned a home in the neighborhood with her husband, Dr. Aaron Carruth, close to where Dirksen's body was discovered. She told the reporter she couldn't believe there would be a drug dealer doing business with anyone around there. The reporter didn't mention that Ms. Carruth looked as if she'd been up for thirty-nine hours, with bloodshot eyes and a massive case of the jitters.

Just as Sinclair expected, more TV reporters came out of the woodwork. When she saw Simon Erickson drive up in a TV van, Sinclair looked at the clock on her desk. The digital readout said 11:37. He'd made it before lunch. The young, dark-haired reporter, who was thin and all of about five-foot-eight, wore black Costco slacks, a rumpled white shirt, and what to Sinclair looked like a yellow clip-on necktie.

"Do you have a few minutes to talk about da drug dealer dat was killed da udder night and how it might be related to da udder shootings at da illegal marijuana fields?" Erickson asked when Sinclair met him at the door.

She obliged and told Erickson pretty much exactly what she had told Wallen.

She was just finishing up the interview with Erickson when another TV van arrived, followed by another. Sinclair didn't get to lunch until almost two o'clock, and by then she was famished.

McCain had seen the newspaper headline and read the article before he and Jack headed up the highway to take one more look at the trail camera photos at Walt Ashford's. He thought about calling Sara to see what the story's reaction had been like, though he thought better of it. He knew the media would be bugging her all day today. She always did a great job talking on TV, he thought, but she still hated it. He'd maybe have to do something nice for her tonight. Dinner out would be good. Flowers might be too obvious after Austin's little thank you the night before.

On his way through Naches, McCain caught sight of a tan-colored delivery-style van pulling off the highway into the Ace Hardware store. It looked similar to the ones he'd been seeing on the trail cameras. He decided it might be worth a look-see, so he turned in and parked next to it.

Two men were piling out of the van as McCain climbed out of his truck. The men wore white overalls with a rainbow of splattered paint on them.

"Hey, guys. I need to get my house painted before winter," McCain said. "Is that the kind of painting you do?"

"Yep. Inside and out, big or small," the van driver said.

"Got a card?" McCain asked.

The driver gave him a card. It read, "Pat's Painting" above a phone number with a local prefix.

"You Pat?" McCain asked.

"That's me."

"I live up in the Nile," McCain fibbed. "You work that far out of town?"

"We have, but it's been a while. We'd probably have to charge mileage in addition to the price of the job. We're working up in Tieton now."

"Okay, thanks. I'll give you a call," McCain said as he put the card in his pocket. "Say, do you have any other trucks in your fleet that look like these?"

"Nope, this is it. Me and Chuck here," he pointed to the other paint-spattered man, "and our van. Why?"

"Just wondered," McCain said. "I've seen a couple very similar vans up by my place coming and going and thought they might be part of your outfit."

"I bought this van used from a public auction a year or so ago. There were like six of them that came up for sale. You're probably seeing one of those."

"Hmmm, probably. You remember the auction house?"

The painter gave McCain a funny look, and then told him

the name of the auction company and the approximate date of the sale.

"Thanks," McCain said, then followed the men into the hardware store. They headed to the paint section, and he went to the hunting department. He needed some steel shot shotgun shells for his upcoming duck hunt with Austin Meyers and figured he could grab them now.

Jack was asleep on the back seat of the truck when McCain climbed back in and turned the key in the ignition. He headed west on SR 12 up the mountain to the Nile. As he drove, he made a mental note to contact the auction company about the vans. He had just hit SR 410 on his way to Walt Ashford's when he took a call on the radio.

"Wildlife 148," the radio crackled.

"Go ahead."

"We have request for an officer up Oak Creek. Dispute between two hunters. Twelve miles up Oak Creek Road."

"Received. I'll be there in twenty minutes."

"I guess the cameras are going to have to wait," he said to Jack, who barely opened his eyes.

McCain hated these calls. He'd had dozens of them throughout his career. He could almost tell what this call was about based on all the past dispute calls. One hunter had shot at a deer, and the deer had run over the hill where another hunter had shot at it. In some cases, the deer dropped at the shot from the second hunter, and in other cases the deer had been hit by the first hunter but continued running, only to bleed out and die somewhere else. The first hunter would claim he hit the deer, and the second hunter would say it was perfectly healthy until he shot. There were different versions of this "I shot, he shot" deal, and the police had to make the difficult decision on who was going to take possession of the deer or elk. Sometimes it was fairly easy to figure out, and other times it wasn't.

McCain drove up Oak Creek and kept an eye on the odometer. When he was about thirteen miles up the road, he saw two rigs parked just off the road and four men sitting on tailgates. All were wearing hunter orange vests or jackets. They all seemed pretty relaxed.

At least it hadn't escalated into fisticuffs, McCain thought. Some of the disputes he'd been called to had erupted in violence, with two hunters throwing punches and rolling around in the dirt.

"Hey, fellas," McCain said as he climbed out of his truck. "You the guys that called in the dispute?"

"Yes, sir," a tall, lanky man of about thirty said. McCain thought if he'd had the right beard, he could pass as an Abe Lincoln look-alike.

"Okay, here's what we're going to do," McCain explained. "First, let me see all your hunting licenses so I know who is who."

After McCain got the licenses, which he kept for the time being, he asked the men to separate into hunting groups. Once he determined that the two younger guys were part of one group, and the other two men were hunting together, he asked the two older hunters to move over and wait by his truck. Then he walked a ways with the two younger guys and said, "Now, I only want the guy who's most involved to do the talking. Tell me what happened."

The hunter was a man of about thirty. He was fit and average height with a square jaw, cropped goatee, sandy hair, and blood on his hands. His name was Devin Young. He told how he had been hunting up the hill when he heard a shot in the next canyon over.

"I sat down and started glassing that way. In a minute or so, there came a nice buck, bouncing along like mule deer do when they're getting out of Dodge."

Young said he saw which way the buck was going, and he headed as quickly as he could to try and cut him off.

"I was just getting to the edge of the next draw when here comes the buck. I got a really good look at him and I swear he was as healthy as the day his momma brought him into this world. No limp, no blood anywhere. So, I set up, waited until he stopped at about two hundred yards, and bang, down he goes."

McCain looked at the other guy and asked, "Were you with him?"

Abe Lincoln said, "No, I wasn't with him. I was down in the bottom of the draw about four hundred yards below. I could see Devin aiming at something. I looked up the draw, saw the buck, and boom, down it went."

"We were all happy about getting the deer, what with them being pretty scarce these days. We had just started gutting the buck when here comes these two guys. One guy looks at the deer, then looks at the other guy and says, 'Yep, that's him. That's my buck.'"

"Now, we're thinking they're joking," Young said. "But they're serious. Of course, neither of us are near our rifles. We'd laid them against a piece of sagebrush to keep them out of the blood and guts. Well, these guys lower their rifles on us and tell us to leave the deer alone, that it was theirs."

"I tried to tell them the deer hadn't been hit, but they were having none of it," said the lanky guy whose name was Travis Hanson. "They told us to leave. So, we grabbed our stuff and left. A deer isn't worth getting shot over. On the way down the hill, we called 911."

"How'd everyone end up together at the rigs?"

"We're not proud of it," Young said, "But we knew where their truck was, so we drove up here, and somehow they accidentally got a flat tire."

"We didn't want them driving off with Devin's buck," Hanson said. "When they got back after dragging the buck down, we were sitting here waiting for them. We told them you were on your way, and we'd get to the bottom of this thing."

McCain told the guys to wait where they were and went over to talk to the two older men. Both were in their forties, and by the look of their attire, including their four-hundred-dollar boots and the newest in high-tech camo hunting pants and jackets, McCain figured they weren't hurting for money.

The two men, John Nelson and Chris Ferris, were from Seattle, and they said they'd been hunting this area for years. Their story matched that of Young and his friend, other than the part where Nelson said he had shot, then saw the deer rear up and take off running. He said they were heading up to look for blood when they heard the shot in the direction the deer had run and figured someone had put the buck he'd wounded out of its misery.

"We've always gone by the sportsman's way of doing things," Nelson said. "First one to put a bullet in an animal, it's his."

"And did you point your rifles at the other men to get them to move along?"

Ferris kind of smiled and said, "Naw, we just brought them off our shoulders to walk down the hill safely."

"Okay," McCain said. "Let me take a look at the deer. You guys stay right here."

When he checked the deer, McCain found one bullet hole. He'd had one of these arguments before where the guys who'd tagged the animal actually shot into the air to make it look like they took the killing shot. In fact, they'd just arrived at the dead animal first. But this time, McCain didn't think it happened that way. He believed the younger men and felt the other guys might just be used to having their way no matter right or wrong.

"What caliber are you shooting, Mr. Nelson?"

"Three-hundred Win Mag."

"And you, Mr. Young?"

"Six-point-five Creedmore."

McCain looked at the entrance hole in the side of the deer and checked out the inside of the carcass. The deer was obviously killed by one shot, and it was shot with a smaller-bore rifle.

"I'm sorry to tell you this, Mr. Nelson, but you missed. I've seen the damage a bullet from a rifle of your caliber will do to a deer, and the one bullet hole in this deer did not come from a three hundred."

"What?" Nelson said angrily. "You can't tell that."

"I can, and I'm telling you, you missed. The deer belongs to Mr. Young. Now, onto the subject of threatening someone with a high-powered rifle."

The two older men were not happy about McCain's decision, but after McCain talked with Young and Hanson and got them to not press charges on the possible assault with a deadly weapon, the two men agreed to end the dispute. It also helped that the two younger men pitched in and changed the tire on Nelson's Denali.

McCain helped with the tire change, too, more than anything to stick around and ensure the men went their separate ways peacefully after the spare was placed on the truck. While they were working on the truck, McCain let Jack out to get a little exercise. The dog headed out, looking for a gray digger to chase.

With the tire changed and the dispute settled, McCain whistled for Jack, who came on the run. They loaded into the truck, went back down Oak Creek, and headed to Walt Ashford's for another look at the cameras.

CHAPTER 21

"A lot of good these are," McCain mumbled to himself as he looked at the blurry images of a van going down Nile Road.

Only one van had appeared in the trail-camera photos since the last time he had checked, and it was blurrier than any of the other photos.

McCain put the SIM cards back in the cameras, then drove down the driveway and knocked on Mr. Ashford's door. The old man didn't answer. McCain didn't see his car and figured Ashford had just gone to town. He jumped back in his truck and headed up Nile Road toward Little Bald Mountain. There was plenty of daylight left, and he could at least look around higher up the road to see if he could spot anything explaining the vans' nighttime activity.

As he drove higher up the mountain, McCain kept an eye on the surroundings. In one spot, he noticed a pine tree had been cut with what looked like a green treetop left nearby. Woodcutters are allowed, with permits, to come and cut up dead and fallen trees, but it's against the law to cut green trees.

McCain decided to give it a closer look. He let Jack out, and they walked up the hill to a ten-foot pine treetop next to a stump. The tree was green and freshly cut. The diameter on the trunk of the treetop was definitely smaller than the stump. Someone had cut a piece right out of the middle of the tree.

Why would someone do that, McCain wondered.

He looked farther up the hill and found another green pine tree with its middle section removed. McCain pulled out his phone, took a few photos, and then called for Jack. When the dog appeared, he told him to heel, and they headed back to the truck.

"That's a weird one," McCain said to Jack. "We'll need to figure that out."

Back in the truck, McCain decided he'd stop and chat with the three old boys who liked poking the campfire with sticks.

Before McCain arrived at the men's camp, he could smell their fire. He loved that smell. It took him back to the days when he and his dad camped up in these mountains, fishing the streams and hunting big game.

As he pulled in, McCain saw smoke spiraling up through the trees. Sure enough, the three men were sitting in the same chairs, wearing what looked like the same clothes, poking the glowing embers of a half-burned log.

McCain got out while telling Jack to stay.

"How you fellas doing today?" McCain asked.

"If I was any better, there'd have to be two of me," the man in the hunter orange hat said.

"Still poking that fire, I see."

"Yes, sir. There's nothing better," said the man in the John Deere hat.

"I thought I would check and see if you ever saw that tan van go by again."

"No, can't say that I did," said MAGA hat.

The other two men agreed. They hadn't seen any vans. And they'd been watching.

"We did see that guy in the white Chevy pickup who asked us about the marijuana fields go by though," John Deere hat said.

"Or we think it was the same guy," orange hat said. "It looked like him."

"You didn't happen to get a license plate, did you?" McCain asked.

"We tried, but we're old and fat and don't move very fast," said the man in the red MAGA hat.

The men talked for a few more minutes. McCain asked if they'd heard of many deer being taken. The men said they'd heard of a couple, but most of the hunters were complaining about seeing very few deer and no bucks.

"Have you heard any chainsaws working up the road a ways?" McCain asked.

"Sure. Seems like all the camping hunters and probably some folks from the city are cutting firewood here and there," John Deere hat said. "It's a common sound in the woods during the fall hunting seasons."

McCain had to agree with that.

"Okay, guys. Thanks for the information. If you do see the guy in the white pickup or the tan vans, please give me a call," McCain said as he handed them a card. "Any time, day or night."

"We'll sure do it," the man in the orange hat said as he poked the fire a couple more times, sending gray and black embers into the sky.

As he was heading down Nile Road, McCain took a call from Sinclair.

"Well, we have one piece of the puzzle figured out," she said after McCain answered.

"That's great. So?"

"We have the shooter of the hunter up in Kittitas."

"In custody?" McCain asked

"No. Well, yes. He's dead. It was Juan Delgado Sr."

"Okay, I didn't see that coming. But I guess it makes sense."

Sinclair said that after Delgado was shot at the Fair Avenue house, the crime scene folks had gone through and found several weapons.

"Some were registered to Delgado, and others were not. There was an AR-15 in the bunch, and after doing a ballistics test and comparing the bullet to the one taken out of Mr. Wallace, it was a match. The fingerprints on the rifle matched Delgado."

"So, that one is solved." McCain said. "Anything on the thirty-caliber rifle?"

"No, but the investigators found a bullet in a wooden mailbox post where the drug dealer Jerome Dirksen was killed. Pretty lucky. It could have disappeared underground in a lawn or ricocheted off the pavement, and we'd have nothing. There was blood trace on the bullet. It has to be the one that went through Dirksen. So, if we can find the rifle that matches the barrel twist on the bullet, we might be able to get that shooter too."

"I wouldn't count on just coming across the rifle. There are probably ten thousand thirty-caliber rifles just in Eastern Washington. We need to learn why the shooter is doing what he's doing."

"I agree. Our search of all the young people who have died of drug overdoses in the last year has given us a list of eighty-three people in Yakima and Kittitas Counties."

"Wow, it's that prevalent. I would have never guessed. Well, at least it's a starting point. I assume you're reaching out to all the families?"

"That's the plan."

"Get me the list too, if you would. I'll look it over and see if there are any names that I might know. I'd be happy to talk to them if so."

"That would be great. I'll bring it home tonight," Sinclair said.

"Need me to grab anything at the store? I'm heading through Naches now."

"We're out of cottage cheese, and the sour cream is past the 'best by' date."

"Sour cream is always sour. Does it really matter?"

"Let me see, um, yes, it does matter."

"Okay, cottage cheese, sour cream, got it. See you in a bit."

McCain pulled into the market, ran in, and headed to the dairy section.

"Hey, Luke!" a voice said from across the aisle.

It was Jim Kingsbury. He was without his hat and had on a white t-shirt with a blue logo and the words: "**THE HOKEY POKEY CLINIC.**" Underneath, it read: "A Place to Turn Yourself Around."

"Oh, hey, Jim. How's it going?"

"Good. Say, I was hoping to run into you. Dugdale and I were up near Kloochman Rock, looking around for some elk sign this morning, and this guy comes up to us and starts asking about marijuana fields in the area."

"Oh yeah? What did he look like?"

Kingsbury gave a description of the guy that matched the one the different people in the camps had given. Tall, thin, fifties, sunglasses, driving a white Chevy.

"Any chance you got a license plate or a photo of the man or his truck or something?"

"As a matter of fact, we did. I've got the license plate number right here. Hope you can read Dugdale's handwriting," Kingsbury said, handing the note to McCain.

"Thanks a bunch, Jim. This really helps," McCain said as he hurried out of the store to his truck to run the plates.

McCain typed the license plate number into the laptop computer on his center console and waited. He was excited that this might be the break they needed. As the computer did its thing, he called Sara.

"We might just have gotten a break on the pot field shooter," he said, even before Sinclair said hello.

He told her about running into Kingsbury and started to tell her about them talking to the guy who was asking everyone about the pot fields when she interrupted.

"What did his shirt say today?"

McCain told her, and she laughed. He went on to tell her about Kingsbury getting the license plate numbers on the guy's truck.

"I'm running the plates now. We can discuss it more when I get home."

"Did you get the sour cream and cottage cheese?"

"Crap," he said. He hung up and went back into the store.

As McCain was driving down SR 12 to his house, the computer screen lit up with the information. The owner of the 2018 white Chevy 1500 pickup was Byron Hendricks, 59, with a home address in Moxee.

When he got home, Sinclair was not there yet. So, it being Jack's dinner time, he fed the dog and then went back to his truck laptop and looked a little more closely at the information on Hendricks. A photo of the man's Washington driver's license popped up on the screen. McCain stared at Hendricks's photo for a few seconds. The face was familiar. He had seen the man somewhere in the not-too-distant past, but he couldn't remember where.

He was thinking on it, now back inside, when someone knocked on the front door. He opened the door to find Austin Meyers standing on the porch.

"Just wanted to make sure we were still on for duck hunting on Sunday?" Austin said. "My mom says I can go. I've been working with Bear every day on his retrieving. I can't wait."

"Yep, we're on," McCain told the young man. "I'm looking forward to it too, and so is Jack. Let's meet here at five thirty, and we'll pack the decoys down to the river. I know a spot where the local ducks like to hang out."

Just then, Sinclair drove into the driveway in her big black Chrysler. Austin told McCain he'd see him Sunday morning and went to say hello to Sara as she got out of her car.

"He's like I was at that age," McCain said, nodding toward the Meyers' house. "He can't wait until Sunday to go duck hunting."

"It'll be fun for both of you," she said. "Did you get the information on the guy Kingsdale talked to?"

"Yep. Did you bring the list of families?"

"Got it right here," she said, lifting her briefcase.

"Perfect. Let's go fix a quick dinner, and then we can jump into the list. It'll be interesting to see if this Byron Hendricks is on it."

CHAPTER 22

Mandy Hendricks had been a star athlete at East Valley High School. She'd played point guard on the basketball team all four years. During her senior year, the team finished fifth in the state. She also played second base on the softball team and hit well over .400 for the season. According to the college scouts, Mandy was not quite good enough to play in the Pac 12, but there were many Division II colleges lining up to give her a scholarship for basketball and softball.

A month before she was to graduate, the East Valley softball team was playing in the regional finals. When an opposing batter hit a pop-up to right-center field, Mandy sprinted out to make the catch. The center fielder was calling for the ball, but Mandy didn't hear her. The two players hit head on, and the collision was so hard Mandy tore her labrum and cracked a cervical vertebra in her neck. Surgery was required to fix both injuries. At that point, the college scholarships started to wither away.

After the surgeries, the doctor had prescribed Hydrocodone for the pain. Later, the doctor tried to wean her off the medication, but the only time Mandy wasn't in pain was when she took the pills. Fearing she had become addicted to the pain relievers, the doctor stopped prescribing the drug. Mandy soon found other sources for the drug she felt could ease her physical pain and mental anguish after losing her college scholarships.

Her parents saw what was happening, and knowing that their daughter was hooked on painkillers, they got her into a treatment program. For a time, it looked like the treatment had worked, but unfortunately Mandy slipped back into drug dependency. She was smoking pot daily and using opioids and cocaine frequently.

One night, she got some cocaine laced with fentanyl. Even though she only used what she thought was enough to dull the pain, it was too much. When her friends found her unresponsive, they called 911. But it was too late. Mr. and Mrs. Hendricks had lost their little girl.

* * *

"He's got to be our shooter," Sinclair said after they went through the list of people dealing with the loss of family members due to drug overdoses. "Although I'm not sure why he would have such a hatred for the pot growers. It doesn't seem from what we're seeing here that pot was an issue."

Sinclair had brought up some newspaper stories on Byron Hendricks's daughter on the computer. They read that Mandy Hendricks was a star athlete who was on her way to play college ball when a freak accident cut her career short. There was a short story about the girl dying of an accidental overdose. The obituary in the paper was particularly sad.

"I can see why a parent would lose it a little and want to blame someone for causing the death of their child," McCain said.

He looked at the photo of Byron Hendricks again. He still couldn't figure out where he'd seen the man.

"Well, we should pay Mr. Hendricks a visit tomorrow,"

Sinclair said. "I don't know if we have enough to get a search warrant for the rifle, but I'm going to try."

They looked through the list of families some more, but with no other names really standing out, they put it away and watched some TV before turning in for the night.

The next morning, McCain was up early. He wanted to get to the office and start pursuing the man who was selling illegal mountain-goat hunts. He and Hargraves had met a few days earlier, and they had talked to a woman with the Department in Olympia who was in charge of watching the internet for any potential illegal hunting and fishing activity. It hadn't taken her long before she found the ad on an obscure hunting site for a guiding business called "Northwest Goat and Sheep Adventures." The ad showed a photo of a smiling hunter with a dead mountain goat. Below the photo was a phone number to call for more information about booking a trip.

Before he left for the office, McCain wished Sara good luck with Byron Hendricks and asked her to call him as soon as she knew anything.

"Will do," she said. "Good luck with the goat guy."

When McCain got to the office, Hargraves was already there.

"Morning, Stan," McCain said as he walked into the inner office where he and Hargraves had cubicles next to each other.

"Morning. You ready to give this guy a call?"

"Yep. Let's do it."

The call went directly to an automated voicemail that said to leave a name, number, and a short message. A man by the name of Richard Benton said he would give them a call back. McCain left a voicemail, saying that he was a hunter from Seattle who'd always wanted to shoot a mountain goat. He said he'd just come into a little inheritance money and thought now might be a good time to try for a goat. McCain said that he was excited about the possible hunt and hoped that Benton would give him a call. He then left a phone number for a special cell phone the department used for these kinds of cases.

"Well, that should get his attention," Hargraves said. "Hope he calls soon."

"Me too," McCain said. "Until he calls, I guess I'd better get up the hill."

McCain took a few minutes to check his emails, input a couple daily report sheets from the past two days, hit send, and then headed out the door. His plan was to collect Jack and then head up into the mountains above Rimrock Lake, near White Pass. He wanted to check on that area's deer hunters, as there'd been no one in that area talking to hunters since Hargraves had been up there on opening weekend.

McCain swooped by his house, picked up a very happy Jack, and headed west to the Cascades. He was just about to the "Y" where SR 12 and SR 410 split when his phone rang. He pushed the answer button on the steering wheel and said, "This is McCain."

"Hey, it's me," Sinclair said. "We went to Hendricks's house, but Byron wasn't there. Mrs. Hendricks told us that her husband spends just about every day in the mountains. She said she has no idea what he does up there, but after Mandy died, it seems to bring him some solace."

"What about the search warrant?"

"The judge wouldn't sign it. Said our evidence was all circumstantial."

"I get that. Well, I'm headed up to White Pass. Maybe I'll run into Mr. Hendricks."

"Maybe. How'd it go with the goat guide?"

"He didn't answer his phone. I left a message."

"He'll call back. Not everyone has ten thousand dollars to spend on a hunt. He has to check out all the potential callers."

"Yeah, you're probably right. We'll see."

After they hung up, McCain started thinking about Byron Hendricks and wondered where, in the tens of thousands of mountainous acres ahead of him, he might be.

As the day went by, McCain and Jack checked nearly two dozen deer hunters. Only one hunter had been successful in filling his tag, and the buck was a young one that happened to have an extra point on the right side of his forked antlers. The man was quite happy to have the deer and the venison for the winter. Most of the other hunters were discouraged over the lack of deer they had been seeing. McCain understood, and when the hunters let loose on him as a representative of the Fish and Wildlife Department, he would listen to their complaints and tell them he would pass it on to his superiors.

What McCain wanted to tell most of them was that just driving the roads would not improve their odds of filling their tags. The people McCain had checked during the season who had been successful, save for the two young guys in Kittitas County whose truck rolled down the hill, had been at least a mile from the nearest road when they found a buck. He figured it would be no use though, as many hunters were not willing to put in that extra effort. When they didn't see enough animals by driving around, they were miffed. To them, it was the Fish and Wildlife Department's fault.

Late in the afternoon, McCain checked one last group of hunters and then headed down the hill. He was about twenty miles east of White Pass when he heard a bell. *Bing bing.*

He couldn't figure out where the bell had come from, then it dawned on him – it was the special phone he'd requisitioned to talk to Richard Benton, the crooked goat guide. McCain looked at the phone and saw he had a voicemail. It took him a minute to remember how to access it. Finally, he was listening to the voice of Benton.

The message said: "Hello, yeah, this is Richard Benton. You

called about a mountain goat hunt? I have a couple of openings in the next two weeks. Give me a call if you're still interested."

The man left his phone number, the same one from the internet ad.

McCain decided to call him now. He punched in the numbers, pressed send, and listened for the ring. The name he had used when he called the first time was Luke Stone. He always used his real first name, so it was easy to remember.

Benton picked up on the second ring and said, "This is Benton."

McCain pushed the speaker button on the requisitioned phone and the record button on his main phone.

"Hi, Mr. Benton. This is Luke Stone. You left me a message a little while ago. I'm the one who called this morning about a mountain goat hunt."

"Sure. Hi, Luke. Yeah, we can still get you out this season. We've been having some pretty good luck."

"Wow, sounds great. I'm not an avid hunter, but like I said in my voicemail, I've come into a little money and was thinking a mountain goat hunt might be cool. I like to hike and climb, so this could be fun."

"If you like to climb, you'll definitely enjoy this."

"Looking at the game laws, it looks like I need to be drawn for a permit though, so how does that work?"

"Well, we have a special deal with the state. They've given us a few special permits that we are allowed to use. The fee includes your hunting license, your tag, as well as handling the animal if you are successful. And you should be successful. We've taken four nice goats already this year."

"Okay, great. Any chance you could send me some of the photos of the goats you got? I'd like to show my wife, so she knows what I'm getting into. It will give me an idea of the terrain we'll be hunting too."

"Yeah, let's get some paperwork handled first," Benton said.

"Sure. So how does the money thing work? I think I'd be a little reluctant to pay the full amount before the hunt."

"No, no, you're right to ask about that. We want half up front, so five thousand dollars, and the other half at the end of the hunt. I'd prefer cash or a money order. We could meet somewhere sometime soon to put the deal together if that would work for you."

McCain was reluctant to meet any place around Yakima. There was too great a chance someone might recognize him and blow his Luke Stone cover. He wanted the guy to believe he was coming from Seattle, so he asked about meeting at the restaurant at the Snoqualmie Pass summit.

"That's about halfway," McCain said after he suggested the location.

"I guess I could do that. We have a three-day hunt open next week, and one the following week."

McCain thought quickly. Two weeks out wasn't great, as that was in the middle of the general elk season. He'd need to be around for that. Plus, he wanted to nail this guy before any more goats were killed.

"Next week would work, I think. When can we meet?"

"How about Sunday?"

McCain remembered he was hunting ducks with Austin on Sunday, but their hunt should be over by noon at the latest.

"I could do that in the late afternoon sometime, say like five o'clock."

"That works. I'll be driving a silver Nissan Pathfinder."

"Sounds great. I'll be in a midnight blue Toyota Tundra. I'm getting excited. Bring those photos if you would. I'd really like to see the animals you've been getting."

"Will do. See you Sunday."

McCain picked up his main phone and pressed the record button again to stop recording. He checked it. It had recorded for three minutes and forty-three seconds. He'd doublecheck it when he got home, but he was sure he had recorded the full conversation. He'd also figure out how to record the meeting with Benton on Sunday.

A few minutes later, he received a call from Sinclair.

"We decided to put a sheriff's deputy in an unmarked car to watch for Hendricks when he came home. I just got a call that he pulled in. I'm heading that way."

"Okay. I'm coming down the mountain. I'll feed Jack. You want me to wait for you for dinner?"

"Naw, go ahead. I have no idea how long this might take."

"Okay. Good luck."

"Thanks, see you soon."

"Okay, Jack. We're on our own for dinner," McCain said. Jack heard his name, and the word dinner – which he'd learned the meaning of at about eight and a half weeks old – and started wagging his tail, banging the back of the front seats.

"Settle down, boy. We need to get home first."

CHAPTER 23

Sinclair got home about eight o'clock. She was more than a little disappointed.

"Hendricks admits to being in the mountains the past several weeks asking campers, hikers, and hunters if they've seen any illegal pot fields. But he says he has had nothing to do with the shootings."

"Did you ask if he was a hunter and had any rifles?"

"Yes. He said he was, and he did. He listed about six different caliber rifles he owns, including a .30-06. He offered them all up so we could check the ballistics. We will test them, but if someone agrees to let them be tested, chances are good that none of them are the weapons used in the shootings."

"He could have another one that isn't registered to him stashed someplace," McCain said.

"True, but when I asked where he was on some of the days and times the killings took place, he had alibis for some, including being out of state the night Delgado was shot."

"Did he say why he wanted to find the pot fields?"

"He said he was going to try to burn them down, and if he couldn't do that, he was going to go to the sheriff's department and turn them in."

"Well, that sounds admirable and all, but it still seems suspicious. He's looking for pot fields while some of those workers are getting killed."

"I agree. I really had the feeling he wasn't telling us everything he knows."

"So, are you going to watch him?" McCain asked.

"Not right now, but we did tell him that if an illegal pot field or two ends up burning down, he'd be the first person we'd be talking with. He agreed to stop looking for them."

"Okay, well, I really thought we had the guy who was doing the shootings. So, what are you going to do now?"

"I'm thinking we need to check out some other angles. I'm going to talk to Miles Carter at the DEA and see what he thinks about this theory of another drug cartel killing the workers to gain a foothold in the region."

Carter was the head of the local Drug Enforcement Agency office. Based on Sinclair's previous work with the man, she knew he'd have his finger on what was happening with the cartels.

"That's definitely worth checking out," McCain agreed.

"And," she continued. "I want to talk to some of the other families on the list that lost kids to drug overdoses. I still think there is something there. And we'll check on your idea that maybe some of the area's legit pot stores got tired of the illegal competition and decided to take the law into their own hands. Hopefully something will shake out."

After a few seconds, she asked, "So, how was your day?"

McCain told her about checking deer hunters with Jack and about the conversation he had with Richard Benton, the goat poacher.

"So, you're going up there on Sunday afternoon. What about your promise to hunt ducks with Austin?"

"Should be no problem. We'll be done hunting ducks by noon."

"You want me to go with you when you meet this guy, pose as the dutiful wife and all?"

"I guess you could. I recorded our phone conversation and got some good audio of him lying about the tags and permits. But I'd like to get video of him accepting my down payment."

"An eyewitness who happens to be an FBI agent should suffice," Sinclair said. "But maybe I can have a small camera on me too."

"Okay, we'll figure that out. It really shouldn't be too hard to nail this guy."

"You won't have to shoot a goat, will you?"

"No. If it gets to the shooting part, I'll miss intentionally. In this case, where he doesn't seem to be a habitual poacher and we can get in and grab him, we should be able to take him down before any more animals are killed."

They talked for a few more minutes about the pot worker killings and the goat poacher. They were just settling in for the night when McCain's phone rang. He didn't recognize the number. He almost let it go to voicemail but decided to answer it.

"Yeah, this is McCain."

"Hello, Officer McCain. This is Milt Shafer. I'm one of the ol' farts you talked to a couple times at the campfire on Little Bald Mountain Road."

"Sure, Mr. Shafer. What can I do for you this evening?"

"Well, you were askin' about those vans comin' and goin' on the road outta the hills here."

"Yes, what about them?"

"We jest saw one headin' up the road. Goin' lickity-split. Thought you'd like to know."

"Yessir, Mr. Shafer. Thanks for the call. I'll head up that way right now."

He hung up and turned to Sinclair.

"Guess I'm going back out. One of the trucks Walt Ashford

has been seeing just went up the road to Little Bald Mountain. If I get up there, I might be able to stop them and finally figure out what's going on."

"Okay. But that wasn't Mr. Ashford?"

"No, it was one of the men I've been talking with who's camped along the road the trucks are using. I asked them to call if they saw them."

McCain put his boots on, buckled his service belt around his waist, grabbed his jacket and cap, then whistled for Jack, who was sleeping soundly on McCain's bed.

"Come on, boy. Our day's not quite over."

"Be safe. Hope you catch them, whatever it is they're doing," Sinclair said.

McCain decided he needed to get up the hill quicker than usual, so he hit his lights and pushed the F-150 to eighty, heading up the four-lane highway to Naches. He slowed going through town, but picked it up again heading west. He called Ashford to see if he'd watch for the truck coming back down on Nile Road.

When Ashford answered, McCain told him what was going on and said, "Can you keep an eye on your road to make sure they don't come back down before I get up there?"

"Sure can," Ashford said. "Glad to help."

"I should be there in about fifteen minutes," McCain said. "I'll honk my horn when I go by, so you know I'm up that far. If I get past your place before they come down, I should be able to find them."

"Good luck. Let me know how it turns out," Ashford said before clicking off.

McCain made good time, blowing past Ashford's place twelve minutes after he'd made the call to the old gentleman. He honked his horn as he went past.

Since Milt Shafer said the truck had gone up the road, McCain knew there was an excellent chance he could stop the rig coming back the same way. It wasn't a dead-end road, but the other roads that might lead them out were really rough and narrow for a bigger truck with a van on the back. His only concern was if the truck had come back down and turned west on Nile Road, instead of east past Ashford's house. If that happened, nobody would have seen them.

McCain turned onto Little Bald Mountain Road and headed up the hill. When he got to the spot where Shafer and the other old boys were camped, he slowed. He decided to quickly pull in and just check with them to see if they had noticed the van coming back down the hill. McCain pulled up to the two trailers and the camper parked there, then jumped out of his truck.

"Hey, Officer McCain," Milt Shafer said as he stepped out of his camp trailer.

"Hello, Mr. Shafer. Thanks again for calling me. Did you happen to notice if the van has come back down the hill?"

"We've been watchin' for it, but nothin' has come down that road since it went up."

"Okay, well, thanks again," McCain said as he climbed back into the truck, turned around, and pulled back out to the road.

"Looks like they are still up here someplace," McCain said to Jack, who was sticking his head between the seats, looking out the windshield.

As he drove slowly up the road, McCain searched both sides, looking for the van or any other activity that would be out of place at nine-thirty at night. McCain kept his window down and listened for anything that might sound suspicious as he drove slowly up the mountain. When he was about eight miles from where Shafer and the two other men were camped, he heard what he thought was a distant chainsaw running. As he continued up the road, the buzz of the chainsaw grew louder and louder. When he came around a bend in the road, the chainsaw stopped. McCain stopped as well.

It was a dark night, but there was still a half moon. McCain turned his headlights off to let his eyes adjust. He sat and looked and listened for a couple minutes. It wasn't long before he heard voices in the distance. McCain glanced back at Jack. The dog's ears were up and alert. He'd heard the voices too, and he was looking to the right, up the hill.

As McCain looked around, he could see just the top of what looked like a van parked off the road around the bend. He put his pickup in gear, turned the headlights on and drove up the road. Sure enough, his headlights illuminated a tan van, almost exactly like the one Pat of Pat's Painting was driving. The roll-up door in the back was open, and McCain could see the butt ends of about twenty logs. Something in the middle of each log made them lay catawampus. They appeared green, like they'd just been cut. Cutting green trees was illegal on public forest lands. Why would anyone want to cut green wood for firewood, McCain wondered.

McCain pulled his rig in behind the truck, let Jack out the back passenger door, took the flashlight off his service belt and went to get a closer look at the logs. Each of them had a gigantic knot somewhere in the middle of the trunk. Then it dawned on him: This was burl wood.

He had seen railings and lamps made out of burl wood and had recently read about how popular the wood was with designers who planned huge log homes being built around the Northwest. Bigger burls can be used in any number of ways, including in decorative bowls, tabletops, and even counter tops, depending on their size. Foresters describe burls as big, fungus-fueled growths on trees. And they can affect many varieties of trees.

The ones McCain was looking at here were from pine trees. He thought back to the downed trees he had seen in this area when he was looking around a week earlier, and it started to make sense. The people running the vans out of the woods at night were, in fact, poachers, but they weren't killing deer and elk illegally. They were harvesting trees illegally.

McCain was counting the trees in the van when Jack started growling. McCain turned just in time to see a man coming down the hill on the run.

"What are you doing?" the man yelled in Russian-accented English. "Get away from truck!"

"State police!" McCain yelled, pulling his service pistol and shining the light on the man. "Stay right where you are."

The man froze. But someone out in the darkness, behind the man, didn't. McCain could hear footsteps heading back up the hill, hurriedly moving through the brush.

"Show me your hands," McCain commanded. "Now!"

The man looked to be in his mid-twenties, and he was big. He stood roughly six feet tall, and McCain thought he was easily 275 pounds. McCain figured the guy could be playing interior lineman for the Seattle Seahawks. He was very fit and looked to be extremely strong, with big shoulders, biceps, and forearms. Around his head, holding down a blonde mullet, was a large headlamp. The man had a big chainsaw in his right hand, and he was moving it around like it was a child's toy.

McCain told him to put the saw down and again asked the guy to show him his hands. The man obliged, setting the saw down and holding up both hands.

Looking again at the size of the man, McCain was glad he'd pulled his pistol. He had no idea where the other person had gone, or if that person was armed. He looked at Jack who was watching and listening to something farther up the hill.

"Come on down here please," McCain said to the man. "What's your name?"

"My name is Dimitri Slavichski," he said as he walked toward McCain.

"Well, Mr. Slavichski. I need to see your driver's license."

The man dug into his back pocket, pulled a license out of his wallet, and handed it to McCain.

"Do you have a permit for cutting green trees here in the National Forest?"

"No, I do not," Slavichski said.

"Okay. For the moment, I'm going to put you in handcuffs until we can get all of this sorted out. You're not under arrest yet. I just need to figure out what is going on here. Who is the other person with you?"

"What other person?" Slavichski asked dumbly.

"Your partner who ran up the hill a minute ago."

Slavichski said nothing. McCain had him put his hands behind his back and turn around. Again, he obliged. When he placed the handcuffs on the man, McCain couldn't believe how thick his forearms were. He hoped the manacles would hold. The last thing he wanted was to brawl with some guy big enough to hunt bears with a switch.

"Stand right there and don't move," he said to Slavichski.

McCain went to his truck, opened the door, and grabbed the radio mic.

"Wildlife 148 requesting assistance," he said into the mic.

"Copy, Wildlife 148," the dispatcher's voice crackled on the radio. "What's your location?"

McCain gave the dispatcher his location and was told a YSO deputy would be headed that way ASAP.

McCain didn't want the person who was still out there to get too far away. On the other hand, he didn't really want to leave the handcuffed Slavichski by himself in the back of his truck. He decided the prudent move would be to just wait for backup from the sheriff's office.

While they waited for the deputy to arrive, McCain tried talking with Slavichski. But the man clearly wasn't interested in talking. McCain asked several questions, but Slavichski basically ignored him.

"That's okay. We'll get it all worked out down at the county lockup," McCain said.

That sparked Slavichski into talking. "What if I tell you something I know about person killing workers in the marijuana fields? Would keep me out of jail, yes?"

"It might, but I can't make any promises. Why not tell me about what you have going here and who your partner is? Then we can talk about the other stuff."

There was a long silence, and McCain could see the big man thinking.

"You don't want to know about killings?" Now Slavichski was the one asking the questions.

"We're getting it figured out," McCain said. "How would you know anyway?"

Slavichski smiled. "Oh, I know things you would like to know. Let me go. I tell you."

McCain was tempted, but instead just sat and looked at him.

"I see man who was at one of the fields. I watch him shoot."

Now McCain was the one not wanting to talk. He hoped Slavichski would keep telling things he might know.

"I there, cutting trees. I see man shoot at man in field."

Dead silence from McCain.

"I know what man look like. I give you good description. Let me go, yes?"

"Sorry, Dimitri. I can't do that."

They went back and forth like that for a bit, until both men quit talking. McCain was glad. He was tired, and he was especially tired of listening to Dimitri Slavichski.

During the conversation, Jack had stood, watched, and listened up the hill. Now, McCain was watching him. If the person who had taken off was over the hill and gone, Jack would have lost interest. But the dog was still on high alert, and if McCain had said go find him, he believed Jack would have been off like a shot.

A couple minutes later, a YSO rig pulled up behind McCain's truck. It was Deputy Williams.

"Hey, Rifleman. Whatcha got going on here?" Williams asked as he climbed out of his SUV.

"We have us a black market burl wood situation," McCain said.

Williams looked puzzled, and McCain quickly explained.

"Right now, we have one perp in hand and another in the bush. If you can accompany Mr. Slavichski down to the county jail, Jack and I are going to round up his partner."

"Ten-four," said Williams. "Mr. Slavichski, right this way."

Williams walked the man to the back seat of the SUV and placed him in the rig.

"He'll try to talk you into letting him go. He says he can ID the guy shooting workers in the pot fields, and wants to trade information for his freedom. I told him we'd talk about it later."

Williams fired up his SUV, turned around, and headed back down the hill. McCain went to his truck, grabbed his shotgun and a headlight, and walked over to where Jack was still watching the hillside.

"Okay, boy. Let's go find him," McCain said. "But E-A-S-Y."

Jack knew that meant he was to go slowly, and he started working up the hill at a deliberate speed.

CHAPTER 24

McCain followed Jack up the hill at a slow but steady pace. He didn't turn on his headlight because he worried whoever was up there would then know his exact position. The person could certainly hear them coming, but a light would make McCain an easy target if the person had a rifle and was of the mind to take a shot at a pursuer.

Jack was following his nose, but it wasn't a true tracking job. The dog never once put his nose to the ground. He kept his head high, smelling the currents coming down the hillside.

They had worked up the hill a good four hundred yards when Jack slowed and started emitting an almost imperceptible, deep-throated growl.

McCain knew that meant they were getting close.

"Easy, boy," McCain whispered to Jack.

Then the dog really started to growl. A second later, there was an explosion from the brush, just ahead and to the right of McCain. He tried to turn on his headlight to see what was coming his way, but he didn't have time. Another large man, bigger than Slavichski, was coming fast. And he had a big piece of wood in his hand.

McCain somehow saw this in the light of the half moon, processed it in a millisecond, and raised his shotgun to try and shield himself from the inevitable blow. But it never came. From the corner of his eye, McCain saw a blur of yellow and watched as Jack jumped and grabbed the man's arm as it was coming down.

"Owwwwww!" the man screamed.

Jack bit hard into his forearm, and the big man lifted the dog off the ground, then spun around, trying to get free. Jack held on tightly. This gave McCain just enough time to pull his taser gun, which he then used to shoot the man in the shoulder as he spun around, Jack still attached to his arm.

The electrical voltage was enough to bring the man to his knees, but it didn't put him down for long. He was starting to get back up when McCain gave him another blast of 50,000 volts. That worked, or at least it worked for a few seconds, as the man fell face-forward. McCain jumped on the man's back, wrestled the big man's free arm around and put a handcuff on his wrist.

"Let go," McCain said to Jack. "Good boy!"

Jack did as he was told, then backed up a bit, still growling. With the man's second arm still free, McCain secured the other half of the handcuff on the second wrist. He'd just clicked the manacles closed when the man tried to get back up.

"You want another blast?" McCain asked. "Or I can get the dog to attack again."

Jack growled a bit louder.

"No, no! No more dog," the man said with a heavy Russian accent.

McCain stood the man up, told him he was under arrest, and read him his Miranda rights. He then asked him if he understood, and after the man said yes, McCain asked his name.

"Sergi Slavichski," the man said as they started down the hill.

McCain stood almost six-foot-five, and Sergi looked him

right in the eye when he was standing. The man had the physique of Dimitri, only with bigger shoulders, bigger arms, bigger chest and bigger legs. McCain was feeling lucky not to have been beaned by the man. It could have killed him. He looked at Jack again and thought his four-legged partner had earned a steak dinner for his quick actions.

"Are you and Dimitri brothers?" McCain asked as they walked.

"Cousin," Sergi said.

"So, how much burl wood have you harvested so far?"

"Nine truck loads. This one number ten."

"How much are you getting for the wood?"

"Good pieces, maybe five hundred. Most around two hundred."

Unlike Dimitri, Sergi seemed happy to tell McCain what they were doing, so McCain kept asking questions as they walked down to the trucks.

"And how many pieces in a truckload?"

"Fifty maybe. Sometimes more."

"Wow, that's pretty good," McCain said.

With that, Sergi smiled and puffed up his enormous chest.

"Dimitri was telling me he saw a man shoot at some workers in a marijuana field a while back," McCain said. "Did you see the man too?"

"No, I at truck with load of wood. He is up cutting wood. He come down in hurry when gun go off."

"I don't blame him. Did he tell you what the man looked like?"

"No, we get in truck and drive."

When they got to his pickup, McCain put Sergi in the back seat, loaded Jack in the front passenger seat, and said, "Guard him."

Again, Jack had no clue what that meant, but since he didn't like Sergi much anyway, he sat and stared at the man, growling a low rumbling growl now and again.

McCain returned to the van and took several photos of the wood inside and outside of the rig, including the license plate. He then pulled the roller door down and secured the padlock that was resting in the catch. He assumed Dimitri had the key.

When he got back in his truck, he radioed dispatch and asked them to send a tow truck equipped to pull a bigger truck. He gave instructions to have the truck towed to the YSO impound lot. Then he started his pickup, turned around, and headed back down the road.

As they were passing Walt Ashford's place, McCain looked over and saw the lights on in the house. He slowed and pulled into the driveway.

McCain was getting out of the truck as Ashford came out onto the porch.

"How'd it go?" he asked McCain.

"Pretty good," McCain said as he walked over to the porch, where Sergi couldn't hear the conversation. "We caught the guys. They were illegally harvesting burl wood."

"Really? I know what that is. I didn't know it was so valuable."

"I guess so. Anyway, we couldn't have done it without you, Walt. I sure appreciate you contacting us."

"Did Jack help you?"

"As a matter of fact, he did. He tracked one of the men, then jumped in and grabbed him as he was about to whack me with a rather large piece of wood."

"Wow, isn't that something? He's one of a kind, that yellow dog."

"I think so. Anyway, I just wanted to let you know we got the guys. I'll swing by sometime in the next few days and grab those cameras off your fence posts."

"That's fine. Please stop in anytime. I'd like to hear the whole story."

"Will do. Have a good night."

McCain hopped back into the truck and turned around. Jack was wagging his tail and looking at Walt as the gentleman waved goodbye.

"We'll be back, boy. You can have a cookie then."

"I don't want cookie," Sergi said from the back seat.

"I was talking to the . . . never mind," McCain said as he accelerated down Nile Road. He was looking forward to getting home.

Processing Sergi Slavichski took a while, and it was after midnight when McCain and Jack finally got home. He had called Sara as they were headed to town to give her a brief recap of what had happened. Once again, she had asked, "Is Jack okay?"

"He's fine. I'm going to grill him a steak for his heroic deed. Oh, and by the way, I'm fine too."

"I'm glad you're okay too," she said and clicked off.

Sara was sitting on the couch in the living room with her legs pulled up to her chest and tucked inside her nightshirt when McCain and Jack came through the front door. As soon as McCain was inside, she jumped up, walked over, and gave him a big hug and a kiss.

"I am glad you're okay," she said, a tear running down her cheek. "I do worry about you. Probably too much. I'm very thankful Jack was with you tonight. I don't know what I would do without you."

McCain couldn't think of anything to say, so he hugged her again, longer and harder.

CHAPTER 25

McCain and Jack were out checking on hunters in the hills west of Ellensburg a couple days later when he got a call from the Yakima County Assistant District Attorney Blake Franks.

"I have another one," Franks said, after McCain pushed the button on his steering wheel to answer his phone.

"Another one what?" McCain asked. He was half-expecting a call from the ADA after the arrest and discussion with Dimitri Slavichski.

"Another jailbird who has the urge to sing."

"Ah, my Russian friend Dimitri suddenly wants to be a good American citizen and help solve a crime?"

"You got it. I know you're busy, but do you think we could meet with him and his attorney at my office later today?"

"I'm working up in Kittitas County. I can be there about four."

"That would be fine. He claims he can ID the shooter in these pot field killings."

"Yeah, he alluded to that the other night, right before his cousin tried to bean me with a club."

169

"Oh, man. His attorney didn't mention that. You okay?"

"Yeah, actually the attorney may not even know about it. Anyway, I wouldn't be so willing to make a deal with the other Slavichski we arrested. Let's see what Dimitri has to say. See you at four."

McCain and Jack continued their patrol, and checked several deer hunters throughout the day. Besides giving warnings to a couple men who were not wearing enough – or in one case, any – hunter orange, everything went fairly smoothly.

Around three o'clock, McCain decided to start heading down the mountain for his meeting with ADA Franks. He was thinking about how he should have cited the guy who wasn't wearing even an inch of hunter orange when his phone rang.

"This is McCain."

"Hey, it's me," Sinclair said. "I heard from the DA's office that this guy you caught with the illegal trees can ID the pot field shooter."

"Yeah, I got a call from Blake Franks. I'm heading that way now to meet with them."

"I'm going to be at the meeting too. Do you think he can really ID the shooter?"

"I think he might have seen the shooter in the mountains, but my guess is he won't be able to give much of a description. He's looking for a get-out-of-jail-free card. You might, just for the fun of it, bring a photo of Mr. Hendricks with you."

"Already have it, along with five other random photos, ready to show Mr. Slavichski."

"It's a longshot, but who knows."

"I'm going to meet with Franks ahead of time to see what the defendant might be asking for."

"Sounds good. I'll see you there."

McCain had just enough time to run Jack by the house, change shirts, and head to the DA's office. When he arrived,

Sinclair was already there, sitting in a conference room with Franks, Dimitri Slavichski, and public defender Adriene Molina.

"Sorry if I'm late," McCain said, looking at his wrist even though, like ninety percent of American men, he hadn't actually worn a watch since 2003.

"No, you're right on time," Franks said. "Everyone else was just a little early. So, let's get going. Ms. Molina, can you tell us why you asked for this meeting?"

Once again, the public defender was dressed in a business suit, black skirt, white blouse, and gray jacket. McCain noticed she wasn't wearing any scarves this time. Her dark brown hair was rolled up and sat in a bun on the back of her head, and her extra large, black-framed glasses were perched on her nose.

"Mr. Franks, my client, Dimitri Slavichski, was a witness to one of the shootings in the mountains west of Yakima where a man was slain in a marijuana field. We believe his description could lead to the identification of the shooter. Because of this, he is hoping there might be some concessions made ahead of the prosecution of his theft charges."

Since the murder cases associated with the illegal marijuana fields were being led by the FBI, Sinclair would be the one making any deals.

"I would say we're open to some discussion," Franks said, looking at Sinclair. "But I'm going to ask Agent Sinclair to ask Mr. Slavichski some questions. Then we'll see where it goes."

Sinclair first asked Slavichski to describe what he saw.

"My cousin and I were cutting wood up in hills. I see man come up hill and aim rifle down hill. I look down hill and see man coming out of bushes. Man on hill shoot. Man in bushes falls. I don't want man on hill to see me, so I turn and run down hill to truck where Sergi is."

"Sergi is your cousin?"

"Yes. I tell him get in truck. We go."

"Were you up above the Little Naches River?" McCain asked.

"Yes, Little Naches."

Based on what he told the group, he had seen the same shooting that Art Duncan and Brad Clark had witnessed. But, as he described where he was in relation to the shooter, he was on the opposite side of the knoll from where the two ATV riders had been.

Sinclair next asked Slavichski to describe the man doing the shooting as best he could.

"He was medium height, medium build, like him," Slavichski said before pointing at Franks.

Franks, who was wearing a blue suit with a light blue shirt and gray-and-blue-striped tie, was about five-foot-ten and probably weighed 190 pounds.

"What was he wearing?" Sinclair asked.

"He wear camo clothing. Pants and shirt. Black hat."

"Could you see his face?"

"Yes. White face with chin beard."

"You mean a goatee? What color?"

"Yes, goat. White."

"No, not his face. His goatee," Sinclair said.

"White."

"What kind of a rifle was he shooting?"

Slavichski looked a bit perplexed at the question.

"Is a rifle. Look like rifle," he said.

McCain quickly pulled up a photo of an AR-15 on his phone. "Like this one?"

"No. Is hunting rifle," Slavichski said.

Again, McCain pulled up a photo on his phone. This time, the photo was of a hunting rifle with a black stock and a black scope, similar to what Duncan and Clark had described. He showed it to Slavichski.

"No, not black, brown," he said. "Rifle is brown."

"Let me show you some photos," Sinclair said. "See if any of these men look like the man you saw."

She put six photos, including one of Byron Hendricks, out in front of Slavichski, who looked at each one closely. After he laid the last one down, he looked at Sinclair and said, "No, the man I see not here."

"Did the shooter have a backpack on?" McCain asked.

Slavichski thought about that for a minute.

"No, no backpack," he said.

They asked several more questions, trying to determine how close Slavichski was to the shooter, where the sun was, and how long he looked at the man. He answered each one quickly, and from what McCain could tell, truthfully.

"So, do you think you have something here that might help?" Molina asked.

"Possibly," Sinclair said. "We appreciate Mr. Slavichski helping us, but until we find the shooter, we won't know what we can do for your client. When we apprehend the man, we would certainly like the option of calling Mr. Slavichski in as an eyewitness. At that time, we might be able to make a deal to help you out."

Molina didn't look happy with that, but still thanked everyone and stood. Dimitri Slavichski looked at McCain, gave him a kind of "help me out" look and followed his court-appointed attorney out the door.

"Well, that didn't help much," Franks said.

"No, it didn't," Sinclair said.

McCain wasn't too sure. They now had two descriptions of the same shooter, yet they were not the same. The man that Duncan and Clark had seen was described as taller and fit. They said he was wearing a backpack and they both described the rifle as black. Eyewitness descriptions of perpetrators often vary from person to person. In this case, where the three men supposedly saw the shooter above the Little Naches, there were two different descriptions of the man, and definitely a different description of the rifle.

Later that evening, Sara and Luke were discussing the meeting with Slavichski.

"Something's not right," McCain said. "The descriptions are off. I mean, I can see that maybe the height and weight of the described shooter might vary some, but what gets me is the two men I talked with the day of the shooting said he had a black rifle. Dimitri was pretty adamant that it was brown."

"Maybe they were just too far away to see the actual color."

"Could be, I guess. But both Duncan and Clark, who were interviewed separately, said it was black. And they both said the shooter was wearing a backpack. One of the men even mentioned a colored logo or patch on the pack."

"Yeah, that's weird. Slavichski said no backpack. Could they have seen two different men, and the man the ATV guys saw was actually a hunter?"

"If he was, he was hunting illegally, because that was out of season. No high-powered rifles and no scopes were allowed. I guess they could mistake a basic rifle for a modern rifle, but still, it shouldn't have a scope."

They both sat and thought about it for a minute.

"Do you think Adriene Molina is attractive?" Sinclair asked.

"What's that got to do with all of this?" McCain asked.

"It doesn't. I just think she is really beautiful, but she seems to be hiding behind the dowdy librarian look, with the big glasses and all."

"Let's just put it this way – she is not nearly as attractive as you are. Isn't that right, Jack?"

Jack was lying on a doggie bed next to a freestanding woodstove that crackled away. He lifted his head and looked at

McCain, then dropped it back down to the floor and returned to sleep.

"See there, Jack agrees. And yes, Ms. Molina is attractive, but she seems to be trying hard not to be. Don't ask me why."

They talked a bit more about the case, including the interviews Sinclair had with more of the family members who had lost loved ones to overdoses. She said nothing there seemed to assist the investigation, other than the fact that a few people – mostly fathers – said they weren't unhappy about a vigilante taking out drug workers.

"They didn't say they were happy to hear it, but they weren't unhappy," Sinclair said.

"Seems like a logical reaction, especially after what they've been through," McCain said. "What about the pot shop owners around the area? What did they have to say?"

"Most seem like they have their hands full with their small businesses. They're kind of like some of the parents I talked to. They're not overly upset about the shootings. On the other hand, a couple were taking extra precautions, thinking that the killer might not just be targeting illegal drug growers and sellers."

"You know, I was thinking that whoever is doing the shooting is a pretty dang good shot. Is there a way to check if any of the family members or pot shop owners has a military background, maybe as a sniper?"

"Hmmm, not a bad thought. I'll do some checking on that."

"What about the DEA guy, Carter is it?"

"I have a call into him but haven't heard back. I'm sure I'll be able to talk to him soon. Now, I'm tired of thinking about all this. Let's go to bed."

CHAPTER 26

BEEP! BEEP! BEEP! BEEP!
McCain opened one eye and looked at the clock. The digital readout said 5:00. He had to think about it a second. What day was it and why . . . oh yeah . . . it was Sunday morning, and he was going to be taking Austin Meyers to the river for some duck hunting. Normally, he would have been awake well before the alarm went off, especially for a hunting outing, but he'd had a long week and felt beat.

"Are you going to turn that thing off?" Sinclair mumbled sleepily.

"Yep, sorry. Go back to sleep."

"You can count on that. Good luck and have fun."

She pulled the blanket up over her shoulder, rolled over, and was out.

McCain threw on the clothes he'd laid out the night before and padded out to the kitchen to start the coffeemaker. Jack wandered in. Being up this early was not part of his daily schedule, so he was a little confused. But as soon as Jack saw the shotgun come out, the dog would be eager to go.

"We're going to try to find a duck this morning," McCain

said to the dog. Jack just turned around and went back to his bed next to the woodstove.

Austin was at the front door at five-thirty sharp, wearing hip waders and carrying the 20-gauge pump shotgun McCain had helped him purchase a year before. Prancing around next to him was his yellow Lab, Bear.

"Looks like you're all set. Let me grab my shotgun, and Jack and I will meet you at the back gate. I have the decoys there ready to go."

As usual, Jack started whining and jumping when McCain pulled his shotgun out of the gun safe.

"Keep it down, boy," he whispered to the dog. "We don't want to wake Sara."

"Too late," came Sinclair's voice from the bedroom.

"Sorry," McCain said. "Bye."

McCain had his decoys in special poncho-style packs that fit over the wearer's head. They carried six decoys in the back and six in the front. He put one on and gave a second to Austin.

"These are cool," Austin said as they walked down the dirt trail to the river. "Thanks for doing this."

"You bet," McCain said. "I have a little spot downriver a ways where the ducks like to sit after they feed at night. Hopefully, they'll come in this morning."

When they got to the river, the first indication of morning lght was just starting to show in the east. McCain and Austin plopped the two dozen mallard decoys in the slow water of a big riverbend. Then they went to the bank and started moving driftwood and tumbleweeds into some long grass about twenty yards from the decoys. As they worked, the two dogs were running, playing, splashing in the water, and having fun. Bear kept trying to retrieve the decoys, and Austin kept telling him "no" before taking them and placing them back in the water.

"He'll figure out pretty quickly the difference between a real duck and a fake one," McCain explained.

They dragged a log over for a seat in their makeshift blind, settled in, and called the dogs to come sit by them, just as it was getting light enough to see. McCain explained where he thought the ducks would be coming from and told Austin to concentrate on the mallard drakes. He told him there was a good chance at having some wood ducks come in too.

A few minutes later, a pair of mallards swooped in over their heads, wings whistling. They turned to settle in to the decoys.

"Take 'em," McCain said to Austin, who stood and fired at the drake.

The ducks flew away unharmed. Bear ran around looking for something to retrieve. Finding nothing with real feathers, he picked up a decoy and dragged it back to the blind. Jack just sat there, looking at the young dog like he'd lost his marbles.

It took two more small groups of ducks coming into the decoys before Austin scored. A fat mallard drake fell out of a group of four that had their wings set, dropping into the decoys. The bird fell with a splash, and Bear raced out to grab it.

"Come on, Bear. Fetch it here!" Austin yelled.

The dog dutifully brought the duck to the young man who was beaming with pride.

"That's the way it's done!" exclaimed McCain. "Way to go."

They sat in the blind for another couple hours, talking about dogs and hunting and even a bit about girls. Occasionally, a single or a double or a small flock would come in, and they would shoot. McCain always let Austin shoot first. When they finally decided to pick up the decoys and head for home, they had four drake mallards, one hen mallard, and two wood ducks – both males.

"Man, that was fun," Austin said as he pulled the decoy poncho over his head. "I think Bear did great, don't you?"

"He sure did. All the training you've done over the summer really paid off. You've got a duck dog for sure."

When they got back to the house, McCain set up his tall

cleaning table and showed Austin how to dress the ducks. He plucked one and then skinned a second, explaining the different ways to prepare them. Then, he watched as Austin cleaned the rest of the birds. Finally, he put the ducks in Ziploc bags to send them home with Austin.

"We'll figure out a time to go chase some pheasants and quail one of these days soon," McCain said. "Bear will really love that."

"I will too. I can't wait. Thanks, Luke."

McCain stood and watched as Austin, with Bear next to him, walked back to the Meyers' house.

"Looks like you had some success," Sara said when McCain and Jack came into the kitchen through the sliding back door.

McCain could smell the bacon frying even before he entered the house. "Yeah, we did. It was fun. I think Austin really enjoyed it."

"I figured you'd be ready for a nice breakfast," she said. "It'll be ready in ten minutes, just enough time for you to go take a shower."

After breakfast, McCain did something he rarely did; he took a nap. He must have needed it, because Sara let him sleep for almost two hours.

"You better get up," she finally said to wake him. "We need to talk about the meeting with the goat poacher." Sinclair never called Benton by his name. She liked calling him a poacher.

Once McCain was up and moving, they sat down and talked.

"I think he'll bring photos of his other hunters," he said. "Hopefully, we can get names to go along with them. We can't push it too much. Still, if we can get some information on at least a couple of the men, we can maybe get enough on this guy without me having to go on a hunt with him this week."

"Okay, do you want me to try and video it?"

"Maybe just act like you're checking your Facebook or emails or something on your phone, and at least get the audio of the conversation. That should be enough. I'll get him to say his name. Plus, like you said, if they can't believe an FBI agent, who will they believe?"

McCain dressed in a nice pair of slacks and a dress shirt. Sinclair wore a dress and looked pretty dang good, McCain thought.

"Should I have a wedding ring?" she asked.

"That would be good, but where are we going to get one?"

"I still have the ring that Stewart gave me," she said.

Sinclair had been engaged several years earlier, before she moved to Yakima. The guy was an idiot, McCain thought. Here he had this beautiful woman ready to marry him, and he went and had a fling with an old girlfriend just before the wedding. The word got out, and Sinclair somehow ended the engagement without shooting the guy. The two of them rarely – no, never – talked about Stewart. McCain figured she had kept the engagement ring mostly out of spite.

"Yeah, that would work. Or you could use this one," he said as he handed her a small box. "I was waiting for the perfect romantic time to ask you, but I guess this is as good as any. I love you more than you'll ever know, and I want you in my life forever. Will you marry me?"

He couldn't tell if she was mad, glad, happy, sad, or pissed. She was making a face he'd never seen before. She erupted in tears. "Yes, you big dummy. I'll marry you. I want you in my life forever too. You and your big yellow dog."

Now tears were streaming down both their cheeks. Jack just sat there and looked at them. He couldn't figure out what all the commotion was about.

When it was time for them to head to Snoqualmie Pass, they'd composed themselves and tried to concentrate on the task at hand. But as they drove, the conversation evolved into when they should set the wedding date, where they should hold the wedding, who all they needed to invite and the like. To McCain's surprise, Sinclair was pushing for something sooner rather than later. He was fine with that. Whatever she wanted.

"Whenever you want, wherever you want, I am totally fine with it," he said to her. "You just tell me when, and I'll be there."

They got to the restaurant near the ski lifts at the top of Snoqualmie about five minutes early. Richard Benton was already there. They pulled in next to his rig, and McCain rolled down the window.

"Mr. Benton," he said after Benton rolled down his passenger window. "I'm Luke Stone, and this is my wife Sara."

"Hey, nice to meet you," Benton said.

"Should we go into the restaurant?" McCain asked.

The three went into the restaurant and got a booth. Sara started fiddling with her phone. Benton watched her.

She looked up and said, "Oh sorry, I just wanted to check some emails. I won't bother you guys."

"So, Mr. Benton, should I call you Rich?"

"It's Richard," Benton said sharply. "Not Rich or Richie or Dick or Rick. It's Richard."

"Sure, Richard, sorry."

"No, that's okay. Those are nicknames from my early days. I don't like them. So, did you bring the money?"

Right on cue, McCain thought.

"Sure did," McCain said as he reached into his back pocket and pulled out an envelope with fifty crisp one-hundred-dollar bills inside that he'd requisitioned from the department. He handed it to Benton. Sinclair fiddled with her phone a bit.

"Did you bring any photos? I want to show Sara the animals and some of the terrain where we'll be hunting."

Benton produced some prints with four different men sitting with mountain goats.

"Wow, those are beautiful animals," Sinclair said as she looked at the photos. "Hey, does that guy work at Boeing? I work at Boeing, and he looks familiar. Mark something is his name."

"I don't know where he works, but his name is Scott Jackman. He had a great hunt. We got that billy on the first day. I really have them dialed in."

"Boy, sure sounds like it," McCain said. "Any chance I could get his phone number or the names and numbers of the other guys? I just want to talk to them about what the hunt was like and how to be ready."

"I can tell you that stuff. In fact, here is a sheet on what you should bring and what to wear."

They talked a bit more about the days they would be hunting and where they would meet. McCain asked again about the permit and the hunting license, and Benton said he would have those for him when they met to start the hunt.

"Listen, not that I don't trust you Richard, but five thousand dollars is a lot of money to me. I really need a receipt and I would like to talk to a couple of the guys who have hunted with you. I mean, you seem like an up-and-up guy and all, but I want to make sure you're not going to just vanish with my money."

"I totally understand. Let me get into my phone, and I'll give you the name and number for this guy," Benton said as he pointed to the photos. "And this guy."

Before they finished, McCain had the names and phone numbers of the two hunters, plus Scott Jackman's name, and he had a receipt with Benton's home address on it for the five-thousand-dollar payment.

After they got back into McCain's truck, Sinclair said, "What a sleeze. I wanted to arrest him right then and there."

"Yeah, me too. But if I can talk to these guys and get a little more information on Benton, I should be able to arrest him at the trailhead before we head out on Tuesday."

"That'd be great," she said. "Now, what would you think about a Thanksgiving wedding?"

CHAPTER 27

Monday morning at work was crazy for both McCain and Sinclair.

McCain was trying to run down the other men who had purchased hunts from Richard Benton. Meanwhile, Sinclair was following up on a call left at her office by someone who might have a security camera photo of the sniper who shot Juan Delgado Sr. on Fair Avenue.

McCain called the first man and got no answer. Instead of leaving a message, he called the second man on the list.

"Hello?" a man named Mike Davidson asked as he answered his phone.

"Yes, Mr. Davidson. My name is Luke McCain. I am a police officer with the Department of Fish and Wildlife."

"Crap. I knew it. I knew it was too good to be true," Davidson said. "You're calling about the goat hunt I took with that pompous ass Richard Benton, aren't you?"

"As a matter of fact, I am," McCain said. "But don't worry, Mr. Davidson. We're not after you or any of the other men who bought hunts. We want him. Are you willing to tell me about your hunt, and if it comes to it, testify against him?"

"In a heartbeat," Davidson said. "The guy is no more a big game hunting guide than I am an astronaut. A real piece of work, that guy."

The two men chatted for a few more minutes, and McCain again assured him that he was not in trouble if he'd help with the investigation. He told Davidson that only he and a couple other people knew about them looking into the illegal hunting activity. If Benton was tipped off and disappeared, they would have to look at the people McCain was talking with now, including him.

"Hey, no problem here," Davidson said. "I'd love to be there when you take that guy down. What a jerk."

"Okay, thanks again. I'll be in touch," McCain said before ending the call.

He was just starting to research a possible contact for Scott Jackman when Sinclair called.

"We think the photo this woman has may actually be of the shooter down by the fairgrounds," Sinclair said. "It's not a great photo. No facial features or anything, but it does give us an idea of what the guy might look like height-and-weight wise."

"And?" McCain asked.

"He looks to be fairly short and very slender, kinda like a marathon runner."

"Hmmm," McCain said as he thought. "Doesn't sound much like the other two descriptions we have. One is tall and slender, another is medium height and possibly a little overweight, and now we have a short, skinny jogger."

"I just emailed a copy of it to you, so you can see yourself. Based on where the guy is standing relative to the building, he just doesn't look very tall."

"Okay, I'll take a look at it. I'm running down the Benton hunters. One guy I talked to is ready to hang Rich Benton by his toenails."

"That's Richard," Sinclair said with a laugh. "Good luck with that."

McCain brought up the email from Sinclair on his computer and opened the attachment of the still shot from a security video. In the photo, a man is walking down the sidewalk, carrying a case big enough to hold a rifle. As Sinclair had said, the man looked very slight and not very tall. McCain studied the photo for a bit longer, but there just wasn't much to identify the man. He decided to get back to nailing down more witnesses against Richard Benton.

A check of the DMV's files brought up seven different Scott Jackmans in Washington. McCain had seen the photo of the man with the mountain goat that Benton had showed him, so he figured he could ID the guy through driver's license photos of various men with the same name. He scrolled through three different driver's licenses and, bingo, there was the Scott Jackman who had been smiling at the camera from behind a recently deceased mountain goat. McCain pressed a couple more buttons on the computer, and soon he had the man's address and phone number.

Scott Jackman Number Three answered the phone almost immediately. McCain identified himself and said he wanted to talk to him about his mountain goat hunt with Richard Benton.

"Yeah, whadaya wanna know?" Jackman said.

"Did you feel it was a good hunt? Everything you expected?"

"It was great. I got my goat the first morning. Benton was a bit of a dick, but for the most part it was a good hunt. The goat's at the taxidermy right now. I've got the perfect spot for it in my trophy room, right next to the Helan Shan blue sheep I shot in the Himalayas."

McCain told him a little about the investigation and gave him the same talk he'd given to Mike Davidson.

"Yeah, I'd testify, if I don't lose my goat," Jackman said. "And don't worry about me calling the guy. He's kind of a dick. If he gets in trouble, and I don't, hey, all the better."

McCain thanked him, told him he'd be in touch and hung up. After the call, he thought it takes one to know one – Jackman seemed to be kind of a dick too.

He tried to call the last hunter on his list again but got no answer, so he decided to go through the list of names Sinclair had given him of the families who had lost family members to drug overdoses. McCain looked at the dates. These were people who had died of an overdose in the past year. What about the families who had lost children in the past five years, he wondered. He knew it would give them close to four hundred names, but maybe there'd be something there.

He picked up his phone and called Sinclair. She didn't answer, so he left a message, asking her to try to get more names from the previous four years. Then he started down the list he had. When he came to Byron Hendricks name, he thought again about the license photo he had seen of the man. He knew he'd seen him before. McCain saw hundreds and hundreds of people during a year in his job. He figured he'd run into the man somewhere along the line as he checked anglers and hunters around the region.

Then he looked at the photo of Mandy Hendricks in the obituary from the paper. She was a very pretty girl and most likely had a boyfriend, McCain thought. What if her boyfriend was the one who was killing the drug workers? Or, McCain wondered, could it be one of the other dead girls' boyfriends? It was something to discuss with Sinclair, for sure. He looked through the rest of the list and noted the names of the girls who had died of overdoses.

When he was finished, McCain decided to try the third man on his Benton goat hunter list again. This time, the man answered.

"Yeah, this is Craig," the man said.

McCain went through the whole deal again. He told the man

he wasn't in trouble, but Richard Benton was, and they'd like his cooperation in prosecuting the man. The hunter, Craig Arenson, said he'd be more than happy to oblige, telling McCain a story similar to Mike Davidson's. None of the men had come away from the experience with warm and fuzzy feelings for Benton.

With the witnesses all lined up, McCain figured that with the testimony of the men and the audio and video he had of the phone call and the meeting with Benton, they had enough to arrest him the next morning. McCain phoned Stan Hargraves.

"What's up?" Hargraves said as he answered his phone.

"I think I've got enough on Benton, the guy running the goat poaching deal. Are you available to help me take him down tomorrow morning?"

"Yeah, I'd love to. Let's get together and figure out how we're going to handle it."

They decided to meet later that afternoon. That gave McCain some time to head into the mountains and check on the special permit elk hunters. The general deer season was over, and some of the special permit bull and cow permit hunts were getting underway.

McCain stopped by his house to pick up Jack, then headed west on SR 12. He planned to drive up Rock Creek off SR 410 and see how the hunters were doing up that way. Over the next four hours, he talked with several hunters. All were seeing elk, but he checked only one hunter with a branch-antlered bull. It was a nice five-point, and the hunter was extremely happy to have it.

He didn't want to be late for his meeting with Hargraves, so McCain dropped off the hill and headed back down 410 toward Yakima. As he slowed to go through Naches, there appeared to be a big gathering of rigs and guys standing around a truck at the hardware store. McCain pulled in to see what was going on.

As he got close to the big group, he could see they were all looking into the back of a pickup where ivory-tipped antlers were sticking up well above the sides of the bed of the truck. McCain parked, got out, and went over to the truck. He had seen plenty of big elk in his day, but this one was one of the biggest.

"Look at the size of that thing," one of the lookie-loos said as McCain walked up.

"Wow, that is a nice one," McCain said as he looked around at the gathered group. "Who's the lucky hunter?"

"I am," said a voice from behind the group. It was Frank Dugdale, Jim Kingsbury's hunting and fishing partner. "I've hunted damn near my whole life, and I finally got a good one."

"You wouldn't have got him if I didn't spot him," said Kingsbury, who had just come out of the hardware store carrying an axe. He was wearing a brown, long-sleeved sweatshirt with big white lettering that read, COW FARTS COME FROM THE DAIRY AIR. A picture of a milk cow, looking back over its behind, sat over the lettering.

"Well, congratulations, Frank," McCain said. "I'm happy for you."

And to Kingsbury, he asked, "What are you going to do with that axe?"

"I'm going to butcher me an elk. I saw a guide in Wyoming do it once. Works pretty slick."

"I'd like to see that, and I'd really like to know how you got this big bugger in the back of the truck," McCain said.

"It wasn't easy," Dugdale said. "Luckily, some young fellers came along and helped us get the thing down the hill. I backed the truck up to the hillside and they rolled him right in."

"Well, congratulations again," McCain said to Dugdale. Then to Kingsbury, he said, "Hey Jim, can I talk to you for a second?"

He and Kingsbury walked over to his truck, where McCain said, "I just wanted to thank you again for getting the license plate of that white Chevy truck a while back. We ran the guy down, thinking he might be the shooter in those pot field killings, but now we're not too sure."

"Yeah, he was kind of weird, asking about those marijuana fields. It was like he was getting paid to find them. Or like he was trying to locate them for someone else."

"Well, I appreciate it. Now, don't go chopping off any toes while cutting up that bull."

McCain climbed into his pickup, touched his hat, nodded at Kingsbury, and headed east for Yakima. He was thinking about the bull, and then he thought about what Kingsbury had said. Was Hendricks scouting out the pot fields for the shooter, he wondered.

"Of course, he was," McCain said out loud to himself. Why hadn't he thought of that?

McCain got on the phone and called Sinclair. She picked up right away.

"Hey, how's it going?" she asked.

"Good. Listen, I've been thinking about the drug worker killings. Do you think you can get the names of families who have lost kids in the last five years to overdoses?"

"Yeah, I'm sure we can."

"Good, our shooter might very well be on that list. Also, I was thinking, what if it was a boyfriend of one of the girls who died, like Mandy Hendricks? They wouldn't be on the list, but still could be seeking revenge."

"That'll be a little more difficult to check out, but it might be worth it."

"Actually, we might be closer than we think on this thing. I was talking to Jim Kingsbury, and he said something to me that makes sense. Remember when he was approached by Byron Hendricks about the whole 'have you seen any pot fields' deal? He said it was like Hendricks was scouting for someone else. I think he's on to something there."

"Hmmm, could be. Let me work on it a bit. I can check with Mrs. Hendricks and see if Mandy had a boyfriend, get his name, and contact information. And I'll work on the list of ODs from the last five years."

"Okay, I have to meet with Stan in a few to go over our plan for arresting Rich Benton – "

"Richard," Sinclair interrupted.

"Whatever. All the men who hunted with him think he's a jerk, and they'll all be glad to testify against him. So, all we have to do is arrest him peacefully tomorrow, and no more mountain goats will be killed."

"That's good to hear. Wish I could be there for that."

"You've got your hands full. I feel like we're getting close on this drug killer."

They said quick goodbyes as McCain pulled into the WDFW regional office to meet with Stan Hargraves.

CHAPTER 28

The meeting place McCain had set up with Richard Benton was on the west side of Kachess Lake, at a Forest Service road that would take them to the Box Ridge trailhead and ultimately to Alta Mountain. McCain had called the Kittitas County Sheriff's office and asked if they could spare a deputy to assist. They were sending Deputy Hernandez.

The plan was to meet with Hernandez and Hargraves a half hour before they were to meet Benton at the Forest Service road. Hargraves, who was in camo hunting attire and was driving his personal truck, was going to act like he was hunting elk nearby. He'd be parked up the road just a ways from where Benton was to meet McCain. Hernandez would stay back for five minutes after McCain was supposed to meet with Benton and then come in her KCS rig. If things changed, he'd call her.

McCain didn't bring Jack on this one. If he had to keep up the charade for any length of time, he didn't want Benton seeing the dog and wondering why he was there.

They were to meet Benton at seven o'clock, and so Hargraves went in five minutes before that. He drove by Benton's Nissan truck and parked up the road, just out of sight. Hargraves could see Benton eyeballing him as he went by, but the officer, all decked out in camo clothing, didn't raise any concern.

At seven sharp, McCain drove around the bend and pulled into a small gravel parking area next to Benton. When the rogue guide saw McCain, he jumped out of his rig with a big smile on his face.

"You ready to go kill a nice mountain goat?" he asked as McCain climbed out of his Tundra.

"Actually, we're not going hunting today, Mr. Benton," McCain said as he pulled his badge out. "I'm a police officer with the Department of Fish and Wildlife, and I'm placing you under arrest."

Benton didn't hesitate for a second. He turned, jumped back into his rig, and fired it up. McCain did the same thing, pressing the number for Hernandez.

Tires squealed and gravel flew as Benton tore off.

"He's running," McCain said into the phone.

"Ten-four," Hernandez said.

McCain was just about to hit the road when Hargraves flew by in his truck. McCain followed. They had the man boxed in, or at least they thought they did. As Benton approached Hernandez, whose rig was sideways in the road to block it, Benton slammed on the brakes, slid sideways, smacked the front end of Hernandez's SUV, and went off the road.

Somehow, Benton got his truck straightened and sped down the bar ditch. The rig canted at about a thirty-degree angle, with its driver-side tires in the ditch and the passenger-side tires up on the pavement.

Seeing what was happening, Hernandez quickly backed off the road to let Hargraves by on the pavement. From McCain's view, it looked like a street race, except one rig was on the street and the other was in the gutter.

McCain closed the distance quickly. In no time, he was at the back end of Benton's Nissan, with Hargraves just ahead of it. McCain saw Benton looking around, trying to figure out what to do. He tried to anticipate the goat guide's next move. As soon as he saw Benton jerk his steering wheel to the right, McCain slammed on the brakes.

In an instant, Benton's rig was literally flying across the road, turning on its side as it went. It missed the front end of McCain's truck by just a few feet, then landed in a shower of sparks on the road before sliding on its side into the opposite ditch.

Hargraves slammed on his brakes and threw it in reverse. McCain jumped out and, with his service pistol in hand, ran to Benton's truck. A cloud of dust was still billowing above the pickup as McCain ran to the passenger side and peeked into the truck. Benton was just sitting there, head down, hands still on the steering wheel.

"Now, as I was saying," McCain said through the open car window. "Richard Benton, you are under arrest. Keep your hands where I can see them and come on outta there."

Hargraves walked up a second later and said, "Well, wasn't that fun. I was worried the state was going to have to buy me a new truck."

"Mr. Benton's insurance company will be paying for some repairs on my rig," Hernandez said as she walked over to the men helping Benton out of the passenger window.

"I don't have insurance," Benton said, brushing himself off.

"We'll just add that to the list of infractions here today," Hernandez said. "You'll be paying on this one for a while."

"Yeah, once you get out of jail," Hargraves added.

After they made sure Hernandez's rig was still drivable, they had her take Benton to the Kittitas County jail. He'd later be transferred to Yakima County. Hernandez would also handle getting a wrecker out to impound Benton's rig. Actually, as those things went, he'd be forfeiting it to the state. They'd try to sell the truck at auction, after all the legal procedures were finalized.

McCain and Hargraves headed back to Yakima. McCain had told Sara he would call her when they had Benton arrested, so he dialed her number.

"How'd it go?" she asked.

"We got him," McCain said. "And we can add a couple more charges to the list, including eluding police and driving without insurance."

"Oh-oh, that doesn't sound good."

McCain told her all about the little car chase and how good it felt to place the cuffs on Richard Benton. As he was talking to Sinclair, he thought about Benton's brother-in-law, the man who had tipped him off to the illegal mountain goat hunting. He'd try to call him next, just to let him know they got him.

"I'm running down those names from the last four years," Sinclair said. "There are over three hundred so far. But I agree with you. I think our shooter may be in there."

"Bring them home tonight, and I'll look at them too. What about the boyfriends?"

"I talked with Mrs. Hendricks. She did say her daughter had a boyfriend, and he was extremely upset when Mandy Hendricks died. In fact, the boy's parents were worried he might take his own life. I have his name and contact information. I'm going to try to talk to him later today."

"There has to be some other boyfriends or girlfriends out there who blame those involved in the illegal drug world for their loved ones' deaths. It's going to take some legwork getting all those names."

"Let's keep working on the names we have now, and then go to the boyfriends if we need to," Sinclair said.

"Sounds good. See you tonight," McCain said and hung up.

As he drove back to Yakima, McCain thought about the

security photo of the man carrying the gun-sized case. The photo showed a man who looked nothing like the description of the shooter Dimitri Slavichski gave. Could there be two different shooters, McCain wondered. Or maybe the man was just walking by with a musical instrument, or a couple of pool cues in a case.

Then he remembered he wanted to call Rod Hudson, the deer hunter who had shot the big two-point buck and told McCain about the mountain goat poaching scam. He had Hudson's phone number in his notebook, so he pulled over at the Indian John Hill rest stop near Cle Elum, looked up the phone number, and placed the call.

When Hudson answered, McCain said, "Mr. Hudson, this is Officer McCain with the Washington Department of Fish and Wildlife calling."

"Oh yeah. Hey there. I'm with the family. Can I call you back in a bit?"

"Sure, call whenever."

As McCain remembered, Hudson had said he would be in some serious hot water with his wife if she knew he was involved in her brother-in-law's arrest. Obviously, the family knew what had happened, and he was playing dumb big time. McCain would wait for the call.

When he got back to the office, he and Hargraves both had to fill out about eleven reports on the investigation and subsequent arrest of Richard Benton. But in this case, McCain was happy to complete them. They weren't often able to take down someone who was so blatantly stealing wildlife from the people of Washington State. There was an excellent chance Benton would serve some time in prison and face tens of thousands of dollars in fines. It definitely felt good, McCain thought.

Sinclair was already there when McCain got home. He walked through the front door and found her sitting in the middle of the living room with piles of papers and files scattered all around her.

"Don't touch anything," she said as he closed the door. "It doesn't look like it, but I know where everything is."

"Hello to you too," McCain said sarcastically.

"Oh yeah, hello. Hope you're not expecting dinner, because I have nothing planned."

"No problem. We'll figure something out."

When Jack heard the word dinner, he jumped off McCain's bed and padded into the living room.

"At least someone is happy to see me," McCain said to Jack. "But the only reason you are is because it's your dinnertime."

Sinclair didn't even hear him. She had a pencil in her mouth and was looking through a file full of papers.

McCain fed Jack, changed into sweatpants and a pullover hoody, and called the only pizza place around that delivered to Lower Naches. He ordered a medium meat lover's pizza and then went back into the living room.

"Are there files I can look at that won't foul you up?" he asked.

"Yeah, that stack over there," she said, pointing to a stack of folders about a foot tall. "I've been through them, but maybe you'll see something I missed."

McCain was about a third of the way through the files when the doorbell rang. He answered it, paid the pizza guy, and took the pizza into the kitchen. He put a couple pieces of pizza on a plate, grabbed a bottle of water out of the fridge, and delivered it all to Sara.

"Thanks," she mumbled, the pencil still crossways in her mouth.

McCain grabbed a couple pieces, put them on a plate for himself, and took the remaining files to the kitchen where he ate and read.

Two hours later, Sinclair said, "I don't know. It seems like there should be something here, but I can't find anything. How about you?"

"No, not really. On the other hand, there could be fifty or a hundred possibilities. How do you know?"

"You don't, but I was just hoping something might stand out, either an arrest of an irate father for harassing a known drug dealer or an inordinate number of complaint calls to the YPD or YSO or something."

"By the way, how'd it go with Mandy Hendricks's boyfriend?"

"His name is Cody Collins. He said he was definitely hurt when Mandy overdosed, blamed himself, and felt like he wanted to die. But he got into counseling and said he is doing much better. He said he still misses her, but is working at getting on with his life."

"Did you ask him if he knows anyone who would want to kill the drug dealers and suppliers in the area?"

"I did, and he said, 'you mean besides Mandy's dad?' But then he said that he didn't think Mr. Hendricks could actually kill anyone. Cody said that Hendricks had totally stopped hunting after Mandy died, saying it would just be too hard to take even an animal's life now."

"But could he be looking for the pot fields so that someone else could pull the trigger?" McCain asked.

"It's the best lead we have so far. Maybe we should put someone on Mr. Hendricks and see who he talks to and hangs around with. He can't be spending every waking moment in the woods."

"I think it's worth a shot," McCain said. "But who are you going to get to do it?"

The Yakima FBI office had one agent, Sinclair, and an administrative assistant. There was no one else.

"What are you doing the next couple of days?" she asked McCain. "You've never met him in person, and if I remember your schedule right, you have a couple days off."

"I was planning on taking Jack down to the valley to hunt some birds tomorrow."

"There'll be lots of time for hunting birds. We need to hunt a killer."

"Okay, only for you," he said. "Now, I'm tired. Can I go to bed?"

"Only if you take me with you," she said. "I'm beat."

CHAPTER 29

It was five-thirty the next morning, and McCain was sitting in his Toyota Tundra, four houses up the block from where Byron Hendricks lived in Moxee. Forty-five minutes later, McCain saw a dressed-for-the-day Hendricks walk out to the newspaper box. Soon after, the garage door rolled up, a white Chevy pickup backed out, and the door closed. Hendricks drove up the road and out to the highway, where he turned west toward Yakima.

McCain stayed within eyeshot of the white pickup without getting too close. He followed Hendricks as he drove to the I-82 freeway and took it west around Yakima until it merged with SR 12. McCain figured Hendricks was going to continue heading west to the mountains, but he pulled off at the last Yakima exit and went into a commercial area with a big grocery store, a couple fast-food places, and a sit-down restaurant. McCain watched from a stoplight as Hendricks pulled into the full-service restaurant, parked, and walked in.

When McCain drove into the parking lot, he could see through the window that Hendricks was sitting with someone. The other man's back was to McCain, so he couldn't see a face.

McCain considered going into the restaurant, but thought better of it and parked in a spot where he could watch the two men.

McCain sat and watched the two men for an hour. Hendricks just had coffee, while the other man had breakfast. Finally, the two stood and headed to the front counter to pay their bill.

When McCain was finally able to see the man following Hendricks out the door of the restaurant, he said "huh" to himself. The man was of medium height, seemed a tad overweight, and sported a white goatee. McCain quickly grabbed his phone and took several photos as Hendricks and the shorter man walked to their trucks. He also shot a couple photos of the unknown man's truck as it backed out. And he jotted down the license plate as each of the men drove off.

Rather than follow, McCain called Sara.

"How's it going with Hendricks?" she asked.

"Good. I think I just saw him meet with the shooter. The guy matches the description that Dimitri Slavichski gave us. Can you arrange for us to meet with Slavichski sometime real soon? I took some photos of the man, and I want Dimitri to look at them. If he can ID the guy, then we might have our killer. I have his truck license and will run that down next."

"Let me call Franks and see if we can arrange something. I'll get back to you."

"Okay, I'm going to run to the office and print these photos. I'll see what I can find on him in the computer."

"I wonder if his name is in our files somewhere," she said.

"I'd bet money on it," McCain said.

"Oh, by the way, I finally talked to Miles Carter at the DEA," Sinclair said. "He gave me some interesting information."

"He did, huh? Like what?"

"Well, it seems like there may be some internal strife within the cartel here locally. The main man running things here, a guy named Enrique Chavez, is evidently taking a bunch of heat from the bosses down in California for losing the workers and the pot fields. The rumor is, according to Carter, they may be ready to remove Chavez and replace him with the guy under him, a dude named Raul Apolinar."

"Hmmm, that must be the Raul the worker at the marijuana field was talking about."

"I asked Carter if there was a possibility that Apolinar could be taking out his own workers to make it look bad for Chavez."

"What'd he say?"

"He said it was a stretch, but that it was possible. He said these guys would do anything, including taking out their own family members, if it meant more power and more money."

"Did you get a photo of Apolinar?"

"No, but I have a description. According to Carter, Apolinar is fairly tall and lean. Chavez is medium height and weight."

"Tall, lean, Hispanic – that could be the shooter those ATV guys saw above the Little Naches. This is just not making any sense."

"Let's keep following the lead on the man you took the photos of, and I'll try to find out more on Chavez and Apolinar," Sinclair said. After a quick goodbye, she hung up.

Before he headed to the office, McCain pulled up the DMV site and punched in the license plate of the truck he had photographed. He sat and waited as the computer did its thing. Thirty seconds later, the information popped up. The black Dodge Ram was registered to a Darrell Browning. His address was in Selah.

McCain then punched Browning's name and address into the site. A few seconds later, a copy of Browning's driver's license appeared on the screen. The information showed that Browning was sixty-two years old. The photo was definitely of the man McCain had seen, only without facial hair.

When he got to his office, McCain downloaded the photos

he'd taken on his phone into the computer and brought them up individually. With a simple program on his computer, he was able to flip through the photos, choose the best one of Browning's face, and enlarge it.

As he was looking at the man's face, McCain had the feeling he'd seen it prior to today too. It was the same nagging feeling he'd had when he first saw Hendricks.

McCain printed an eight-by-ten of Browning's cropped photo, then searched through a WDFW photo file. He found photos of five other men in their fifties and sixties with white beards or goatees. If Dimitri could pick Browning out of that bunch, McCain thought, they might just have their man.

After spending an hour taking care of some internal emails and filling out a couple more daily activity reports, McCain was ready to do something to pass the time. He knew not to bug Sinclair, who was already doing all she could. He decided he'd run up to Walt Ashford's and pick up the trail cameras he'd left there. It would only take him a half hour, but McCain knew he'd better not arrive without Jack. Ashford would be disappointed, and Jack would miss out on eating the gentleman's cookies.

After picking up Jack, who was always happy to be going somewhere because it got him out of the boring back yard, McCain headed up the highway to the Nile. Fall had arrived, and now the cottonwoods along the Naches River shimmered with golden leaves, surrounded by the bright foliage of sumac. He rolled down his window as he drove, breathing in the crisp autumn air.

Jack stuck his head around McCain's shoulder, trying to get a snoot-full of the air coming in the window too. McCain could only imagine what all the dog was smelling. It had to be sensory overload.

Walt Ashford was mowing the lawn when McCain pulled into the driveway. The old gentleman stopped the mower and wiped his brow with a red handkerchief he'd pulled from his brown corduroy pants. McCain let Jack out, and the two of them walked over to Ashford.

"I believe this will be the last mowing of the year," Ashford said.

Jack walked up to Ashford and nuzzled his hand.

"You're quite the hero dog, aren't you, Jack?" Ashford said as he scratched Jack's ears. "I think I have a cookie in the house if you would like to come in."

McCain followed Ashford and Jack up the stairs to the front deck and then into the log house's spacious front room.

"So, tell me how you caught those guys stealing the burl wood," Ashford said as he went into the kitchen.

A minute later, he came out with glasses of lemonade for McCain and himself, along with his now-trademark small plate of cookies. McCain went through the whole deal, play-by-play. When he got to the part about Jack jumping in and grabbing Sergi Slavichski's arm, Ashford's eyes got big, and he said "Ooooo."

The whole time McCain was telling the story, Jack sat next to Ashford and enjoyed having the man rub his ears and neck. Occasionally, the old gentleman would slip Jack a piece of cookie.

"So, you shouldn't have any more vans running up and down your road in the middle of the night," McCain said after he finished telling the story. "And if you do, please call again. We wouldn't have known about all this if you hadn't come into the office."

"I'm just glad you caught them," Ashford said.

A minute later, McCain's phone started buzzing. He looked at the caller ID and said, "I'm sorry to cut our visit short, Walt, but I need to call this person back. I'll grab the cameras on my way out. I'll stop back by when I'm up this way."

McCain drove up the drive, jumped out, and ran to the cameras, pulling them off the posts. He then jumped back into the rig and headed back toward town. The cell service in that area was spotty, and he had been surprised to see Sinclair's call come through when he was at Ashford's house. He waited until he had strong service before he called her back.

"Hey," Sinclair said. "Where are you?"

"Just leaving the Nile. I'll be back in Yakima in twenty-five minutes."

"Good, because we have a meeting with Franks and Molina and Dimitri Slavichski in an hour. Did you get those photos printed out?"

"Yes, I did. And I have the ID on the man. His name is Darrell Browning. I got the basics on him, but it would be good to find out if he was in the military. Any way you can check on that?"

"Do you know his date of birth?" she asked.

McCain pulled off the highway at a wide spot and looked at the printout he had of Browning's driver's license. He gave her the birthdate and said, "See you at Franks' office in an hour."

He had just enough time to swing by his house and drop Jack off. When he got there, Austin Meyers was working with Bear in the front yard of his house. He asked McCain if Jack could stay with them.

"I want Bear to watch how good Jack is," Austin said.

McCain agreed to leave Jack, ran in the house, put on his regular work shirt – which included his WDFW police badge – and then headed to the prosecuting attorney's office.

This time he was the early one, so he sat in the lobby for a few minutes until Sinclair showed up. Once they were both there, Franks had them come into his office.

"Are you willing to give this guy some kind of reprieve on the theft of the trees if he gives a positive ID on your guy?" Franks asked Sinclair.

She looked at McCain and asked, "What do you think? It's your bust."

"I'd say we'd be open to something, but we need Dimitri to be there for the positive ID in the courtroom if it comes to that. Then we might be willing to offer a little leniency."

Sinclair looked at Franks and said, "There's your answer."

Two minutes later, they were in the conference room, sitting across the table from Dimitri Slavichski, his large forearms, and the very professional-looking Adriene Molina.

"So, what is it you would like to ask my client?" Molina asked, peering through her giant, black-rimmed glasses.

"Officer McCain has some photos he would like Mr. Slavichski to look at. We're hoping your client can identify the man he claims shot the pot field worker above the Little Naches River. Is he willing to do so?" Franks asked.

She looked at Dimitri, and he nodded his head.

McCain spread six photos of white-bearded Caucasian men in front of Slavichski, who picked them up and studied each one intently.

Finally, Slavichski said, "Yes, I see man who shoot worker in pot field."

"Can you tell us which one it is?" Sinclair asked.

"What you do for me?" Slavichski asked.

"That's not how this works," Franks said. "You tell us who it is and then, when we get him into court, we will have you give an eyewitness statement. Then we can see what we can do for you."

Slavichski didn't look happy about that.

"Let me have a few minutes in private with my client," Molina said.

Franks, Sinclair, and McCain stood up and left the room. Three minutes later, Molina stuck her head out the door and said, "My client is ready to assist you."

"Wonder what she said to him," Sinclair whispered to McCain as they walked to the door. McCain just shrugged his shoulders as if to say, "beats me."

"Can you positively identify the gunman who you saw shoot the man in the marijuana field above the Little Naches River on October seventh?" Franks asked.

"Yes," Slavichski said, pointing to the photo of Darrell Browning. "This the man."

CHAPTER 30

McCain and Sinclair agreed to meet at her office to discuss how they'd proceed with Darrell Browning. As he drove, McCain thought about the two men who had told him about the shooting and their subsequent descriptions of the shooter. Originally, the men had reported to McCain that they witnessed a hunter shooting an elk with a high-powered rifle. Were they too far away to really see the shooter? Or, as Sinclair had asked earlier, did they actually see a different person?

He thought about that for a bit, then decided it would be too much of a coincidence. But why would they give such a different description? Their description more closely matched the cartel lieutenant Raul Apolinar.

What if Dimitri Slavichski was just pointing a finger at someone and had no idea who the real shooter was? He could be doing it just to earn an early jail release or smaller fines. But how did he pick the one guy who could possibly be the shooter?

McCain got to Sinclair's office right behind her. After parking their rigs, the two walked into her office together.

"I've been thinking about all of this," McCain said. "I have more questions now than I did before."

"I know," Sinclair said. "It's crazy. I think we need to bring Mr. Browning in."

McCain told Sinclair what he'd been thinking on the way to her office and she, unfortunately, had no answers. Not that he expected her to.

"Let me check to see if the information I requested on Browning has arrived," she said as she sat down at her computer. She scrolled through a few emails and said, "Here it is."

"Well, it looks like Mr. Browning is a fine, upstanding citizen," Sinclair continued. "No service record and no criminal record. From what I can tell, he doesn't even have any speeding tickets."

"That worries me a bit," McCain said. "Dimitri Slavichski better not be lying to us."

"I didn't get that feeling," Sinclair said. "He was very sure of his description earlier, and he was positive when he checked out the photo. I think I better go find Mr. Browning and bring him in for some questions."

"You do that, and I'll head home and feed Jack. Let me know how it goes."

It was still a little early for Jack to have his dinner, so McCain decided he'd return the trail cameras from Walt Ashford's to the office. When he got there, just for the heck of it, he decided to pull the SIM cards and take a quick run through the photos.

He was only half paying attention to the photos as he scrolled through dozens of shots of cars and trucks and SUVs. Occasionally, there'd be a shot of a squirrel on the side of the road. Another showed a raccoon. And there was a shot of a doe walking between the fence and the road. Then, a photo caught his eye. There was a black truck pulling a trailer with a side-by-side. He wouldn't have given it a second thought, but it looked like the black Dodge Ram that Browning was driving.

McCain knew there were hundreds of black Dodge Rams

out there, but this one had a sticker in the back window. Hunters Fighting Hunger, the large decal read. McCain quickly grabbed his phone and pulled up the photos he'd taken of Browning's truck that morning. Sure enough, there was the Hunters Fighting Hunger sticker.

McCain couldn't see the truck's license plate in the trail camera photos, but it had to be the same truck. Knowing the other trail camera was taking shots from a different angle, he quickly put the second SIM card into the computer's receiver and started scanning them.

On the first card, the black truck appeared at 8:58 a.m. on October 17. He scrolled ahead to October 17 and scanned the photos around nine o'clock. McCain squinted to see the driver. Feeling stupid for not doing it earlier, McCain worked the mouse and clicked a couple of buttons to enlarge the photo. He zeroed in on the driver behind the windshield. White goatee and all, there was Darrell Browning.

Of course, Browning just driving along on a public road was no big deal. What was a big deal was who sat next to Browning in the truck. It was none other than Art Duncan, the man who had reported the shooting.

Isn't that interesting, McCain thought to himself. When he zoomed back on the photo to see the whole shot, it suddenly dawned on him. That day, when Duncan and Brad Clark had told him about the pot field shooter on the ridge above the Little Naches River, there was a second side-by-side with them. The men in the second ATV were wearing helmets and stayed in the background. But now, as he thought about it, McCain remembered looking at the men.

"Damn," McCain said to himself. He remembered now. The driver was Byron Hendricks, and the passenger was Darrell Browning.

He called Sinclair. She didn't answer. Crap. She needed to know about this.

"Listen," McCain said, leaving her a voicemail. "Call me as soon as you can. I might have this whole thing figured out."

He didn't know what to do next. He could go try to find her, but he just sat there for a few minutes, thinking about everything, hoping she'd call. He tried her phone again. Voicemail again. This time he didn't leave a message. Finally, he decided to go feed Jack. He grabbed the two SIM cards and headed out the door.

When he got home, Jack wasn't in the back yard. McCain started to panic. Then he remembered leaving the dog with Austin Meyers. He walked across the street to the Meyers' front door and knocked. Austin opened the door, and two yellow dogs shot into the yard and ran in circles, Bear chasing Jack.

"I guess you didn't totally wear them out playing with them," McCain said.

"They were passed out in the front room two minutes ago," Austin said.

"Thanks for watching Jack. He really enjoys being with you and Bear."

"No problem. I like having him around, and so does Mom. Bear likes having someone to play with too. I heard you guys caught some men up in the Nile stealing weird trees."

McCain told a quick version of the Slavichski cousins' take-down, explaining to Austin what burl wood was. When he got to the part where Jack flew in and saved McCain from getting conked on the head by the giant Sergi Slavichski, Austin smiled.

"Good thing Jack was there," Austin said as he watched the two yellow dogs running and playing.

"Yes, it was," McCain said. "I'm going to cook him a steak one of these days when I'm not so busy. And I want to take you and Bear down to the valley to hunt some pheasants sometime soon."

"Sure, just let me know when," Austin said.

The two talked for a couple more minutes. McCain got

an update on Austin's relationship with Ashlee, his date for the homecoming dance. To McCain, it sounded promising.

"She doesn't think I'm a jerk or anything," Austin said. "We're talking about going to the winter formal dance in December."

"Well, that's good. I'll let you know about bird hunting. I better go feed Jack and figure out what we're doing for dinner. Come on, Jack. Thanks again, Austin."

McCain and Jack headed home, and just as they were walking in the door, Sinclair called.

"We can't find Browning," she said. "His wife says he's up at an elk camp with some buddies."

"I might know who the buddies are," McCain said.

He told her about getting the cameras from Walt Ashford's, and on a whim, looking through the photos and finding the shot of Browning and Art Duncan, driving together down Nile Road.

"I think Browning, Duncan, Hendricks and Brad Clark are all in on it. Browning might be the shooter, but the other guys are involved."

"Okay, I can see that. I asked Mrs. Browning if they had lost a loved one anytime in the recent past, and she said their son had died three years ago from an overdose."

"I'm guessing the other two men have a similar story. So, did you get his phone number?"

"Yes, and Mrs. Browning tried it while I was there, but he didn't answer. I've tried a couple more times, same thing. The phone is either turned off, or it's in a poor service area. She said that he can usually only call out when he gets high enough on a mountain to get service."

"Is there anyone Mrs. Browning knows who could locate their camp? This time of year, there'll be a couple hundred camps up in the mountains. I wouldn't know where to begin."

"She's checking with a couple people who she thinks might have been to their camp at one time or another. She's asking them to call me."

"Did she wonder why the FBI wanted to talk to her husband?"

"I just told her the truth, that we wanted to chat with him about the killings of the men in the marijuana fields. I said he might have some information that could help us. She said he might, since he seemed to be very interested in it and spends a great deal of time in the mountains."

"There you go. Well, I'm home, just about to feed Jack. What's your plan?"

"I'm headed that way. See you soon."

Jack, who was sitting and just staring at McCain as he talked on the phone, started barking when he heard the words "feed Jack."

"Oh, for crying out loud," McCain said between barks. "You'd think you hadn't eaten in a week."

When Sinclair got home, she had two big bags of Mexican food, including chips and salsa and two giant chicken burrito dinners with rice and beans. As they ate, they talked about the four men. McCain wanted to go back through and see if he'd missed Duncan or Clark's names. They hadn't known Browning's name until today, but it was his guess that the name would be in the files.

"I hope we get a call on their camp," Sinclair said. "I know it's an FBI investigation, but I would like you to go too if we figure out where it is. We'll also need some assistance from the sheriff's office."

Sinclair didn't hear anything that night. But she would soon, from an unexpected caller.

CHAPTER 31

When Browning got high enough on the mountain, he called his wife. She told him that a lady FBI agent had been to the house. She wanted to talk to him about the killings in the illegal marijuana fields. Browning told his wife there was nothing to worry about, then got the FBI agent's phone number from her. Afterward, he went back to camp, where he and the three other men had a little confab.

Duncan had a small cabin on the south side of Rimrock Lake, and when the men got up the next morning, they jumped into Clark's Ford Expedition and drove off the mountain to the cabin. There, they retrieved three rifles that had been hidden under the floorboards and stowed them in Duncan's eighteen-foot Lund boat. They hitched the boat to Clark's rig and took it down to the public boat launch off Tieton Reservoir Road and launched into Rimrock Lake. The men brought fishing rods so that anyone who had questions about the men in the boat would think they were just some buddies fishing for kokanee.

When the men got to the deepest part of the lake, a spot 120 feet deep according to the boat's depth-finder, they carefully dropped each of the three rifles overboard. It would be almost impossible to find the weapons now. After that, the men puttered around in the lake, keeping up the smokescreen of some good old boys going fishing. Finally, they motored back into the launch, loaded the boat up, and took it back to Duncan's cabin.

When they were done putting everything away, they drove back up the hill, past their camp to a high spot on the hill where there was decent cell service. Browning pulled out his phone and dialed the number his wife had given him.

"Sinclair," she said, answering her phone.

"Yes, Agent Sinclair. This is Darrell Browning. I understand you want to talk to me."

"I do, Mr. Browning. Thanks for calling. Is there a time when we can meet?"

"Well, I'm up here at elk camp and wasn't planning on being back in town for ten days or so. I'd be happy to meet you up here?"

"I think we can arrange that. Tell me where your camp is, and I'll come up about noon or so. Would that be okay?"

"That should be just fine."

Browning gave her the directions to their camp up a Forest Service road above Clear Lake and told her goodbye.

Sinclair called McCain.

"Well, I have the location of Browning's elk camp," she said when McCain answered.

"Great. Who called?"

"Browning."

"You're kidding. Did he seem nervous or evasive?"

"Not in the least. He sounded like a man without a care in the world."

The two talked about what they might expect in going up to the camp.

"If Browning is our shooter, he's a good shot," Sinclair said. "He hit both the Delgados at long distance."

"Yeah, and the younger Delgado was a moving target. That's a really difficult shot at long distance," McCain said. "We need to consider the possibility of an ambush."

They called the sheriff's office for backup and were told that Williams and Garcia were available to assist.

At eleven o'clock, the group met at the grocery store in Naches. Sinclair was in her big black Chrysler sedan, McCain in his state F-150 pickup, and Williams and Garcia each in their YSO SUVs. They decided to all drive separately, in case they had to transport four men off the hill. Or heaven forbid, they ran into any major issues.

"I think I should hustle up there ahead of you and do a little scouting around," McCain said. "I'm pretty familiar with that country, and I think I can go in, hike to a little higher ground, and check it out. I'll radio if I think we're clear to proceed."

"That sounds like a good plan," Williams said.

"I don't know," Sinclair said. "But I guess it's better than just driving four police rigs in there without any idea what's waiting for us."

"I get the feeling they aren't going to be any trouble," McCain said. "Just by what you heard in the tone of Browning's voice, I believe we're going to be fine."

They agreed to McCain's plan, loaded up in their rigs, and headed west on SR 12. McCain ran his lights and pushed the F-150 up the two-lane highway at a good pace, passing the few rigs on the road as they pulled over for the flashing blues. He made it to the Clear Lake turn-off at 11:26 and slowed on the road up past the lake.

When he was just about where Browning told Sinclair their elk camp was located, McCain pulled over, jumped out, and climbed the slight hill to the east of the road. He kept trees between him and the skyline and worked his way to a spot where he could look down on the road and the place where he thought Browning's camp was set up.

McCain peeked over the rise in the hill. Through the trees and brush, he could just see the top of a white wall tent and some gray smoke curling into the air. McCain backed off the rise and circled up the hill, staying on the far side where he couldn't be seen from the road, then walked the distance he had estimated it would take to be above the camp.

As he snuck along through the trees, McCain kept his eyes peeled for anything that might be out of the ordinary, like maybe a man with a rifle pointed at the road. But he found nothing like that. Again, he quietly walked up the hill to the rise and slowly looked over.

There, below him about two hundred yards, was a camp. Browning's black Dodge Ram was parked there, as was Hendricks's white Chevy pickup. Two other rigs were also parked near a large canvas wall tent. Two other smaller canvas wall tents were placed next to the larger tent.

McCain watched with binoculars but couldn't see anyone. The smoke he'd seen coming up from the camp originated from a stove pipe that popped out of the large white wall tent. He watched for a couple minutes, but nobody was moving around.

Before he called Sinclair and the deputies, McCain did another perimeter search, checking all around the camp for a couple hundred yards with his binoculars. Again, he saw nothing out of the ordinary. He backed down the hillside so he couldn't be seen and started hoofing it back to his truck. When he got to the rig, he radioed Sinclair, Williams, and Garcia, and gave them a quick report on what he'd seen. They all agreed to drive into the camp.

Two minutes later, Sinclair's black sedan pulled up behind McCain, followed by the two YSO rigs. McCain put his truck into drive and rolled slowly up the road. The whole time, his head was on a swivel, looking left and right, up and down. When he got to Browning's camp, he pulled in right behind the black

Dodge, and the other three officers parked in a way that would make it tough for the other rigs parked at the camp to leave in a hurry.

Sinclair got out of her car and hollered at the tent, "Mr. Browning, could you please come out of the tent? And ask Mr. Hendricks and whoever else is in there to come out too?"

"Don't shoot," Browning yelled from inside the big canvas tent. Then he laughed. "That's what they say in the movies, isn't it?"

Sinclair found no humor in the statement.

"Just come on out," she yelled. "We're only looking to talk for a couple minutes."

Browning's head popped out the tent's zipper flap, followed by the rest of his body. A second later, Byron Hendricks, Art Duncan, and Brad Clark emerged. They looked around and saw the four rigs and smiled.

"Geez, you brought out the cavalry," said Duncan. "Including you, Officer McCain. Nice to see you."

Sinclair ignored Duncan and said, "Mr. Browning, can I please speak to you privately? Maybe we can go over there," she said pointing to Williams' SUV.

When they reached the rig, Browning said, "Agent Sinclair, I have an idea why you want to talk to me. You think I might be the person who shot those men involved in growing and selling drugs, right?"

"That's right, Mr. Browning. I have a witness who can put you up on the mountain when one man was shot."

"The shooting up on the Little Naches?"

"Yes, that's the one."

"I was up there in that country, but I didn't shoot anyone. In fact, I saw Officer McCain that afternoon on the Little Naches road. The four of us were hunting up that way. Art and Brad saw the shooter."

"We understand they gave a report to Officer McCain that day," Sinclair said. "And I talked with them later. But we have another eyewitness who tells a different story. He's identified a photo of you as the shooter that day."

"Well, he's a liar then, because I was hunting over a mile away from the shooting. Byron will tell you right where we were. We were hunting together."

"Can you tell me where you were on the following dates?"

She ticked off the dates of the shootings in the pot field in Kittitas County, along with the dates when the Delgados were killed.

"I'd have to think on that a bit and maybe ask my wife. I have trouble remembering where I was yesterday. Oh wait, did you say September 28th? Me and the missus were at the beach in Oregon, down by Lincoln City. I'll have to check the other dates with her."

"Anyone see you in Oregon?"

"Only about thirty members of my family. We go there every year for a big family reunion."

Sinclair asked him where they stayed and got the information on how many days they were there and who all attended.

One by one, Sinclair talked to the other three men. She asked them the same questions and received similar answers. Hendricks said he was hunting with Browning over a mile from where Duncan and Clark were when they saw the man shoot down toward the marijuana field. Duncan and Hendricks had seemingly strong alibis for the dates the men were shot in Kittitas County. Clark and Hendricks had alibis for the date the first Delgado was killed in Yakima. And Duncan and Clark had alibis for when the younger Delgado was killed and crashed into the Tieton River.

After talking with the men, Sinclair asked McCain to come over for a chat.

"We have some serious issues with this," Sinclair explained.

"Browning has an airtight alibi for the Kittitas shootings, and Hendricks claims the two of them were hunting a mile or more away from the shooting where Slavichski claims Browning took the shot. Duncan and Clark are sticking to their stories too."

"Did you check the other men's whereabouts on the other dates of the shootings?"

"They mostly have alibis for the different shootings. We'll have to check them, of course, but I don't know how we can make an arrest right now. I was sure we had our guy."

"Me too," McCain said. "What do you want to do next?"

"I'll ask them to get me all their information on where they were and who they were with on the dates of the shootings, then wish them good luck hunting, I guess."

"It still feels like they're involved," McCain said. "But besides keeping them under surveillance and waiting for Browning or one of the other men to shoot someone, what can we do?"

Browning, who was walking toward McCain and Sinclair, said, "I have a big gun safe full of rifles. If it would help, I'd gladly turn them all over so you can check them out. The other guys would be glad to help in that way too."

"We might just take you up on that, Mr. Browning. Let me do some more work on this first," Sinclair said. "We'll get back to you."

She thanked the men for their time, wished them good luck with their hunt, and headed to her car. The two sheriff's deputies did the same.

McCain waited a bit for the deputies and Sinclair to leave, then walked over to the four men.

"I don't see anything hanging from the meat pole, so no luck yet?" he asked.

"Three of us aren't hunting right now," Duncan said. "Byron doesn't hunt much anymore, and Darrell and I only have muzzleloader tags. Brad has a multi-season permit, so we're up here helping him. Besides, it's just fun to come up to elk camp. We've been doing it for twenty-seven years."

"We're seeing elk every day, but no spikes," Clark said.

"Listen, Officer McCain," Browning said. "As you already know, or will find out if you look into it, all four of us have lost children to drug overdoses. We hate the system that allows these people to produce and sell illegal drugs. Yes, we know our kids are partially to blame, but if the drugs hadn't been so easily obtained, we might have them here today. We're certainly not upset at what's been happening around here. If one dealer or grower dies, it could be saving the lives of someone else's kid. We're okay with that. But we haven't been doing any of the killing."

"So, do you have any thoughts on who actually might be shooting the drug workers?" McCain asked.

The men all rubbed their chins and thought about the question.

"Rival gangs?" Duncan suggested. "Or jealous pot shop owners?"

"We've thought about that, and the FBI is looking into it," McCain said. "But I'll be honest with you guys – you were looking like our best suspects."

"Sorry to disappoint you," Browning said.

The men chatted for a few more minutes, and then McCain thanked them for their time, wished Brad Clark good luck with his elk tag, and headed to his truck.

As he drove back to town, he thought about the meeting with the men. He still wasn't sure they were on the up-and-up with him. It would be good to discuss all of this with Sara, he thought.

Chapter 32

After McCain was gone, the four men moved back inside the wall tent.

"You think we're clear?" Clark asked the group.

"How can we not be?" Duncan said. "Everyone has an alibi for the shooting up on the hill above the Little Naches. The rifles will never be found, and if they are, we'll be dead and gone. But where in the hell did the guy who saw Darrell take the shot come from?"

"Maybe they were fishing, just telling us they had an eyewitness," Hendricks said.

"But they pegged Darrell," Clark said. "What are the odds they'd pick the right one of us?"

"Twenty-five percent," Browning said. "Only, they were one hundred percent right."

"One eyewitness against two eyewitnesses who saw something else, plus all our alibis," Duncan said. "With the rifles gone, believe me, we're in the clear."

"Well, it's put the fear of Jesus in me," Hendricks said. "I think we need to take this as a sign to call it quits."

The three other men nodded in agreement.

"What about the protégé?" Clark asked.

"We'll leave it up to him," Hendricks said. "We can't stop him if he's set his mind on it."

"But we're done, right?" Browning asked one more time.

They all agreed.

* * *

McCain was almost to Yakima when his phone buzzed. He pressed the answer button on the steering wheel and said, "McCain."

He was half expecting it to be Sinclair, but a man's voice said, "Officer McCain, this is Rod Hudson, the guy who shot the big two-point, whose brother-in-law is the goat poacher."

"Oh yeah. Sure, Mr. Hudson. How are you?"

"I'm fine. Sorry I couldn't talk when you called the other day. My wife and sister-in-law were with me. Anyway, I'm glad it worked out. Sounds like Richie is going to do some time for this one."

"Oh, he's definitely going to jail, and we confiscated his truck which he won't be getting back. Plus, he'll be paying a big fine, prorated over who knows how many years to come. I called just to thank you again for the tip, and I wanted to make sure you get your bonus points for next year's special hunt draws."

"I appreciate that. If I have any issues with the points, I'll give you a call."

McCain told him thanks again and clicked off.

After thinking more about the men and what Sinclair had told him about the cartel situation, he really wanted to talk with her again. He called and asked if she had time to meet. She said she was heading into a Zoom meeting with her boss and some other FBI big wigs in D.C. but could meet later.

"How about 3:45?" she asked.

"That'll work. See you at your office?"

"Sure, see you then."

McCain ran to his office to kill some time. He wanted to doublecheck Rod Hudson's information to make sure he'd get the extra ten bonus points applied to his special big game applications the next year. And he wanted to look through the files on the people who'd died from drug overdoses again, to see if there might be anything else there that would point to someone being the shooter.

At 3:30, he jumped in his rig and headed to Sinclair's office. When he arrived, Sinclair's administrative assistant, Kirsten Day, told him that Sinclair was still in the Zoom meeting and asked him to take a chair.

According to Sinclair, Day was in her mid-thirties, but McCain thought she looked about twenty-two. She was fairly short, with straight brown hair, blue eyes, and a slim figure. He thought she should be heading to Yakima Valley College for an English class.

She chatted with McCain for a few minutes, until Sinclair walked out of her office and said, "Well, there's ninety minutes of my life I'll never get back."

"That good, huh?"

"It comes with the territory. So, let's chat. Did you find out anything after I left?"

"I'm not sure I'm buying into the story that those four guys aren't involved. How'd you do on getting a bead on this Apolinar guy that Carter told you about?"

"Nothing yet. But I'll call him again now to see what I can find out," she said and picked up the phone to call the DEA agent.

"I'm going to take off. See you at home," he said as he walked out the door.

That night, as they ate grilled sockeye salmon McCain had

caught on the Columbia River earlier in the summer, they talked about the case. Sinclair hadn't heard back from Carter yet, so they rehashed the meeting with the four men up near White Pass earlier that day.

"Are you going to ask for their rifles?" McCain asked.

"We could, but again, if they have the rifle or rifles used in the killings, they aren't just going to hand them over. My guess is they're way too smart to use their own registered hunting rifles."

"Well, it's definitely worth checking out their alibis for the different days of the shootings."

"Kirsten is helping me with that."

Kirsten was much more than a phone-answerer. She assisted on many of the minute details of the investigations the Yakima office was involved in.

"It'll be interesting to see what's going on with this Apolinar and the cartel too," McCain said.

CHAPTER 33

Miles Carter called Sinclair the next morning. They chatted more about the ever-changing illegal drug trade in Eastern Washington. Sinclair brought him up to speed on their investigation into the pot field killings, and told him they wanted to look more closely at the theory that the killings might have come from within the cartel.

"I can see that happening," Carter said. "Some of these guys would sell their sister if it meant more power and more money."

"So we've heard," Sinclair said.

She asked Carter if there was any more talk of a possible coup going down.

"There's some scuttlebutt out there, but nothing that makes us believe anything might be happening at this time. But I'll certainly keep my ears to the wall."

Carter never came out and said he had a mole inside the cartel, but Sinclair assumed he must. Or, at the least, he was paying someone on the inside for information on occasion.

"The killings of the workers and the destruction of the pot fields at the hands of law enforcement had to have hurt," Sinclair said. "But would it be enough that the cartel would look to change leadership?"

"I'm guessing if this persisted into the growing season next year, they'd definitely do something," Carter said. "If history tells us anything, they'll take things into their own hands if law enforcement can't catch who is doing this."

"Any chance you can get me Apolinar's information?" Sinclair asked. "Right now, he's a person of interest, and I'd at least like to talk to him."

"Let me see what I can do," Carter said, and told Sinclair he'd call her later.

Sinclair called McCain and told him about the conversation she'd had with Carter. After discussing that for a bit, McCain told her he was going to grab Jack and head back into the Cascades to do some more checking on elk hunters. He told her to call if there was anything he could help with.

Jack was raring to go when McCain got to the house. He decided he'd head up and work some of the country in the Bald Mountain area off SR 410. Over the next several hours, McCain stopped and talked with a couple dozen elk hunters, checking their licenses and tags. Two hunters had killed spike bulls. Several others reported seeing some elk, but no legal bulls. The rest of the hunters hadn't seen any animals. Those, McCain surmised, were the ones just driving the roads.

McCain had an elk tag, but he hadn't had the time to go hunting yet. Most years, he would have a chance to hunt a day or two out of the two-week season. But other years, he didn't get time. This was shaping up to be one of those years.

If he could get away for even a day, he knew exactly where he would go. There were a couple big, deep, dark canyons in the Wildcat area, where the elk went after being pressured by the archery and muzzleloader hunters. It was a tough hunt, with lots of hiking up and down steep terrain, but the elk go there because the hunters don't.

Hopefully, he'd get a free day to check it out. He was driving back to Yakima, dreaming about the possibility of an elk hunt, when Sinclair called.

"Hey, how's your day going?"

"Pretty good. We have a line on Apolinar. Carter is hearing that with the loss of the workers, Enrique Chavez has ordered Apolinar up into the woods to handle the last marijuana harvest before everything freezes."

"They've been lucky," McCain said. "Normally, we'd have had a good freeze by now. Does he have any idea where the pot's being grown?"

"Somewhere near White Pass, he thinks. If he figures it out, he'll let us know."

"So, what's next?"

"We'd like to catch Apolinar at the illegal grow, arrest him, and then squeeze him about the shooting deaths of the growers and the Delgado men."

"Sounds like a plan. I like it."

"I'll request some assistance from YSO. With their help, we should be able to grab Apolinar and get some more information. Maybe if he confesses, we could wrap this thing up."

"Perfect. Not to be too selfish, but that should give me a day or two to go elk hunting before the season ends."

* * *

McCain was all set to go try to find that elk two days later. He'd taken care of some paperwork that was hanging over his head and planned to head up into the Wildcat for an afternoon hunt. So much for best laid plans.

Sinclair, with the help of Miles Carter, got the license plate and description of the SUV Apolinar drove. Local officers from the YPD and some deputies from the YSO took turns watching the rig around the clock. When Apolinar took SR 12 west out of Yakima, Deputy Garcia, who was on surveillance at the time, called Sinclair and let her know Apolinar was headed to the mountains.

"Stay with him," Sinclair told Garcia. "I'm coming your way. Hopefully, I can catch up with you."

She called the sheriff's office and asked them to send Deputy Williams as quickly as possible.

Garcia was in an undercover rig, which allowed him to stay within eyeshot of Apolinar's black Cadillac SUV. He kept his distance, and when Apolinar finally parked off a Forest Service road on the south side of Rimrock Lake and started hiking up the hill, Garcia watched from a good distance with binoculars. As soon as Apolinar was over the hill, Garcia radioed Sinclair and Williams.

When they all arrived at Apolinar's black SUV, they parked their three rigs around the Cadillac, boxing it in so there was no way he could drive off, even if he happened to get back before Sinclair and the deputies arrested him.

Sinclair made sure the two deputies had their handheld radios, and then said to Garcia, "Lead the way."

The deputy found the spot where Apolinar started hiking up the hill and followed the man's tracks the best he could.

"Where's McCain when we need him?" the out-of-shape and slightly overweight Garcia asked.

"He's hunting elk not too far from here," Sinclair said.

The trio continued hiking up the hill. With the three of them looking for tracks, they moved along up the hill, Garcia bringing up the rear.

"This is where I saw Apolinar go over the hill," Garcia said, breathing hard from the hike.

They all stopped and slowly advanced a bit at a time, looking down the hill with binoculars.

"There he is," Williams whispered. "Almost to the bottom.

He's standing with a couple other guys, right next to what looks like a small pot field."

Sinclair and Garcia looked, and in short order they both spotted the tall, thin Apolinar talking to two other men.

"So, what's the plan?" Williams asked.

"Well, I don't think there's any need for us to go rushing down there," Sinclair said. "Let's just watch for a while and see what transpires. Apolinar will have to come back up this way to get to his rig. Maybe we should just wait for him here."

"I like that idea," said Garcia. He really didn't want to have anything to do with the hill they were now looking down from.

They settled into some small pine trees and had been watching the men for a few minutes when Apolinar suddenly slumped to the ground. A half-second later, they heard the distinct crack of a rifle to their right.

"Crap," Sinclair said as she turned toward the sound of the shot. "Apolinar's been shot. Try to locate the shooter!"

Sinclair's command was unnecessary, as the deputies had already turned toward the shot and were searching the trees and rocky crags on the ridgeline with their binoculars.

"There he is. Gray jacket, black pants, black baseball hat," Williams said before he took off running in the direction of the shooter.

"Got him," Sinclair said. "Garcia, you head back to the rigs and drive up to see if you can cut off any vehicles coming down the road. And call the shooting in."

"Ten-four," Garcia said. But Sinclair didn't hear him. She was already hustling down the hill toward the downed Apolinar.

When Sinclair got to Apolinar, he was already dead. From what she could tell, it was a clean shot through the heart. The two other men had scattered at the shot and were nowhere to be found.

Sinclair radioed Garcia. "Apolinar is dead. We **REALLY**

need to find the shooter."

"Roger that," Garcia said. "I have medics on the way, but maybe I should send the coroner instead?"

"Affirmative," Sinclair said. "Send the coroner, cancel the ambulance. And if either of you can get a phone signal, please call McCain and try to get him up here with Jack."

"Roger," said Williams, breathing heavily. "I have a signal and will call now. I've lost the shooter. He was heading down toward the road the last time I saw him."

"Ten-four," Garcia said. "I'm driving that way now."

Chapter 34

McCain was on his way up the highway, headed for the Wildcat for an afternoon hunt when his phone rang. "Yeah. McCain," he said, answering his cell.

"This is Williams," the deputy said between fast, labored breaths. "We need you and Jack up here behind Rimrock. Apolinar's been shot. FR 1205. Sinclair will meet you at her rig. You'll see it."

"Wait, what? Who shot him?"

"Don't know. I'm trying to catch up to the shooter now. Garcia is trying to cut him off at the road."

"Okay, I'll get there as quick as I can."

McCain sped through the grassy median that separates the two lanes going east and west, then headed back to his house. He was already dressed for hiking the hills, but he needed his to-go pack, and more importantly, he needed Jack.

When he got home, he put his service belt on, grabbed his pack, called Jack from the back yard, and the two of them jumped into McCain's WDFW pickup. As soon as he was on the highway, McCain hit the blue lights and pushed the Ford up the road as fast as he could.

It took him twenty-three minutes to get to Sinclair's car, but when he arrived, she wasn't there. He decided to drive up the road a bit to see if he could find Garcia.

McCain had driven about a mile when he spotted a blue sedan parked behind a silver Mercedes SUV. Garcia was standing outside the blue car, talking on a handheld radio. McCain pulled in at an angle, up close and just ahead of the Mercedes, effectively blocking the rig from moving.

When McCain jumped out of the truck, he heard Garcia say, "Yeah, McCain's here now."

Sinclair's voice came over the radio, "Let me talk to him."

Garcia handed the radio to McCain.

"Sara, what is going on?"

She gave him a quick version of what happened and then asked if Williams had a copy.

"Copy, yes," Williams said. "I'm on the ridge above the road, but I haven't seen the guy for some time. If Garcia is at his rig, the shooter must still be on foot."

"Do you have a confirmed spot where you last saw him?" McCain asked.

"I can get you close," Williams said.

"Okay, Jack and I will head up the hill. I'll look for you when I get to the ridgetop. What's your plan, Sara?"

"I'm hiking back to my rig now to wait for the coroner."

"Okay, stay alert and keep your pistol ready. There's a chance the shooter doubled back that way."

McCain went and let Jack out of the rig, grabbed his state-issued .223 Springfield semi-automatic rifle and his pack, and started up the hill.

"You stay alert too, Paul," McCain said to Garcia. "It would be a pretty good guess that the shooter is heading this way to try to get to his car."

"Will do," Garcia said. "Go get him."

McCain hiked up the hill at a fast pace. He had worked out

many mornings to be ready to hunt these hills for elk and deer. Now he was really glad he'd put in the work.

It took him about fifteen minutes to get to the top of the big hogback ridge that overlooked the road. He kept Jack close as he went, not wanting the dog to get too far away if they happened to stumble into the shooter.

When he made it to the top, he stopped and took a breather. He pulled out a water bottle and took a big drink. Then he radioed for Williams.

"Yeah, go ahead," Williams voice crackled over the radio.

"I'm on the ridgeline. Where are you?"

"I kept walking south on the ridge, looking down both sides to see if I can see the guy, but so far no luck. Let me look back the way I came."

McCain stood up on a big stump and looked up the ridgeline to the south with his binoculars. He saw Williams about the same time Williams saw him. Then he saw a man dressed in gray and black right behind Williams.

McCain keyed the radio mic and said, "LOOK OUT!" But it was too late. The man struck Williams in the back of his head with the butt of his rifle. Williams crumpled.

"Shit," McCain said, and took off running in that direction. As he ran, he said into the radio, "Garcia, Williams is down. Get an ambulance up here right away."

He'd watched the man in gray and black turn and run off the ridge, down in the direction of the road, but right now he needed to go check on Williams. He'd catch up with the shooter soon enough.

When he got to the deputy, McCain could see Williams was still breathing. Within a few seconds, Willimas was starting to move around a bit.

"Whaaad, happened?" Williams mumbled.

"You got ambushed by the shooter. Luckily, he just thumped

you in that rock-hard head of yours. If he'd have shot you, well, I really didn't want to have to pack you off this mountain, so I'm glad he didn't."

"You're such a good friend," Williams said softly, rubbing the big goose egg forming on the back of his head.

"Listen, you probably have a concussion, so I think you should just take it easy while I try to run down the shooter. Here's a bottle of water. We've got an ambulance on the way."

"You got any Jack Daniels to go with this?" Williams asked as he opened the bottle of water.

"Seriously, stay here," McCain said. "I'll be back shortly."

"How about some Advil?" Williams asked.

McCain just shook his head, patted his hip to get Jack to heel, and started down the hill, following the fresh prints in the dirt. He didn't need Jack to track the man. As far down as he could see, the hill was torn up from where the guy had scrambled down toward the road.

At almost a run, McCain descended the hill, watching ahead as far as he could, through the trees and brush. Jack stayed right at his side.

As he went, McCain replayed the sequence in his head of the man sneaking up on Williams. He was trying to decide if the man looked like Browning or any of the three other men from the ATVs. He didn't think it was Browning. The build wasn't right. But it could have been Duncan. He wasn't sure.

He kept hustling down the hill. When McCain had the road in sight, he slowed. It looked like the tracks went all the way to the dirt road, but he wanted to make sure the shooter wasn't waiting to ambush him too. Seeing nothing, McCain proceeded slowly to the road. He let Jack stay a bit ahead of him, figuring the dog would alert him to any danger. When they hit the road, McCain saw that the man's tracks were headed downhill, toward where his Mercedes SUV and Garcia's car were parked.

"He's coming down the road toward you, Garcia," McCain said into the radio.

"Ten-four," Garcia said.

McCain was walking down the road, following the tracks when the near-silence exploded with a gunshot.

"Crap," McCain said to himself and started running that way.

"I hit him," Garcia said over the radio. "Or I think I did."

"Are you okay?" McCain asked.

"Yes, he's still headed down the road."

Ten seconds later, McCain rounded the corner and saw Garcia standing behind McCain's truck, looking down the road. When he reached Garcia, the deputy gave him a quick recap of what had happened.

"After you radioed, I decided to hide over there in those trees," Garcia said. "I saw him coming down the road and looking back over his shoulder. When he got to his car, I could see he was pissed. We had him blocked in. So, I stepped out and told him to freeze, that he was under arrest. He took off running and started to swing his rifle around at me, so I shot. I'm pretty sure I hit him in the arm because he dropped the rifle."

Garcia lifted the rifle and showed it to McCain.

"Okay, Williams is up on the ridge with a big bump on his head. You think you can go up and assist him down the hill while Jack and I track the shooter?"

"I'll head that way," Garcia said.

"Go up the road about four hundred yards. You'll see where we came down the hill. Just follow the tracks up, and it will lead you right to Williams. Did you recognize the shooter?"

"No, never seen him before. He's Hispanic, dressed pretty nicely for a walk in the woods."

"He wasn't here for a hike. He was here to kill someone," McCain said before heading back down the road.

The shooter's tracks were obvious in the dusty dirt road, especially because they were laced with drops of blood. Knowing the man was now without his rifle spurred McCain on. He jogged along, staying on the tracks while watching ahead.

"Sit-rep?" Sinclair said over the radio.

"I'm headed up the hill to assist Williams," said Garcia. "And McCain is following the shooter down the road toward you. Be alert."

"Ten-four," Sinclair said.

The shooter's tracks stayed on the road, and McCain figured he and Jack had to be catching up to him. They jogged up a little rise, and when they were able to see down the road, McCain froze. The shooter was standing in the road, and Sinclair was a few yards away with her pistol pointed at him. But the man wasn't standing still. He was gradually moving toward her.

McCain started to raise his rifle to take aim at the man as Jack took off like a puma. The dog was a yellow blur, racing down the road. When he hit the man, it was like he'd been undercut by an NFL linebacker. The man's feet flew up in front of him, and he landed hard on his back and head in a cloud of dust.

Sinclair was on the man in an instant, rolling him over and putting handcuffs on his wrists. Jack was standing in front of the shooter, teeth bared, growling.

As McCain hurried down to where Sinclair was now helping the man to his feet, she said, "Jack saved this guy's life. I was just about to shoot him. I was telling him to stop, but he kept coming at me."

"He was about to get it from both directions," McCain said as he lifted his Springfield rifle.

McCain loaded the man into the back of Sinclair's sedan and then said to Sinclair, "Keep your pistol ready and shoot him if he moves. I'm going to head back up to help Garcia with Williams."

He and Jack took off, back to where they had come off the

hill. When they were about halfway up the hill, they ran into the two deputies. Garcia was holding Williams' arm, keeping him steady as they worked down the hillside.

When they got Williams to McCain's truck, they loaded up and headed down to where Sinclair and the deputy's rigs were parked. The ambulance had just arrived, and Sinclair was talking to the medics about checking out the shooter's gunshot wound.

"We've got another one for you here," McCain said out the driver's window as they pulled up.

The medics checked out Williams and told him to get into the ambulance. They had dressed a superficial wound in the shooter's upper arm, and told Sinclair the guy was cleared to go to wherever she needed to take him.

A check of the man's ID showed his name was Enrique Chavez.

"Place Mr. Chavez under arrest, and then escort him to the county lockup if you would," Sinclair said. "I want to stay here until we get Apolinar out."

"Will do," Garcia said, reading Chavez his rights before he loaded him into the back seat of Williams' SUV.

The dust was just settling from Garcia rolling down the road when the coroner arrived.

"I keep meeting you at these things," coroner Dan Duchovy said to McCain. "Are you going to tell me I'm going to get my steps in again today?"

"And then some," McCain said.

Duchovy opened the back of his van, grabbed the portable stretcher, pulled a backpack over his shoulders and said, "Let's go."

CHAPTER 35

The headline in the *Yakima Herald-Republic* the next morning read: KILLER CAUGHT IN ILLEGAL MARIJUANA WORKER MURDERS.

The story told of how Enrique Chavez was caught after shooting a worker in a pot field above Rimrock Lake. The reporter quoted Agent Sara Sinclair as saying that she and two Yakima County Sheriff's deputies had witnessed the killing of Raul Apolinar, who was known to local law enforcement agencies as a top producer and dealer of illegal drugs in the region.

Sinclair described how the FBI, with assistance from the DEA and other local police agencies, had tailed Apolinar to the pot field near White Pass with intentions of arresting him, only to watch him get shot by Chavez. A chase ensued and, according to the story, a sheriff's deputy was knocked out by Chavez, who was then shot by a second deputy before being overpowered and arrested.

The story went on to say the FBI was still doing their due diligence, but Agent Sinclair was hoping this would be the end of the killings in the illegal pot fields in the mountains west of Yakima.

The reason for the murders was still unclear, but one unnamed law enforcement official believed it may have been part of a power play within the drug cartel.

Another man, a hunter in Kittitas County, was now believed to have been killed by Juan Delgado, who in turn was one of the men killed later in a shooting in southeast Yakima. There was no mention in the story of the drug dealer Jerome Dirksen being killed mysteriously in an affluent neighborhood in West Valley.

McCain read the story aloud to Sinclair at the breakfast table.

"Sounds pretty close to the truth," McCain said. "You didn't tell the reporter about you stopping Chavez and Jack tackling him?"

When he heard his name, Jack's tail began banging against the hardwood floor.

"No, those are details they really didn't need to know," Sinclair said.

"You know who will be calling first thing this morning?"

"Yeah, good old Simon," Sinclair said. "And probably several others."

"Well, I'm going to go elk hunting."

"Have fun," Sinclair said before he closed the door. "GOOD LUCK!"

McCain had been right. Simon Erickson showed up at Sinclair's office shortly after ten o'clock and asked her the same questions the newspaper reporter had the night before.

"So, how did you know dat Apolinar was going to be going to da illegal pot field?" Simon asked. "And did you see da udder man dat shot him actually pull da trigger of da rifle?"

Sinclair patiently answered all his questions, and soon Simon was thanking her.

"I'm going to be up der in da mountains doing my live report tonight. Can you tell me where da shooting was exactly?"

Sinclair gave him the Forest Service road number, and the

energetic reporter – camera and tripod in tow – headed out the door.

* * *

McCain was happy to be hunting finally. He loved being in the woods, testing his skills against creatures who lived every second of their lives successfully avoiding danger. Their senses were way more acute than those of a human, and it took everything McCain had to keep from being seen, heard, or smelled by the deer and elk he pursued. Frankly, it didn't work all that often.

He also liked the solitude of hunting the mountains where he'd grown up. It was the perfect place and time to think about things. While he was constantly looking and listening for elk, he was also thinking about Sara and how he was soon to be married to a smart, talented, beautiful woman. It seemed like it had all happened overnight.

He thought about it some more and realized he wasn't at all anxious. He was happy and looking forward to it. He was feeling like a very lucky man.

McCain mulled over the killing of Raul Apolinar by Enrique Chavez. Even though everyone knew Chavez was Apolinar's killer, because Sinclair and the deputies had witnessed it, the truth was neither McCain nor Sinclair believed Chavez was the killer of any of the other men. If anything, Apolinar most likely killed the workers to put Chavez in the hot seat with the cartel.

As he sat on a bluff, glassing the dark timber below him and looking for the flicker of an ear or a tip of an antler, McCain started thinking about the four men on the ATVs. He knew they had alibis for the killings. Well, sort of. As he thought about it, at the time of the pot field killings, the Delgados murders, and the drug dealer death in West Valley, there was always one of the four men who didn't have a good alibi. It was never the same man, but it meant that each of them could have done a killing. If it wasn't Apolinar who killed the men, it was certainly possible that the four men had taken turns.

Then there was the positive ID of Darrell Browning by the burl wood poacher Dimitri Slavichski. He had picked Browning out of a photo lineup with no hesitancy. How could that be, McCain thought, if he hadn't seen Browning do the shooting? Unless Slavichski had seen Browning somewhere else in the woods. Maybe Slavichski had a run-in with Browning about something or another and wanted to pin the shooting on him.

The crime lab investigators were going to test the rifling and the bullets from Chavez's rifle to see if they matched the bullet taken from the mailbox post in the doctor's yard in West Valley. McCain figured it wouldn't be a match. There was no good reason, he thought, why Chavez would want to kill one of his best customers. Unless, that is, Jerome Dirksen had owed the cartel money.

Sinclair had gathered up the thirty-caliber rifles from Duncan, Clark, Hendricks, and Browning to check the ballistics against the bullet in the post. Again, McCain figured it was an exercise in futility and was just one more reason to not suspect the men.

McCain had the nagging feeling that the headline in the paper that morning was not correct. Yes, Sinclair had caught a killer, but it was Apolinar's killer, not the killer of the other men at the illegal marijuana grows in the Cascades, or in Yakima.

He was just starting to turn it all over again in his head when he caught a slight movement in the trees below. Was it a squirrel jumping from a log to a tree, or was it the ear of an elk, wiggling to shake a pesky fly away? McCain looked closely with his binoculars. It was an elk's ear. And the ear sat right below the base of an antler. The antler was a single spike about twenty inches long. He could see a matching antler on the other side of the elk's head. And when the young bull stepped clear of a fir tree, McCain made the perfect shot.

As any elk hunter knows, the sheer excitement of a successful shot gives way quickly to the realization that now the real work begins, especially for a person hunting by themselves. McCain walked down to the bull, spent a minute or two admiring the animal, and then rolled up his sleeves and started the colossal task of breaking it down into packable sizes of meat.

While he worked, he thought about Jim Kingsbury and his axe, and wondered if he could do the job quicker if he had a similar tool. No, McCain thought. His knife worked just fine. He really didn't want to have to pack another ounce of weight out of the hole he was currently sitting in. An axe would not be a welcome addition, he concluded.

It took him six hours and three trips to dress the elk and pack the meat up the hill. McCain had checked his phone, but he had no service down in the big canyon where he'd killed the bull. When he'd arrived at his truck with the first pack full of meat, he checked for service again, but still he had none. Now, as he drove up over the hill and down to the highway, he looked periodically at his phone. When he finally had two bars, he stopped and called Sara.

"Hey, I thought you might be lost," she said.

"Yeah, sorry. I got an elk and I've been packing meat for the last five hours."

"Congratulations."

"I'm on the road now and should be home in an hour."

When they hung up, McCain put the truck in drive and headed down the hill. He was as tired as he had been in a long time, both physically and mentally. But, as he thought about everything he'd been through in the past month, he concluded it was definitely a good tired.

* * *

Two weeks later, McCain and Sara hosted Thanksgiving dinner at their house. In addition to the traditional turkey with all the fixings, McCain had prepared an elk roast for their guests. McCain's parents were there, as were Sara's. The topic of discussion during the gathering was the impending wedding, set to take place on December twelfth.

Worried that Walt Ashford might be all by himself for the holiday, McCain had invited him to join in the festivities, but he had declined. He was traveling to Seattle to spend some time with his daughter and his grandchildren.

A few days before Thanksgiving, the State Patrol crime lab had sent out their findings on the rifles they had tested. As McCain had surmised, neither the rifle taken from Enrique Chavez nor any of the thirty-caliber rifles given to Sinclair from the four men on the ATVs matched the bullet taken from the mailbox post.

For days and days after they had taken down Enrique Chavez, McCain and Sara had discussed the investigation. They tried to convince themselves that Raul Apolinar was the person who had killed the Delgados and the workers in the pot field. But in the end, neither could bring themselves to believe it. Especially when factoring in the killing of the drug dealer, Jerome Dirksen. Sinclair continued to poke around, looking for something, anything, that might give them a true answer. But in the end, there was nothing much more they could do.

As they got closer to the wedding and Christmas, their focus turned to more important things. There had been no more killings, and Sara and McCain hoped there would be no more.

"It's disappointing to not know for sure who the killer is, or was," Sara said to McCain one night just before their wedding. "I guess I'm always going to wonder."

McCain agreed. Although he was pretty sure he knew who the killer was. Or, more correctly, who the killers were. He'd keep an eye out for the four men as he patrolled the Cascades in the weeks and months ahead, but he believed they had ended their mission of revenge. And, while he never could condone murder, if he'd lost Sara or a child to the evils of illegal drugs, he might do exactly what he believed the men had done.

"Whatcha thinking?" Sara asked, as McCain continued to mull it over.

He smiled at her. "I'm thinking about the wedding. About how wonderful it will be with everyone there for the big day. Me in my suit, and you beautiful in your wedding dress."

"You liar!" she exclaimed. "Men never think about that stuff."

"Okay, you caught me. I was thinking about my elk hunt. But I do think you'll be the most beautiful bride ever! Isn't that right, Jack?"

The yellow dog lifted his head off his bed next to the crackling fireplace, looked at Sara and McCain, and laid it back down.

McCain got up, went over and kissed Sara, and said, "I might not be thinking about the wedding, but I can guarantee you I'll be the happiest man in the world come Saturday."

"Good save," she said and kissed him back.

EPILOGUE

Five months later

Jackson Thomas had been dealing meth and crack cocaine for over a year. He was making good money selling the stuff to whoever could afford a hit. Thomas mostly worked around North First Street in Yakima, where people met him at the little spot he had established in the alley behind an abandoned restaurant.

Business had been slow on this particular Tuesday night, so when a man walked up to him, Thomas was happy to see a potential new customer. He wouldn't be happy for long.

As soon as the young man was close enough, he punched Thomas in the solar plexus. The punch came hard and fast, the impact aided by a roll of nickels in the man's hand. Thomas went down in a heap, and before he could move, the man had scrunched Thomas's sleeve up to his bicep and had pushed a needle into his lower arm.

The drug dealer was found the next morning, dead from an apparent overdose.

Two days later, another known pusher was found dead in Southeast Yakima. The police were called, and the body was sent to the coroner, who later listed the cause of death as an overdose of cocaine and fentanyl.

A week later, in a new illegal pot field in the Cascade Mountains near Chinook Pass, Estaban Cruz stepped out of his tent to see what kind of weather the new day would bring. It had been rainy for several days, but with no clouds in the sky, today was going to be a good day to do some spraying.

As he looked around, he couldn't believe how lucky he was. Two years ago, he was working in Mexico, putting in twelve hours a day away for two hundred pesos. Now he was making the equivalent of that every hour. And he was doing it in such a wonderful place.

He gazed up at the ridge above him, taking in the beauty, when he caught the glint of something in the trees. He looked, and there it was again. The sun was shining off something bright. What was that, he wondered.

It was the last thing Estaban Cruz ever thought. He was dead before the sound of the rifle reached his limp body as it hit the ground.

Up the hill, the shooter checked the dead man's body in his scope one more time, just to make sure. Then he packed up and headed back to his truck. As always, he'd been extra careful to make sure no one had seen him. He'd spent many hours with his mentors. He'd learned to shoot and how to cover his tracks. He had learned well. And, if he paid attention and didn't get too cocky, he was positive he would be able to continue his work. Their work.

It had taken him a while to come to grips with the idea that he was taking a human life. But when he figured out just how many other people he was actually saving, he was able to justify it. Besides, he owed it to his beloved girlfriend Mandy Hendricks. If only he could have been there to save her. Maybe he was saving some other person from the heartache he lived with every single hour of every single day.

Maybe he was crazy, Cody Collins thought to himself.

Although none of the doctors who had offered hours and hours of grief counseling after Mandy's death had come to that conclusion. No, he was just doing what needed to be done. And whenever he questioned himself and the work he was doing, he would turn to his Bible and re-read Deuteronomy 32:35.

Vengeance is Mine, and recompense;
Their foot shall slip in due time;
For the day of their calamity is at hand,
And the things to come hasten upon them.

ACKNOWLEDGEMENTS

To my advance readers Terri, Kyle, and Kevin Phillips, and the very passionate Sue Durr, thanks for your suggestions and encouragement.

And thanks again to Gene Beireis for his help in logistics and terminology.

CPSIA information can be obtained
at www.ICGtesting.com
Printed in the USA
BVHW082106250121
598623BV00001B/4